TRUTH
OR
D**I**E

Also by James Patterson

STAND-ALONE THRILLERS

Sail (*with Howard Roughan*)
Swimsuit (*with Maxine Paetro*)
Don't Blink (*with Howard Roughan*)
Postcard Killers (*with Liza Marklund*)
Toys (*with Neil McMahon*)
Now You See Her (*with Michael Ledwidge*)
Kill Me If You Can (*with Marshall Karp*)
Guilty Wives (*with David Ellis*)
Zoo (*with Michael Ledwidge*)
Second Honeymoon (*with Howard Roughan*)
Mistress (*with David Ellis*)
Invisible (*with David Ellis*)
The Thomas Berryman Number
Murder House (*with David Ellis, to be published July 2015*)

A list of more titles by James Patterson is
printed at the back of this book

TRUTH OR DIE

JAMES PATTERSON

& HOWARD ROUGHAN

CENTURY

2 4 6 8 10 9 7 5 3 1

Century
20 Vauxhall Bridge Road
London SW1V 2SA

Century is part of the Penguin Random House group of companies whose
addresses can be found at global.penguinrandomhouse.com.

First published in Great Britain by Century in 2015

www.randomhouse.co.uk

A CIP catalogue record for this book is
available from the British Library

Hardback ISBN 9781780892856
Trade paperback ISBN 9781780892863

Printed and bound by Clays Ltd, St Ives PLC

Penguin Random House is committed to a sustainable future
for our business, our readers and our planet. This book is made
from Forest Stewardship Council® certified paper.

For Dr. Susan Boulware and Gail Pond

PROLOGUE

OLD HABITS DIE HARD

ONE

AT PRECISELY 5:15 every morning, seven days a week, Dr. Stephen Hellerman emerged from his modest brick colonial in the bucolic town of Silver Spring, Maryland, and jogged six miles. Six-point-two miles, to be exact.

Depending on whether it was Daylight Saving Time or not, it was either still dark or just dawn as he first stretched his calves against the tall oak shading most of his front yard, but no matter what the season, Dr. Hellerman, an acclaimed neurologist at Mercy Hospital in nearby Langley, rarely saw another human being from start to finish of his run.

That was exactly how he wanted it.

Although he'd never been married, dated sparingly, and socialized with friends even less, it wasn't that the forty-eight-year-old doctor didn't like people; he simply liked being alone better. Being alone meant never being tempted to tell someone your secrets. And Dr. Stephen Hellerman had a lot of secrets.

A brand-new one, in particular. *A real dandy.*

Taking his customary left turn out of his driveway, heading north on Knoll Street, Hellerman then hung a right onto Bishop Lane, which curved a bit before feeding into the straight shoot of Route 9 that hugged the town's reservoir. From there it was nothing but water on his left, dense trees on his right, and the weathered gray asphalt beneath his Nike Flyknit Racers.

Hellerman liked the sound the shoes made as he ran, the consistent *thomp-thomp-thomp-thomp* that measured off his strides like a metronome. More than that, he liked the fact that he could focus on that sound to the exclusion of everything else. That was the real beauty of his daily run, the way it always seemed to clear his mind like a giant squeegee.

But there was something different about this particular morning, and Hellerman realized it even before the first beads of sweat began to dot the edge of his thick hairline.

The *thomp-thomp-thomp-thomp* wasn't working.

This new secret of his—less than twelve hours old—was unlike all the others encrypted inside his head, never to be revealed. The facts that Hellerman moonlighted for the CIA, was paid through an offshore numbered account, and engaged in research that no medical board would ever approve were secrets of his own choosing. Decisions he'd made. Deals he'd cut with his own conscience in a Machiavellian trade-off so big that it would garner its own wing in the Rationalization Hall of Fame.

But this new secret? This one was different. It didn't belong to him.

It wasn't his to keep.

And try as he did, there simply wasn't enough *thomp-thomp-thomp-thomp* in the world to let him push that thought out of his head, even if only for an hour.

Still, Hellerman kept running that morning, just like every

morning before it. That was what he did. That was the routine. The habit. Six-point-two miles, every day of the week. The same stretch of roads every time.

Suddenly, though, Hellerman stopped.

If he hadn't, he would've run straight into it.

TWO

A WHITE van was parked along the side of Route 9 with its hood open, the driver hunched over the engine, which was hissing steam. He had his back turned to Hellerman. He hadn't heard him approaching.

"Dammit!" the guy yelled, pulling back his hand in pain. Whatever he'd touched on the engine was way too hot. As if the steam weren't a giveaway.

"You okay?" asked Hellerman.

The guy turned with a look of surprise to see he wasn't alone. "Oh, hey," he said. "Yeah, I'm fine, thanks. Wish I could say the same for this piece of shit van, though."

"Overheated, huh?"

"I think the coolant line has a leak. This water should at least get me through my route," the guy said, pointing to a bottle of Poland Spring perched on top of the grille. He smiled. "Unless, of course, you're a mechanic."

"No, just a humble doctor," said Hellerman.

"Oh, yeah? What kind?"

"Neurologist."

"A brain doctor, huh? I've never met one of those before." The guy poured some water on the radiator cap to cool it down before giving it a second go. "My name's Eddie," he said.

"Stephen."

Hellerman shook Eddie's hand and watched as he emptied the Poland Spring into the radiator. He looked pretty young, thirtyish. Good shape, too. Hellerman, as an MD *and* a running fanatic, tended to notice such things. Anytime he first met someone, they were immediately classified as either "fit" or "unfit." Eddie was fit.

"Yeah, that oughta do it," said Eddie, rescrewing the radiator cap.

Meanwhile, Hellerman glanced at the side of the white van. There was no logo, no marking of any kind. Eddie, nonetheless, was dressed in matching gray shorts and a tucked-in polo, much like a driver for FedEx or UPS.

"You mentioned having a route," said Hellerman. "Are you a delivery man, Eddie?"

Eddie smiled again. "Something like that," he said before slamming the hood. "But my real specialty, Dr. Hellerman, is pickups."

Hellerman's toes twitched inside his Flyknit Racers. Never mind that he hadn't told Eddie his last name. Just the way the guy delivered the line—hell, the line itself—was enough to set off every warning bell in his head.

My real specialty is pickups? That could only mean one thing, thought Hellerman.

He was the package.

The sound he heard next only confirmed it. It was the van's side door sliding open. Eddie wasn't alone.

Out came a guy who could've been Eddie's brother, if not his clone. Same age, just as fit. The one major difference? The gun he was holding.

"You know," said the guy, aiming at Hellerman's chest, "one of the first things you learn in field training is that the only habit you should have is to have no habits. You never eat lunch at the same restaurant, you don't have a favorite park bench...and for the love of stupidity, you never jog every day at the same time along the same route. But, of course, you're not actually a field agent, Dr. Hellerman, are you? You're just a civilian recruit." He motioned to the van. *"Get in."*

It took Hellerman all of one second to consider his options. There weren't any. None, at least, that didn't end with his taking a bullet.

So into the windowless van he went. It was empty in the back. Save now for him. "Where are we going?" he asked.

"That depends," said the one with the gun. "Can you keep a secret?"

He let go with a loud laugh that immediately became the most annoying and terrifying noise Hellerman had ever heard in his life. Even after the sliding door was closed in his face, he could still hear it loud and clear. Until.

Pop! Pop-pop!

It sounded like firecrackers, but Hellerman knew that wasn't what it was. Those were definitely gunshots. Three of them.

What the hell...?

THREE

THE ONE with the gun wasn't the only one with a gun.

Before Hellerman could even begin to figure out what had happened outside the van, Eddie opened the driver's side door and quickly climbed behind the wheel. He slid his Beretta M9 into one of the cup holders so casually it could've been a grande mocha from Starbucks.

"You're safe now," he said, starting the engine. "But we need to get out of here. Fast."

"Eddie, who are you?" asked Hellerman.

"My name's not Eddie," he said, shifting into drive and punching the gas simultaneously.

The tires screeched, kicking up gravel from the side of the road, as Hellerman frantically grabbed the back of the shotgun seat to hold on. As he watched the speedometer hit forty, then fifty, then sixty, he waited for Not Eddie to elaborate, but nothing came.

"In that case, who was that with you?" Hellerman asked.

"He's the guy who was going to kill you," Not Eddie answered. "Right after he got what he wanted."

"Which is what?"

"You tell me."

Oddly enough, Hellerman knew exactly what Not Eddie meant. This was all about his new secret, it had to be. *Are we talking about the kid?*

"Yes, exactly...the kid. Where is he? We need to get to him before they do."

The speedometer was pushing seventy now. The posted speed limit on Route 9 was thirty-five.

"Wait a second," said Hellerman. He was back to full-blown confused. "Who's they?"

"The ones who developed the serum. That's what the kid told you about, right? That's what he uncovered. The serum."

"How do you know?"

Finally, Not Eddie was ready to explain. "I'm FBI," he said.

Had Hellerman actually been sitting in a seat, he would've fallen out of it. He couldn't believe what he was hearing. "You're telling me the FBI has an agent working undercover in the CIA?"

"Someone has to keep them in line."

"By killing one of them?"

"It was either you or him, so I think the words you're really looking for are 'thank you.'"

"I'm sorry," said Hellerman. "Thank you."

"You're welcome. But now you've got to help me," Not Eddie said. *Where is he? Because we can't protect him if we don't know where he is.*

Hellerman couldn't argue with the logic. After all, he was living proof of it. Mr. Not Eddie—or whatever his real name was—had just saved his life.

So he told him what he knew, that the kid had travel plans.

"Are you sure?"

"Yes," said Hellerman.

"And what did he want you to do?"

"Spill the beans internally. Later this morning, I'm supposed to meet with the assistant director."

Not Eddie, whose real name was Gordon, glanced back at Hellerman in the rearview mirror. "Thanks," he said with a nod. "I appreciate your telling me the truth."

"As do I," said Hellerman.

"Yeah, about that . . . there's something else I need to tell you."

"What's that?"

Gordon pulled off the road with a sharp tug on the wheel. He turned back to Hellerman and shrugged. "That stuff about me working for the FBI? *I lied.*"

And just like that, without the slightest hesitation, he reached for his grande mocha Beretta M9 and shot Hellerman in the head.

Then he turned the van around and went back to pick up his partner, whom he hadn't really killed.

That was a lie, too.

BOOK ONE

WHAT THE TRUTH KNOWS

CHAPTER 1

HAD IT been anyone else, any other woman, the moment might have registered upward of a 7.6 on the Emasculation Scale, or whatever number it takes to rattle a man's self-confidence until he crumbles.

But this wasn't any other woman. This was Claire.

"What's so funny?" I asked.

Right in the middle of our having sex, she'd burst out laughing. I mean, really laughing. The whole bed was shaking.

"I'm sorry," Claire said, trying to stop. That just made her laugh harder and do that little crinkle thing with her nose that in a weird and wonderful way always made her look even prettier.

"Damn, it's the sex, isn't it? I'm doing it all wrong again," I joked. At least, I hoped I was joking.

As I propped an elbow on the mattress, she finally explained. "I was just remembering that time when you—"

"*Really?*" I said, immediately cutting her off. "That's what you were thinking about?"

There was a certain something simpatico between Claire and me that allowed each of us to know what the other was about to say or do, based on nothing more than our shared history. For the record, that history was two years of officially dating, followed by the past two years, during which we were just friends (with benefits) because our respective careers had put a major strain on the officially dating thing.

Oddly enough—or maybe not—we'd never been happier together.

Claire wrapped her arms around me, smiling. "Just so you know, I always thought it was cute," she said. "Endearing, even."

"And just so you know, it happened over three years ago and I'm pretty sure I was drunk."

"You weren't drunk," she said.

"Okay, but it was definitely over three years ago. Shouldn't there be some kind of statute of limitations?"

"On a man's first attempt to talk dirty in bed? I don't think so."

"How do you know it was my first time?"

She shot me a deadpan look. *"I want to spank you like Santa Claus?"*

All right, she had me there.

"Fair enough," I said. "Rookie mistake. In my defense, though, it was right before Christmas."

"Of course," said Claire, "because that's the first rule of talking dirty in bed. *Keep it topical.*"

"Okay, now you're just mocking me."

"No, I'm pretty sure I was mocking you before that," she said. "Tell you what, though, I'm willing to give you a second chance."

"No way."

"Why not?"

"Charlie Brown and the football, that's why," I said.

"I promise I won't laugh this time."

"Sure thing, Lucy."

"No, really." Claire lifted her head off the pillow, gently kissing my lower lip. "Let's see what you've got, Mr. Mann."

I stared at her, waiting for her to say she was only kidding. Calling me by my last name was sometimes a tip-off. Not this time, though.

"You're stalling," she insisted.

"No, just stumped. Not a lot of holidays in June."

Claire chuckled, playing along. She always played along. "You've got Flag Day next week," she said. "Maybe something about your pole?"

"Very funny."

"Speaking of half-mast, though."

I glanced down beneath the sheets. "Well, whose fault is that?"

Claire suddenly grabbed my backside, rolling me like a kayak. Next thing I knew, she was on top and pushing her long auburn hair back from her eyes.

"Sometimes it just takes a woman," she said.

She then leaned down to my ear and whispered a request that was easily the dirtiest thing I'd ever heard her say. Just filthy. X-rated. Obscene.

And I loved it.

But before I could show her just how much, we both froze to a horrible sound filling the room.

Now I really couldn't believe my ears.

CHAPTER 2

CLAIRE UNATTACHED herself from me, for lack of a more delicate way to describe it, and reached for "the Stopper" on my bedside table. That was my nickname for it. When it rang, everything else stopped.

"I'm sorry," she said before taking the call.

"You and me both," I said under my breath.

In all, Claire owned three cell phones. The first, her iPhone, was for personal use. Friends and family.

The second, a BlackBerry, was for work. Claire S. Parker, as her byline read, was a national affairs reporter for the *New York Times*.

Her third phone, an old Motorola, was also for work. Except this phone and its number were for a very small and select group. Her sources.

Which was another reason why the Stopper was a good name for this phone. The identity of these sources stopped with her, cold, end of story. Not her editor, not the executive editor, not even Judge Reginald McCabe had ever been told the name of a single source of Claire's.

As far as that last guy, Judge McCabe of the United States District Court, was concerned, he went so far as to charge Claire with contempt when she refused to identify a source after being subpoenaed in a criminal homicide case involving an American military attaché assigned to the UN. That got her thirty-six days and nights at the Taconic Correctional Facility in Bedford Hills, New York. I have to say, she rocked the orange jumpsuit they made her wear.

"Hello?" Claire answered.

The unwritten ground rules for when she took these calls were simple. If I had been at her place downtown, I'd have gotten up and given her some privacy. Since we were at my place, though, I had squatter's rights. If she needed privacy, she'd be the one leaving the bedroom.

But she remained sitting there on the edge of the bed. Naked, no less.

She listened for a few moments, the beat-up old flip phone pressed tight against her ear. Then, her voice high-pitched with surprise, she asked, *"Wait, you're here in the city?"* Quickly, she began tapping her thumb and forefinger together, twisting her wrist in the air. If I'd been a waiter in a restaurant, I would've been bringing her the check. But I knew what she actually wanted.

I leaned over to the bedside table closest to me, pulling out the drawer. After handing her a pen, I was about to offer up some paper when I saw her reach for a yellow legal pad that was sitting atop a tall stack of books on the floor, also known as my to-read pile. Mostly biographies. Some historical fiction mixed in as well.

As Claire scribbled something on the pad, I stared at the

freckles on the curve of her shoulders, hundreds of them. My eyes drifted down her spine and I smiled, thinking of the trip we took to Block Island a few summers ago, when I rubbed suntan lotion on her bikinied back and sneakily left bare a small stretch of real estate spelling out my initials, TM.

"Trevor Mann!" she screamed later that afternoon when she caught a glimpse in the mirror as she stepped out of the shower. After delivering a punch to my shoulder—with more wallop than her thin frame would ever have suggested—she broke up laughing. "I've been trademarked!"

Even now, squinting a bit in the dimness of my bedroom, I could still sort of see most of the *T* and some of the *M*. Or so I'd convinced myself.

"Okay, don't go anywhere," Claire said into the phone.

Damn.

I was hoping she'd hang up, turn around, and say, "Now, where were we?" but I knew that was beyond wishful thinking. By the time she looked back at me over her shoulder and all those freckles, I already knew.

"You have to go, don't you?" I said.

She leaned over and kissed me. "I'm sorry."

Those same unwritten ground rules had it that I wasn't supposed to pry. But as I watched her dress, and saw the bounce in her step, I couldn't help myself.

"You've got something, don't you?" I asked. "Something good."

She nodded with a touch of giddiness.

I stared at her, waiting for something, anything that hinted at what it might be. I must have looked like a dog sitting at the edge of the dinner table, silently begging for scraps.

"I know," she said finally. "But we have to keep some mystery between us, don't we?"

Buttoning the last button on her navy-blue blouse, she returned to the side of the bed and kissed me one last time before leaving.

"Call me in the morning," I said.

She smiled. "Promise."

A little over two hours later, I was jolted awake by the sound of my phone. It was just shy of one a.m.

Claire's older sister was calling from Boston. She was crying and couldn't get the words out. She didn't have to. It was as if I knew the second I picked up the phone. *There was a certain something simpatico between Claire and me.*

Something terrible had happened.

CHAPTER 3

DETECTIVE DAVE Lamont shook my hand firmly in the front waiting area of the Midtown North Precinct on West Fifty-Fourth Street and led me upstairs to the far back corner of a squad room that was empty and silent, save for the baritone hum of the fluorescent lighting overhead.

"Have a seat," he said, pointing to a folding metal chair in front of his desk. "You want some coffee?"

"No, I'm okay. Thanks."

He grabbed a mug with a faded New York Giants logo on it that was sitting on top of some overstuffed folders. "I'll be right back."

I watched him as he walked off. Lamont was a tall man, filled out by age, but still with a build that suggested a degree of athleticism somewhere in his past. Given the Giants mug, I was thinking there was probably an old high school yearbook out there with the word *linebacker* next to his name.

Claire once showed me her high school yearbook. Her senior

quote was from Andrew Marvell: "Had we but world enough and time..."

Christ, this is really happening, isn't it? She's really gone. Just like that. I feel numb. No, that's not right. I feel everything. And it's hurting like hell.

Claire's sister, Ellen, had given me Detective Lamont's name and number. He'd made the call to her up in Boston, breaking the news.

I wasn't next of kin, husband or fiancé, or even the last person to see Claire alive, but when I'd told Lamont my name over the phone I'd been pretty sure he'd agree to see me right away.

"You were that ADA, weren't you?" he asked.

"Yeah, that was me," I answered.

Me, as in that former Manhattan assistant district attorney. Back when I played for the home team. Before I changed jerseys.

Before I got disbarred.

I knew he knew the story. Most every cop in the city did, at least the veterans. It was the kind of story they wouldn't forget.

Lamont came back now and sat behind his desk with a full mug of coffee. He took a sip as he pulled Claire's file in front of him, the steam momentarily fogging the bottom half of his drugstore-variety glasses.

Then he shook his head slowly and simply stared at me for a moment, unblinking.

"Fuckin' random," he said finally.

I nodded as he flipped open the file to his notes in anticipation of my questions. I had a lot of them.

Christ. The pain is only going to get worse, isn't it?

CHAPTER 4

"WHERE EXACTLY did it happen?" I asked.

"West End Avenue at Seventy-Third. The taxi was stopped at a red light," said Lamont. "The assailant smashed the driver's side window, pistol-whipped the driver until he was knocked out cold, and grabbed his money bag. He then robbed Ms. Parker at gunpoint."

"Claire," I said.

"Excuse me?"

"Please call her Claire."

I knew it was a weird thing for me to say, but weirder still was hearing Lamont refer to Claire as Ms. Parker, not that I blamed him. Victims are always Mr., Mrs., or Ms. for a detective. He was supposed to call her that. I just wasn't ready to hear it.

"I apologize," I said. "It's just that—"

"Don't worry about it," he said with a raised palm. He understood. He got it.

"So what happened next?" I asked. "What went wrong?"

"We're not sure, exactly. Best we can tell, she fully cooperated, didn't put up a fight."

That made sense. Claire might have been your prototypical "tough" New Yorker, but she was also no fool. She didn't own anything she'd risk her life to keep. *Does anyone?*

No, she definitely knew the drill. Never be a statistic. If your taxi gets jacked, you do exactly as told.

"And you said the driver was knocked out, right? He didn't hear anything?" I asked.

"Not even the gunshots," said Lamont. "In fact, he didn't actually regain consciousness until after the first two officers arrived at the scene."

"Who called it in?"

"An older couple walking nearby."

"What did they see?"

"The shooter running back to his car, which was behind the taxi. They were thirty or forty yards away; they didn't get a good look."

"Any other witnesses?"

"You'd think, but no. Then again, residential block...after midnight," he said. "We'll obviously follow up in the area tomorrow. Talk to the driver, too. He was taken to St. Luke's before we arrived."

I leaned back in my chair, a metal hinge somewhere below the seat creaking its age. I must have had a dozen more questions for Lamont, each one trying to get me that much closer to being in the taxi with Claire, to knowing what had really happened.

To knowing whether or not it truly was... *fuckin' random.*

But I wasn't fooling anyone. Not Lamont, and especially not myself. All I was doing was procrastinating, trying hopelessly to avoid asking the one question I was truly dreading.

I couldn't avoid it any longer.

CHAPTER 5

"FOR THE record, you were never in here," said Lamont, pausing at a closed door toward the back corner of the precinct house.

I stared at him blankly as if I were some chronic sufferer of short-term memory loss. *"In where?"* I asked.

He smirked. Then he opened the door.

The windowless room I followed him into was only slightly bigger than claustrophobic. After closing the door behind us, Lamont introduced me to his partner, Detective Mike McGeary, who was at the helm of what looked like one of those video arcade games where you sit in a captain's chair shooting at alien spaceships on a large screen. He was even holding what looked like a joystick.

McGeary, square-jawed and bald, gave Lamont a sideways glance that all but screamed, *What the hell is he doing in here?*

"Mr. Mann was a close acquaintance of the victim," said Lamont. He added a slight emphasis on my last name, as if to jog his partner's memory.

McGeary studied me in the dim light of the room until he put my face and name together. Perhaps he was remembering the cover of the *New York Post* a couple of years back. *An Honest Mann*, read the headline.

"Yeah, fine," McGeary said finally.

It wasn't exactly a ringing endorsement, but it was enough to consider the issue of my being there resolved. I could stay. I could see the recording.

I could watch, frame by frame, the murder of the woman I loved.

Lamont hadn't had to tell me there was a surveillance camera in the taxi. I'd known right away, given how he'd described the shooting over the phone, some of the details he had. There were little things no eyewitnesses could ever provide. Had there been any eyewitnesses, that is.

Lamont removed his glasses, wearily pinching the bridge of his nose. No one ever truly gets used to the graveyard shift. "Any matches so far?" he asked his partner.

McGeary shook his head.

I glanced at the large monitor, which had shifted into screen saver mode, an NYPD logo floating about. Lamont, I could tell, was waiting for me to ask him about the space-age console, the reason I wasn't supposed to be in the room. The machine obviously did a little more than just digital playback.

But I didn't ask. I already knew.

I'm sure the thing had an official name, something ultra-high-tech sounding, but back when I was in the DA's office I'd only ever heard it referred to by its nickname, CrackerJack. What it did was combine every known recognition software program into one giant cross-referencing "decoder" that was linked to practically every criminal database in the country, as well as those from twenty-three other countries, or basically all of our official allies in the "war on terror."

In short, given any image at any angle of any suspected terrorist, CrackerJack could source a litany of identifying characteristics, be it an exposed mole or tattoo; the exact measurements between the suspect's eyes, ears, nose, and mouth; or even a piece of jewelry. Clothing, too. Apparently, for all the precautions terrorists take in their planning, it rarely occurs to them that wearing the same polyester shirt in London, Cairo, and Islamabad might be a bad idea.

Of course, it didn't take long for law enforcement in major cities—where CrackerJacks were heavily deployed by the Department of Homeland Security—to realize that these machines didn't have to identify just terrorists. Anyone with a criminal record was fair game.

So here was McGeary going through the recording sent over by the New York Taxi & Limousine Commission to see if any image of the shooter triggered a match. And here was me, having asked if I could watch it, too.

"Mike, cue it up from the beginning, will you?" said Lamont.

McGeary punched a button and then another until the screen lit up with the first frame, the taxi having pulled over to pick Claire up. The image was grainy, black-and-white, like on an old tube television with a set of rabbit ears. But what little I could see was still way too much.

It was exactly as Lamont had described it. The shooter smashes the driver's side window, beating the driver senseless with the butt of his gun. He's wearing a dark turtleneck and a ski mask with holes for the eyes, nose, and mouth. His gloves are tight, like those Isotoners that O. J. Simpson pretended didn't fit.

So far, Claire is barely visible. Not once can I see her face. Then I do.

It's right after the shooter snatches the driver's money bag. He swings his gun, aiming it at Claire in the backseat. She jolts. There's no Plexiglas divider. There's nothing but air.

Presumably, he says something to her, but the back of his head is toward the camera. Claire offers up her purse. He takes it and she says something. I was never any good at reading lips.

He should be leaving. Running away. Instead, he swings out and around, opening the rear door. He's out of frame for no more than three seconds. Then all I see is his outstretched arm. And the fear in her eyes.

He fires two shots at point-blank range. *Did he panic?* Not enough to flee right away. Quickly, he riffles through her pockets, and then tears off her earrings, followed by her watch, the Rolex Milgauss I gave her for her thirtieth birthday. He dumps everything in her purse and takes off.

"Wait a minute," I said suddenly. "Go back a little bit."

CHAPTER 6

LAMONT AND McGeary both turned to me, their eyes asking if I was crazy. *You want to watch her being murdered a second time?*

No, I didn't. Not a chance.

Watching it the first time made me so nauseous I thought I'd throw up right there on the floor. I wanted that recording erased, deleted, destroyed for all eternity not two seconds after it was used to catch the goddamn son of a bitch who'd done this.

Then I wanted a long, dark alley in the dead of night where he and I could have a little time alone together. Yeah. *That's* what I wanted.

But I thought I saw something.

Up until that moment, I hadn't known what I was looking for in the recording, if anything. If Claire had been standing next to me, she, with her love of landmark Supreme Court cases, would've described it as the definition of pornography according to Justice Potter Stewart in *Jacobellis v. Ohio*.

I know it when I see it.

She'd always admired the simplicity of that. Not everything that's true has to be proven, she used to say.

"Where to?" asked McGeary, his hand hovering over a knob that could rewind frame by frame, if need be.

"Just after he beats the driver," I said.

He nodded. "Say when."

I watched the sped-up images, everything happening in reverse. If only I could reverse it all for real. I was waiting for the part when the gun was turned on Claire. A few moments before that, actually.

"Stop," I said. "Right there."

McGeary hit Play again and I leaned in, my eyes glued to the screen. Meanwhile, I could feel Lamont's eyes glued to my profile, as if he could somehow better see what I was looking for by watching me.

"What is it?" he eventually asked.

I stepped back, shaking my head as if disappointed. "Nothing," I said. "It wasn't anything."

Because that's exactly what Claire would've wanted me to say. A little white lie for the greater good, she would've called it.

She was always a quick thinker, right up until the end.

CHAPTER 7

NO WAY in hell did I feel like taking a taxi home.

In fact, I didn't feel like going home at all. In my mind, I'd already put my apartment on the market, packed up all my belongings, and moved to another neighborhood, maybe even out of Manhattan altogether. Claire *was* the city to me. Bright. Vibrant.

Alive.

And now she wasn't.

I passed a bar, looking through the window at the smattering of "patrons," to put it politely, who were still drinking at three in the morning. I could see an empty stool and it was calling my name. More like shouting it, really.

Don't, I told myself. *When you sober up, she'll still be gone.*

I kept walking in the direction of my apartment, but with every step it became clear where I truly wanted to go. It was wherever Claire had been going.

Who was she meeting?

Suddenly, I was channeling Oliver Stone, somehow trying to link her murder to the story she'd been chasing. But that was crazy. I saw her murder in black and white. It was a robbery. She was in the wrong place at the wrong time, and as much as that was a cliché, so, too, was her death. She'd be the first to admit it.

"Imagine that," I could hear her saying. "A victim of violent crime in New York City. *How original.*"

Still, I'd become fixated on wanting to know where she'd been heading when she left my apartment. A two-hundred-dollar-an-hour shrink would probably call that sublimated grief, while the four-hundred-dollar-an-hour shrink would probably counter with sublimated anger. I was sticking with overwhelming curiosity.

I put myself in her shoes, mentally tracing her steps through the lobby of my building and out to the sidewalk. As soon as I pictured her raising her arm for a taxi, it occurred to me. *The driver.* He at least knew the address. For sure, Claire gave it to him when he picked her up.

Almost on cue, a taxi slowed down next to me at the curb, the driver wondering if I needed a ride. That was a common occurrence late at night when supply far outweighed demand.

As I shook him off, I began thinking of what else Claire's driver might remember when Lamont interviewed him. Tough to say after the beating he took. Maybe the shooter had said something that would key his identity, or at least thin out the suspects. Did he speak with any kind of accent?

Or maybe the driver had seen something that wasn't visible to that surveillance camera. Eye color? An odd-shaped mole? A chipped tooth?

Unfortunately, the list of possibilities didn't go on and on. The ski mask, turtleneck, and gloves made sure of that. Clearly, the bastard knew that practically every taxi in the city was its own little recording studio. So much for cameras being a deterrent.

As the old expression goes, show me a ten-foot wall and I'll show you an eleven-foot ladder.

The twenty blocks separating me from my apartment were a daze. I was on autopilot, one foot in front of the other. Only at the sound of the keys as I dropped them on my kitchen counter did I snap out of it, realizing I was actually home.

Fully dressed, I fell into my bed, shoes and all. I didn't even bother turning off the lights. But my eyes were closed for only a few seconds before they popped open. *Damn*. All it took was one breath, one exchange of the air around me, and I was lying there feeling more alone than I ever had in my entire life.

The sheets still smelled of her.

I sat up, looking over at the other side of the bed...the pillow. I could still make out the impression of Claire's head. That was the word, wasn't it? *Impression*. Hers was everywhere, most of all on me.

I was about to make a beeline to my guest room, which, if anything, would smell of dust or staleness or whatever other odor is given off by a room that's rarely, if ever, used. I didn't care. So long as it wasn't her.

Suddenly, though, I froze. Something had caught my eye. It was the yellow legal pad on the end of the bed, the one Claire had used when she took the phone call. She'd ripped off the top sheet she'd written on.

But the one beneath it...

CHAPTER 8

I ALL but lunged for the pad, gripping it beyond tight while staring at the indentations she'd left behind.

Another impression.

I could make out a letter here, a letter there. An *S* followed by something, followed by a *B*. Or was that a *6*?

I flipped on the nearby lamp for more light, angling the pad every which way, trying to decipher the ever-so-slight grooves in the paper. It could've been a name, but all my money was on it being an address. It was where Claire was going. It had to be. But I still couldn't make it out.

I thought for a few seconds, racking my brain. Before I knew it, I was dashing across my living room and into my office, grabbing a pencil, followed by a piece of paper from my printer tray. *This could work*, I thought.

Laying the paper over the pad, I began gently making a rubbing, like people do with tombstones and other memorials. But the printer paper was too thick. I needed something thinner. I knew exactly where to find it, too.

It was an invitation I'd just received to a legal aid benefit being held at the New York Public Library. Pretty hard to miss the irony, given that Claire would have been my plus-one.

The invitation itself was on a thick stock, but all I could see in my head was what had been inserted to protect the embossed type: a piece of vellum as thin as tracing paper. Perfect.

I riffled through my pile of mail, finding the invite and the vellum. Laying it on the legal pad, I again began gently rubbing the pencil back and forth. Like magic, the letters started to appear before my eyes. Letters *and* numbers.

It was an address, all right. Downtown on the West Side. She'd also written *1701* below it. Was that an apartment number?

I turned on my laptop, grabbing my keys and throwing on a baseball cap while waiting for it to power up. Quickly, I Googled the address.

The first result was the only one I needed to see. This wasn't someone's home. Claire had been heading to the Lucinda Hotel, room 1701.

Now I was, too.

CHAPTER 9

AN INTERRUPTION.

That was what Owen Lewis was waiting for in room 1701 of the Lucinda Hotel. The tiny camera, no bigger than a lipstick cylinder, was taped to the exit sign above the entrance to the stairwell, wirelessly transmitting to his laptop the same image of the long, empty hallway outside his door. It was monotony in black and white. A continuous loop of stillness and silence, over and over. Uninterrupted.

For anyone else, it would've been the most boring movie of the century. To Owen, it was easily the scariest. Especially how it might end.

She said she'd be here in twenty minutes. That was hours ago. Did they get to her? Am I next?

He'd thought about leaving town, but it was already so late. There were no buses, trains, or planes he could catch at this hour, and he knew you had to be twenty-five to rent a car. His driver's license couldn't get him a beer, let alone a Buick.

All in all, the only real option was a taxi, but that didn't feel like a good idea, for some reason. Just his gut instinct.

No, he would wait it out until morning, stick with his plan.

It was a good plan, extremely well thought out, with the highest attention to every detail. Of course, when you're sporting an IQ that approaches the boiling point of water, anticipation is your stock in trade. You see the future before others do. You live it, too.

"The Boy Genius!" declared his hometown paper back in Amherst, New Hampshire, in a front-page story when Owen was only four. By then, he had memorized the periodic table, could read and write in three languages, and was doing complex algebra. The photo accompanying the article showed him shaking hands with Steve Jobs at a "Pioneers of Tomorrow" conference at Apple's headquarters in Cupertino.

For an entire year after that, Owen wore only a black mock turtleneck everywhere he went.

Elementary school was finished at age six, junior high at eight, and then high school when he was eleven. At fourteen, he was the youngest ever to graduate from Cal Berkeley, earning summa cum laude and salutatorian honors. He would've been valedictorian if it hadn't been for a B+ in comparative Russian literature. Even geniuses have their blind spots.

Next up were combined MD and PhD degrees from Harvard Medical School and MIT at age seventeen, after which Owen spent nearly two years at Eidgenössische Technische Hochschule Zürich, aka the Swiss Federal Institute of Technology in Zurich, studying what had become his true passion: artificial neural networks.

That was when the two men first approached him, one night as he was leaving the library. They were Americans.

"How would you like to help save the world?" one asked.

Owen laughed, not taking him seriously at first. "Only if I get to wear a cape," he said.

A predilection for sarcasm commensurate with sapience, read the extensive psych profile of Owen that the two men had already seen.

"No, I'm afraid there's no cape or even a skintight suit," said the other man. "However, you will get to be a part of the digital age's equivalent of the Manhattan Project."

Owen liked the sound of that. Loved it, to be more precise. It was his chance to make history. And who doesn't want to do that?

But that was then.

Now, less than a year later, here he was hiding out in a cramped hotel room—in Manhattan, no less—hoping against hope that he'd live to see another sunrise.

Turned out, Owen Lewis had the one problem he never thought he'd have. Not in a million years. Or certainly, at least, not before his twenty-first birthday.

It was why they wanted to kill him, the Boy Genius.

He knew too much.

CHAPTER 10

WITHOUT ONCE taking his eyes off his scuffed-up laptop and the live feed from the hallway, Owen bit off another triangle of the twelve-dollar Toblerone from his minibar and dialed Claire Parker's cell for a third time. And for the third time the call went straight to voice mail.

Something was wrong. He just didn't know what. There were a few plausible explanations as to why she hadn't shown up at his room, ranging from the relatively harmless to the absolute worst-case scenario. He could speculate all he wanted, but that was all it would be. Speculation. The important thing now was whether or not she was the only one who knew his location.

She wasn't.

Two minutes later, the image of the man stepping off the elevator at the other end of the hallway told Owen so much at once that his brain tingled with overload, which was no small feat.

Male . . . solo . . . decent physique . . . running shoes . . . baseball cap with curled bill . . . no room key in hand . . . no suitcase or carry-on . . .

The man paused by the elevator bank to look at the directional sign for the rooms on the floor. If he'd just been checking in, thought Owen, he'd almost certainly have had luggage. If he'd been staying at the hotel already, he'd have had no need to look at the sign.

Plus, with that curled bill on his baseball cap, he could shield his face from any security cameras in the hotel.

But most incriminating of all?

None of that mattered.

The guy could've been a blind midget wearing a clown suit, and it wouldn't have changed anything. It was four in the morning and he was heading straight toward room 1701. Thirty yards away and closing.

As if his chair had springs, Owen jumped up and slap-closed his laptop, stuffing it in his already packed backpack along with the wireless receiver for the transmitting camera outside in the hallway.

He sprinted into the bathroom, where he'd already filled the tub to the brim with water, not an inch of porcelain left dry. With a hard yank, he turned the shower on full blast.

As for the hotel's hair dryer, it was already plugged in, the surge protector dismantled and the outlet rewired to deliver the maximum current possible. Suffice it to say, that sort of thing doesn't get a chapter in *Electrical Wiring for Dummies*.

Quickly backing out of the bathroom, Owen took one last look at the setup before shutting the door, his eyes darting about to make sure all the elements were in place.

The shower curtain drawn closed, tucked inside the tub.

The cord of the hair dryer knotted around the towel bar to ensure that it would remain plugged into the outlet no matter what.

And the floor mat strategically placed on the tile floor to ensure that Owen wouldn't slip when he came barging in behind the guy.

From the room next door.

This was the plan, all right. Based on two things Owen knew as surely as he knew that sunrise was only a few hours away.

The first was primal. Sometimes in life it's as simple as kill or be killed.

Second, professional hit men aren't exactly suckers. You can't expect them to fall for the "I'm in the shower" trick simply because you've got the door to the room cracked open and have the water running. They'll search the rest of your room first, top to bottom.

So hiding behind the armchair in the corner or squeezing yourself under the bed? Probably the very last dumb idea you'll ever have.

No, if you want the true element of surprise, you need to think outside the box. Better yet, come up with your own box.

Just make sure there's a connecting door.

"I'd like two rooms," he'd told the clerk at the front desk when he checked in. "And they need to be adjoining."

Owen slipped through the double doors separating room 1701 from 1703, pulling the first one closed behind him. His heart was pounding like a jackhammer against his chest, but he couldn't help noticing that it wasn't just fear. As crazy as it sounded, he also felt a twinge of excitement, a sort of in-the-moment buzz of anticipation that came from an intellectual curiosity always in hyperdrive. A prodigy's conceit, if you will.

In other words, he desperately wanted to know if his plan would work. And there was only one way to find out.

Pressing his ear up against the door, all Owen could now do was wait and wonder.

"Will you walk into my parlor?" said the Spider to the Fly.

CHAPTER 11

I OWNED only one cell phone, as opposed to Claire's three, and it was pinned to my ear as I entered the lobby of the Lucinda at four in the morning, pretending to be completely engrossed in a conversation.

The lobby—which sadly looked as if it hadn't been updated since the Koch administration—was completely empty, as it should've been, given the hour, save for a wary-eyed woman behind the front desk in a turquoise blazer who was clearly in the midst of deciding whether or not to ask me if I was a guest of the hotel.

That was when I delivered the clincher to my imaginary friend on the other end of the imaginary line.

"Yeah, I'm heading up to my room now," I announced.

As I walked past the front desk, walking straight toward the elevators, the woman didn't say a word. I was in.

Then I was up...to the seventeenth floor. With a tug on my baseball cap, I stepped off the elevator and stopped briefly before the sign telling me which rooms were in which direction, left or right.

Room 1701 was to the right.

I walked down the long, narrow hallway, the beige carpet blending in with the beige walls to form a seamless tunnel of blandness, the only splash of color coming from the glowing red exit sign announcing the stairwell at the very end. The odd-numbered rooms were to my left.

1723…1721…1719…

I was repeating them silently in my head, like a countdown. To what, though, I wondered?

And what was I going to say after I knocked? Whoever was on the other side of the door was expecting Claire, but that was hours ago. Now it was the middle of the night, and I was a complete stranger with a lot of explaining to do. This, after first breaking the news that Claire was dead.

1709…1707…1705…

My vision was so trained on the room numbers that I didn't even notice it at first. My hand was literally in the air, knuckles tucked and ready to knock, when I saw that the door was open. Not open like see-into-the-room open, but rather the door was just shy of the frame, as if someone had forgotten to close it all the way.

If I wanted to step inside, all I had to do was push.

Instead, I stepped back. There was a bad vibe racing through me, head to toe. Something wasn't right.

I stood there on the beige carpet, my feet frozen, while my brain sifted quickly through the options. Bad vibe or not, leaving wasn't one of them. In fact, that door being open—be it ever so slightly—just made me all the more curious. For better or worse.

I knocked. Softly, at first, on the outside chance that whoever was in there was still awake at four in the morning.

Very outside chance. After ten seconds of silence, I knocked again. This time, louder. Then louder still.

Oh, shit. Too loud.

The jarring sound came from directly behind me, a dead bolt sliding on the door to another room. I'd woken somebody up, all right, just the wrong person.

Suddenly, I was in no-man's-land, and my only thought was that I couldn't afford to be seen. Call it instinct or sheer panic, but I was done knocking on the door of room 1701.

I was now *in* room 1701.

And I wasn't alone.

CHAPTER 12

IT WAS pitch black; I couldn't see a thing. But there was no mistaking the sound of running water. It was the shower.

Meanwhile, there was the other sound behind me. A door opening and closing out in the hallway. Whoever I'd woken up was going back to bed without laying eyes on me. One bullet dodged.

Now what?

I could practically hear myself playing lawyer with the police, telling them this wasn't breaking and entering because technically the door was open. The trespassing charge, however, would be a little harder to argue.

No, this was an easy decision. I'd slip back outside the door and wait for whoever was in the shower to get out. I'd knock again, and this time Claire's source would hear me. It would be as if I'd never set foot in the room.

But as I turned to reach for the handle, I felt the squish beneath my shoe. The carpet was wet. Soaked, actually.

From there, it was all a blur.

Immediately, I slapped my hand blindly against the wall until I found the nearest light switch. The entryway lit up as I rushed into the bathroom, the water splashing up beneath my feet.

Again, I felt around for a light and found the switch. But it wasn't working. I couldn't see anything beyond shadows.

Reaching for my phone, I hit the flashlight app and waited for my eyes to adjust. When they did, I literally jumped back, almost tripping over myself.

Half his body was in the bathtub; the other half—his legs—dangled over the side. Also dangling was the cord of the hair dryer that was submerged in the water. It didn't take a genius to put it together. This was no accident. Claire's source had been murdered.

I took a step forward, the light from my phone edging up toward his face. It was like a grotesque freeze-frame of the electrocution. Every muscle contracted, his mouth ovaled as if midscream. The stuff of nightmares.

I knew what I was supposed to do next. It was what all the stupid characters in movies somehow decide not to do right before things spiral hopelessly out of control. *Go to the police.* In the big scheme of things, it didn't matter how or why I was there in that room.

As a forensic psychologist once told me in a deposition, with a slow nod of his bearded chin, "A dead body changes everything."

Problem was, all I could really think about in that moment was Claire. Whatever story she was chasing, it was the kind someone else didn't want told. *Really* didn't want told.

And just like that, the random act of violence that had ended her life—a taxi robbery—didn't seem so random.

CHAPTER 13

THE NEXT thing I knew, I was holding off a minute on calling the police.

Yes, it was a crime scene. Yes, I was aware I shouldn't be touching the victim. But I was in that hotel to find out whom Claire had been coming to see, and I still didn't know. Right or wrong, the answer was only a few feet away.

Angling my phone near the sink, I spotted and grabbed a face towel to prevent my leaving any fingerprints as I turned off the shower. I knelt down at the edge of the bathtub and began looking for a wallet, or anything else that would ID the guy. One hand was still holding my phone for light, the other searching his pockets. It would've been a lot easier if he hadn't been wearing jeans.

The front two pockets didn't turn up anything except perhaps a measure of guilt. Most of Claire's sources were people doing the "right thing" in one way or another. Whistle-blowing on corruption, setting the record straight, things like that. Some of them risked their lives in doing so. Now here was one, it seemed, who'd paid the ultimate price.

Until I searched his back pockets.

At first, I thought it was his wallet I was feeling. It wasn't, but it was certainly a form of ID. Even drenched and bunched in a ball as it was, I knew right away what I was holding in my hand. A ski mask. Looked like the same one from the taxi surveillance video.

This wasn't the guy Claire had been going to see.

This was the guy who killed her.

All at once, the rest of the pieces came together before my eyes. Underneath the guy's gray sweatshirt was the same black turtleneck I'd seen in the video. There was also a black baseball cap on the tile floor next to the tub.

There was no doubt this was him, whoever he was, and all I could think of, all I wanted to do in that very instant, was to bring him back to life just so I could kill him again myself.

I'd never known such a feeling. Vengeance was an abstraction to me, the melodramatic word that always seemed a bit too much. Now it wasn't nearly enough. *Where have you taken me, Claire?*

I stood up, looking at the cord of the hair dryer knotted around the towel bar. The tub had been full, the water running. As a plan, it was brilliant in its simplicity. Claire's source had known he was in danger, and had known enough to turn the tables. Damn good for him. Now if I only knew where he'd gone.

Claire would've been all over me for assuming that only a guy would've had the wherewithal to outwit a killer, and she would've been right. He could've easily been a she.

Any proof either way, though, was nowhere to be found as I searched the rest of the room. It was spotless. The two queen beds were made, the wastebasket was empty, nothing had been disturbed. Except for the dead guy in the bathtub, of course. *Now* it was time to call the police.

But before I could even reach for my phone again, I suddenly had a brand-new problem. It was the distinct sound of things about to spiral hopelessly out of control.

Someone was knocking on the door.

CHAPTER 14

THE FIRST thing I did was freeze. There was no second thing. At least, not right away. I had no idea what to do.

Instead, it was all about what not to do. There was no way I was opening that door. No way I was asking, "Who's there?"

But I did need to know. If it was anyone from the hotel, they weren't necessarily going away if no one answered.

About twenty feet of that beige carpet separated me from the door, the final few feet drenched with water. I had to time it just right.

Quickly, I tiptoed right up to the door of the bathroom. Then I waited. I couldn't cover up the squishing sound of my last footsteps on my own. It would take some help, and I knew it was coming.

The second knock on the door—even louder than the first—was all I needed to get right up next to the peephole. I held my breath and took a fast look before peeling off to the side.

Damn. There were two possibilities. One, the peephole was somehow broken. Two, it was working just fine.

Either way, all I could see was black. As I reached over and oh-so-silently swung the door guard closed, I was betting my entire stack on the perfectly working peephole...and a hand in the hallway placed over it.

Ten seconds passed. Twenty. Half a minute. I remained with my back plastered against the wall, inches away from the hinges, hoping the next thing I'd hear would be footsteps fading away toward the elevator.

If only.

It was more like the exact opposite as the sound of the key card sliding into the lock was followed by a click and a beep. The door opened, only to be stopped short by the door guard. Little hard to pretend no one was in the room now.

I waited for the voice of hotel security, or at least someone who worked at the hotel. Anyone. I didn't care. Let it be room service or housekeeping. My mouth was half open, ready to respond to whatever was said. But nothing was. *What's taking so long?*

No, wait...a far more pressing question.

What's that smell?

CHAPTER 15

IT WAS straight out of an Ian Fleming novel, something Q would've given 007. Jutting through the two-inch opening in the door was what looked at first glance like a common pair of pliers. The only difference being what they were doing, literally melting the metal loop of the door guard. Silently, no less.

This wasn't someone from the hotel.

A starter's pistol went off in my head, but I had nowhere to run. I looked over at the windows, which didn't open, and the bed I'd be a fool to hide under. Ditto for the one and only closet as I pictured myself trying to duck behind a hotel robe. The ultimate indignity. *Dying while stupid.*

The only real shot I had was erecting the world's quickest wall of furniture. Basically, I'd lodge everything in the room that wasn't bolted down against the door. It could work. It had to work. Question was, how much time did I have left?

I stared back at the door, those pliers cutting through the

metal as the smell of sulfur continued to overwhelm the air. I had to step back just so I wouldn't cough.

As I slid along the wall, it was my hand that felt it first—the connecting door to the next room. My eyes had passed right by it, and I couldn't blame them. Countless times, if only for shits and giggles, I'd been in a hotel room and opened the first door, only to see the door behind it, leading to the adjoining room, staring back at me, shut tight as a drum and locked. Here goes nothing…

I opened the door on my side, peeking around the edge, and in one, beautiful skip of a heartbeat, it was as if Al Michaels were broadcasting my life instead of the US men's Olympic hockey team. "Do you believe in miracles? *Yes!*"

The second door—the door that was never open, not ever—showed a sliver of daylight, or whatever kind of light was coming through from the other side. Given the odds I was beating, it might as well have been the burning bush.

As silently as I could, I slipped into the adjoining room, closing both doors behind me and locking the one now facing me. I knew immediately I wasn't barging in on anyone. The room was empty, with a neatly made king bed and no luggage lying around. I peeked into the bathroom. No dead body, either.

Let's keep it that way, I thought.

My first instinct was to strip down to my boxers, crawl beneath the sheets, and simply play dumb should there be a knock on the door. I'd answer it while rubbing the sleep from my eyes and convince whoever owned those magic pliers that I was nothing more than an innocent bystander. A pissed-off one at that, for having been woken up.

There was just one problem. *Who the hell flipped the door guard shut in the other room? The guy in the bathtub?*

No, I had to get out of this room, too. Too risky, otherwise. And again, I had to time it just right.

Listening through the walls, I paced and waited. It was like a surreal game of musical doors instead of chairs, and it would've been funny if I hadn't been so pessimistic about the penalty for losing.

Finally, the sound came. The door opening in the next room, and more importantly, the same door closing. That was my cue. As quietly as I could, I slipped back into the hallway. To hell with the elevator. The stairs were right there, and I didn't have to wait for them. I was out of there, lickety-split. At least, I should've been.

I couldn't help myself, though. As I passed the door to room 1701, I stopped and listened. I could hear a guy's voice. At first, I thought he was talking to someone else in the room, that he hadn't come alone. Then he made it clear he had. He was talking on a phone or some kind of radio.

"The kid's still alive," he said. "I repeat, the kid is still alive."

CHAPTER 16

I DIDN'T need any added incentive for what I planned to do next, but there she was anyway as I walked as casually as possible through the lobby of the Lucinda and out to the street.

The same wary-eyed woman behind the front desk wearing a turquoise blazer watched me step by step. Still, she didn't say a word. That would change, of course, once she learned of the dead body in the bathtub seventeen floors up. She'd have plenty to say then, a description of me sure to be included.

"Did you notice anything or anyone out of the ordinary?" the crime scene detectives would ask her. With the help of Forensics, they would've already determined the time of death as during her shift, and quite possibly between the times I came and left.

Safely down the block, I dialed my own crime scene detective. As they say in both PR and politics, *always get ahead of the story.*

"Wait, slow down," said Detective Lamont from behind his

desk. I could hear him through the phone shuffling papers, probably moving Claire's file back in front of him.

I apologized. I was getting *too* far ahead of the story, talking a million words a minute. My heartbeat, still racing, was acting like a metronome for my mouth.

I stopped, took a deep breath, and began again to detail what had happened since I shook his hand on my way out of the Midtown North precinct house. "Talk to you soon," Lamont had told me. He'd had no idea just how soon.

I could tell now that I was trying his patience. The fact that Claire had left my apartment to go see a source did nothing to challenge what he knew—or, at least, thought he knew—to be true: that she was in the wrong place at the wrong time in the back of that taxi.

And why *wouldn't* he believe that? I certainly had. The incident was designed that way, caught on video for all to see.

I told him about the phone call Claire had received, and how I'd figured out the address.

Lamont interrupted me. "Where are you going with all this?" he asked, wanting me to move the story along.

"To the Lucinda Hotel," I answered.

"Hurry up and get there."

I couldn't blame the guy. It was late and he was tired. But I knew all would be forgiven with one sentence about room 1701.

"The guy in the bathtub is the guy who killed Claire," I said.

I could literally hear him sit bolt upright in his chair.

"Where are you right now?" he asked. No, *demanded.*

"Eighth Avenue and Thirty-Fourth."

"Don't move, I'll have it radioed right now. A cruiser will be there shortly," he said. "I'll meet you at the hotel."

"Hold on, there's one more thing," I said.

I was back to talking a million words a minute as I tried to explain the guy with the magic pliers. The more I listened to myself, the more I realized how crazy it must sound to Lamont. If it did, though, he didn't let on. Instead, he cut to the chase, the only thing that mattered at the moment.

"Good guy or bad guy?" he asked.

"Bad guy," I said.

He paused for a moment. "Aren't they all?"

Click.

CHAPTER 17

FROM THE moment I first got the call from Claire's sister, Ellen, so much had changed, and then changed again. Still, in some ways, I couldn't help thinking I was right back where I'd started. With more questions than answers.

The kid is still alive.

As I waited for the cruiser courtesy of Lamont, I kept repeating the line in my head. It couldn't literally be a kid, could it? I didn't think so, but anything was possible. The night so far was a testament to that, and here we were rolling into the next day.

A few minutes later, I caught a flash of red and blue lights out of the corner of my eye. I turned to see my escorts pulling up along the curb on Eighth Avenue. The officer riding shotgun stepped out. He looked like a very young version of Kiefer Sutherland, albeit on some serious steroids. The guy was ripped and he knew it. Had the sleeves on his uniform been rolled up any higher, he would've officially been wearing a tank top.

"Trevor Mann?" he asked.

"Yeah."

He nodded at the door to the backseat. "Let's go."

I climbed in and answered a rapid-fire succession of questions from him while his partner, a guy who didn't resemble any actor I knew, took the turn onto Thirty-Fourth Street, driving slowly toward the front of the Lucinda.

Basically, I was confirming everything I'd told Lamont. The room number. The guy in the bathtub. The other guy who still might be in the room.

"And this other guy, you never actually saw him?" asked the officer.

"No, I just heard him through the door."

"What did he sound like? Black? White? Hispanic?"

"White," I said.

He turned to his partner behind the wheel and smirked. "Shoot the white guy."

They both chuckled as we pulled up in front of the hotel. Engine off, battery on. I reached for the door handle, thinking I was going inside with them. Silly me.

"Stay here," I was told.

It made sense. Of the three of us, I was the only one who didn't have a 9mm pistol strapped to my belt. Besides, I was happy never to set foot inside the Lucinda again.

"Do me a favor, though," I said. "Could you turn off the flashers?"

The cop behind the wheel smiled and nodded. He understood. There might not have been a lot of foot traffic on the cusp of dawn, but there was still no need for me to look like a perp sitting in the backseat. Off went the flashers.

The two disappeared into the hotel as I did my best to keep my eyes open. I was exhausted, my lack of sleep suddenly crashing down on me. Point being, I had no idea how much time had passed when I was jolted awake by the sound of knuckles rapping on the window. Kiefer's doppelganger was waving for me to join him on the curb.

I stepped out, glancing quickly at his name plate. OFFICER BOWMAN, it read. The moment seemed to suggest that it was time I knew that.

"Was the other guy in the room gone?" I asked.

He nodded. It was the way he nodded, though. There was something else, more to it.

"How long did you wait before you called this in?" he asked.

"I didn't wait," I said. "It was right away."

He nodded again. The same kind of nod.

"Follow me," he said.

CHAPTER 18

SO MUCH for my never setting foot in the Lucinda again.

I followed Officer Bowman through the lobby, where his partner was questioning—who else?—the wary-eyed woman in the turquoise blazer behind the front desk. I kept waiting for her to glare at me as we passed by, but it didn't happen.

On the ride up in the elevator, I kept waiting for Bowman to give some clue about what was going on. But that didn't happen, either.

We walked the long, beige hallway in silence, and as we reached the door of room 1701, he stepped inside first and immediately spun around to look at me. Only in hindsight did I realize what he was doing. Gauging my reaction.

I turned and stared into the bathroom, my jaw literally dropping. *It was as if nothing had happened.*

The light was working. The hair dryer was unplugged and sitting on the shelf beneath the sink, the cord neatly wound. There wasn't a drop of water on the floor or in the tub.

Also not in the tub? The guy who killed Claire. He was gone.

I stared back at Bowman, who was still watching me like I was a science experiment, or more accurately, a science experiment with the title "Is This Man Telling the Truth?"

"You don't seriously think I've made this up, do you?" I asked.

"Of course not," he said. "That would make you crazy."

Of course, the way he said it made clear that he was leaving the door open. Speaking of which . . .

"You did notice the sheared-off door guard behind me, right?" I asked. I certainly had as I walked in.

Bowman nodded. "Yep, saw it," he said. "I can also feel the squish beneath my feet. The carpet's definitely wet."

He left it at that. I knew what he was thinking, though, if only because I was thinking the same thing. There was no dead body in the bathtub, and the combination of a sheared-off door guard and some wet carpet didn't prove there ever had been.

"They must have moved the body and cleaned up afterward," I said.

"*They?*"

"I heard only one voice through the door, but that doesn't mean there was only one person."

"You're right, it doesn't," said Bowman before checking his watch. "And about how much time would they have had to do this?"

"Apparently enough."

But even I was doing the math in my head. Ten minutes. Fifteen, tops. I looked back into the bathroom at the neatly folded dry towels, and especially the dry floor. In addition to the magic pliers, was there also a magic mop?

I could see how Bowman or anyone else would be a bit skeptical. That didn't concern me. Truth was, it didn't matter

64

how it'd been done. It had been done. Quickly. Quietly. Professionally. And that combination could mean only one thing. The story that Claire was working on was getting bigger by the minute.

The kid is still alive.

The words were echoing again in my head. Someone had checked into this room and maybe even the room next to it. All I could look at now was the other thing strapped to Bowman's belt besides a pistol. His radio.

"Your partner downstairs," I said. "Did he get the name of who was staying in this room?"

"Yeah, he got a name," came a voice from behind me. I knew right away it wasn't Bowman's partner.

I turned to see Detective Lamont. Quite the sight. His glasses were askew, his tie loosened to the point of looking like a noose. His suit jacket, meanwhile, had more creases than an unfolded piece of origami.

Still, for a guy so disheveled, he somehow maintained an aura of complete control. You can't fake experience.

After silently studying the sheared-off door guard for a few seconds, Lamont stepped past me, gazing inside the bathroom as if confirming what he'd already been told in the lobby. There was no dead guy in the tub.

All the while, I was waiting for him to say the name of whoever it was who'd been staying in the room. He didn't.

"Is it supposed to be some kind of secret?" I finally asked. I couldn't help the sarcasm.

"No," said Lamont, bending down to touch the wet carpet. "No secret. It's just not his real name, that's all."

"How do you know?"

He stood up, looking at me for the first time. "Because I graduated high school in 1984."

"What's that supposed to mean?" asked Bowman. "Besides the fact that you're old."

Lamont ignored him. He was also ignoring the notepad clutched in his hand, suggesting that he'd never even bothered to write down the name.

Instead, he simply recited it, as if from memory. "*Winston Smith.*"

Bowman looked at both of us and shrugged. I looked at Lamont and nodded.

"You're right," I said. "That's not his real name."

CHAPTER 19

"WHY CAN'T Winston Smith be his real name?" asked Bowman.

"It's from a book," said Lamont, straightening his glasses with a professorial nudge. Class was in session. "George Orwell's *1984*. Everyone in my high school had to read it that year. They practically made us memorize it. The name of the main character was Winston Smith."

Bowman shrugged again. "What? So no one else can have that name?"

"They could, but Winston Smith was supposed to represent Everyman," I said. I caught Lamont's eyes and cracked a smile. "It was a few years later, but I read it in high school, too."

"Good for you both," said Bowman, getting his Bronx up. "I wasn't even born in 1984."

I was really starting to dislike this guy. "Anyway," I said, "Winston Smith is simply a more clever version of John Doe."

"Not to mention that our Mr. Smith also paid in cash for this room and the one next door," said Lamont.

As if having prompted himself, he took a walk through the connecting doors to look at the other room. He was back within seconds.

"Do me a favor, Bowman," he said. "Give Mr. Mann and me a few minutes, will you?"

Bowman was more than happy to oblige. "I'll be in the lobby," he said.

As he walked out, Lamont closed the door behind him. He turned and made a beeline for the minibar fridge, grabbing a Diet Coke.

"What do you think they charge for this?" he asked, digging a fingernail under the tab. He popped open the can with a loud snap and grinned. "I guess we'll just have to put it on Mr. Smith's bill."

After taking a long sip, he stepped back and settled into the armchair in the corner. He was in no rush, and whether or not that was calculated I didn't know. He surely had questions for me. I just didn't expect his first one to be the same one I had.

"So what happens now?" he asked.

"I'm not sure what you mean," I said.

"Well, I know what *I* need to do," he said, pointing at his chest. "I need to eyeball all the exits and hope that the security cameras aimed at them were actually recording. I also need to get a description of our Mr. Smith from the clerk who actually checked him in, since the beady-eyed woman downstairs told me it wasn't her."

He was right. I had the wrong word. The woman at the front desk was more beady-eyed than wary-eyed.

Lamont paused, taking another sip. "Then maybe, just maybe, we can start piecing this whole thing together. Because until then, we've got a little problem."

Yes, we did, and he didn't need to spell it out. I'd learned it in law school; he'd learned it at the police academy.

No body? No crime.

"So, like I said, what happens now?" he asked. "What do *you* need to do?"

"You mean, besides getting some sleep?"

"That's a good start," he said. "But yeah, besides that."

I was stalling because I had no idea what he was getting at. Of course, that was his point.

"You tried to trace Claire's footsteps tonight and look where it got you," he said.

"I know her killer is dead, don't I?"

"Yes, and if it wasn't for those dumb doors being open to the next room, you could've been next."

"Is this your way of saying *let us do our jobs?* "

Lamont winced. "God, I hope not. They only say that on cop shows. What I'm saying is this: *Stop trying to do hers.*"

I was about to shake my head, tell him he was off base. No, worse. Delusional. Like Donald Trump with a comb.

But Lamont knew that was coming and was way ahead of me. He'd already reached into his pocket and was now holding it in the air, Exhibit A.

"Where the hell did you get that?" I asked.

He broke into a smile, and as he did, I could practically see the canary feathers caught in his teeth.

"Did I mention you're a lousy liar, Mr. Mann?"

CHAPTER 20

LAMONT WAS holding Claire's cell phone, the old Motorola she used strictly for her sources.

The Stopper.

"Why didn't you say anything back at the precinct?" he asked.

"I wasn't sure that was what she was doing," I said.

"Still, what the hell were you planning? Hop the fence later this afternoon at the Whitestone Pound and search behind the backseat?"

"It was really there, huh?"

"The second you wanted to watch that part of the recording again, I knew you saw her do something," said Lamont.

"Only I didn't know it was her phone she was hiding."

"You know why she would, though, don't you?"

He had me dead to rights on everything, right down to my waiting until the taxi had been cleared by Forensics, then shrink-wrapped and flatbedded from Lamont's precinct to, yes, the Whitestone Pound in Queens, where it would eventually be claimed by whoever owned the medallion for it.

The only part the detective got wrong was the timing. Screw the afternoon. Way too risky. Criminal trespassing is better left for the dark, no? I wasn't planning on hopping that fence until well after midnight.

"She was just protecting her sources," I said. "That phone was for them exclusively."

With that, I cocked my head, and he immediately shook his. He knew what I was about to ask.

"Counselor, we both know I can't turn it over to you, at least not yet," he said. "Pretty damn impressive, though, her presence of mind. Even in that moment…wanting to shield them." He flipped open the phone. "Of course, I can see why. There are a lot of boldfaced names in the directory, at least those I could decipher. Most were just listed by initials."

"Was there a W.S., by any chance?"

"No such luck," he said, pointing at the table between the two beds. Winston Smith had called from the phone in the room.

The kid was still alive, and we still had no way of contacting him.

Like a kick in the head, though, it occurred to me. What about the people who wanted to kill him? What about contacting them?

I took out my own phone, quickly sending an anonymous text to a number I knew by heart.

Lamont's eyes narrowed to a suspicious squint. "What are you doing?" he asked.

Something you're definitely not going to like, Detective.

CHAPTER 21

ONE GOOD setup deserved another. Only mine had to be better, because I'd already discovered theirs.

Less than three hours later, I was sitting on one of the concrete benches lining the perimeter of Bethesda Terrace by the Lake in Central Park. I'd tried to get a little sleep beforehand back in the spare bedroom at my apartment, but it was impossible. Closing my eyes just seemed to magnify everything, if that makes any sense.

In my lap now was a Nikon D4, the 300mm lens peeking out beneath the bottom of the *Daily News*. With the weather warm and breezy and no clouds in sight, I couldn't have asked for a more picture-perfect day.

About thirty yards in front of me was the famous fountain known as the *Angel of the Waters*, the lily being held in the bronze statue's left hand representing the purity of the circular pool around her. Claire had told me that. I suspected it was why I'd chosen the location. That, and the crowds of people. There were joggers passing by, locals sipping coffee and hanging out, even some early-bird tourists looking in their guidebooks or just looking lost. All in all, safety in numbers.

Claire had cleverly hidden the Stopper behind her seat in the taxi, but her other two phones had been in her purse, which had disappeared with her killer. He sure didn't have it when he showed up dead in the tub at the Lucinda. Question was, who had the phones now?

I'd sent the text to Claire's BlackBerry, the phone provided and paid for by the *Times*. I was posing as a confidant— someone she knew and trusted—and as roles go, it was hardly a stretch. The tough part, in every sense, was acting as if she were still alive. Timing was everything. The text had to be sent before her death had made the morning news. Same thing for the meeting.

R u up yet? Need to c u asap. Think kid might be telling u the truth. Meet me in park, far end of Bethesda Fount at 9. Something to show u.

Ten minutes later, after I'd left the Lucinda, the reply came. A text from Claire's BlackBerry.

Ok, c u there.

Even if Claire had still been alive, I would've known the reply wasn't from her. She hated the shorthand of texting, countless times complaining to me that it was dumbing down kids and adults alike. Not only would she never use shorthand, but she made fun of me whenever I did.

Ok, see you there, she would've typed. Not a vowel or consonant less.

Either way, the time and place had been set. All that was left was the guest list. My end was simple. It was just me.

I could've told Lamont about it, but that would've changed everything.

Police detectives might not have the equivalent of a Hippocratic oath, but there was no way Lamont would've allowed me to set this trap alone. He'd either have to handcuff me to a large inanimate object far from the park or be right next to me by the fountain. Most definitely with backup.

That was the difference, really. Why I hadn't told him. His job was to arrest people for what they did, not *why* they did it. If I had involved him, he'd immediately have brought this person in for questioning. Possession of stolen goods, at the bare minimum, with an eye toward accessory to murder.

Or was it accessories? Who knew who could show up, or how many? That was their end of the guest list.

So I had to be patient. Take pictures. Not take them in for questioning. Be their shadow. Identify them, follow them, and figure out the *why*. Because if you want to get some real answers from people, the last thing you do is let them know you're watching them.

I pulled back my shirtsleeves, checking my watch. Two minutes after nine. As much as I didn't know who I was looking for, I knew it wasn't the elderly man and woman deep in conversation who'd been sitting by the far side of the fountain since I'd arrived.

Turning the page of the *Daily News* spread between my hands, I continued to pretend to read. Through dark sunglasses, I kept peeking above the paper, my eyes scanning for anyone who might be approaching, or at least looking in the direction of, the elderly couple on the bench.

The minutes kept ticking away. No one looked suspicious or out of place. Then again, neither did I. Or so I thought.

I was about to check the time again when I felt the quick,

short vibration of my cell. It was an incoming text. Only it wasn't from Claire's phone. In fact, I didn't know whose phone it was from. The sender was anonymous.

Get out of there! it read.

But it was too late.

CHAPTER 22

HE CAME out of nowhere. A man wearing sunglasses even darker than mine, walking around the curve of the fountain and heading straight toward me.

Not fast. Not slow. Just walking. The click of his heels with each step now the only sound in the world.

How had I missed him?

He was dressed in a dark suit with an open-collared white shirt. He looked to be in his thirties. Short-cropped blond hair and in good shape. I couldn't see his eyes behind those sunglasses, but I had little doubt they weren't aimed at anyone else. I could literally feel his stare.

Or was it just the rush of fear shooting up my spine?

Suddenly, I didn't know what to do with any part of my body. My feet were stuck to the ground, my hands frozen and locked in the air, the newspaper pinched between my fingertips feeling as heavy as one of those lead blankets they cover you with before an X-ray.

He had a newspaper, too.

I didn't see it at first, the way it was tucked neatly under his left arm. Now it was all I could look at. There was something about it, how it was folded so tightly as if there was something... *shit.*

Inside it.

His right arm was a blur as it swung across his body, his hand outstretched with his fingers spread. All at once, his left arm loosened, the paper holster sliding down to his elbow while beginning to open. The way he caught the gun in midair, I was instantly sure of two things. One, he'd done this before. And two, I was simply done.

It's not true what they say. You don't see your life flash before your eyes. You see your death. In slow motion, no less.

He'd come to a complete stop, ten merciless feet in front of me, with the *Angel of the Waters* rising up behind him. But she wasn't looking my way.

Others were, though. There was a woman screaming to my left, her high pitch and volume sending nearby pigeons scattering in the air. To my right, there was the sound of feet scampering, someone literally running for his life. *Gun! Gun! Gun!*

I heard it all. Still, I couldn't move.

His arm began to unfold, the barrel of the gun lining up with my head. It was the only thing I could see. Until, out of nowhere, there was something else.

It was another blur, I couldn't see what exactly. More importantly, neither could my executioner. He was being blindsided, someone tackling him at full speed.

Like a linebacker.

CHAPTER 23

I WATCHED as both bodies slammed against the pavement and rolled, a tumble of arms and legs hurtling over and over. I couldn't tell who was who, but I was convinced I knew one of them. *Lamont!* It had to be him.

But it wasn't. As the bodies separated, both sprawling on the ground, I could tell this guy was younger. He was at least half the detective's age. And not nearly as big.

Big enough, though. I certainly wasn't complaining.

He pushed himself up, standing quickly, if not a little wobbly. "The gun!" he barked, pointing.

I hadn't seen it go flying, but there it was, matte black against the terra cotta of the Roman bricks around the fountain. It was closer to me than to him. As for the gun's original owner, he was somewhere in between and staring right at it.

Then at me.

Then right back at the gun.

It was up for grabs.

I sprang from the bench into a headfirst dive while my camera, launched from my lap, shattered to pieces. Scooping up the gun, I whipped my arm and locked both elbows, and dammit if the view wasn't so much better from this angle.

"Stay down!" I yelled, jabbing the barrel of his Beretta M9 straight at his chest. With its fifteen-round staggered box magazine, he and I both knew I could remind him over and over who had the upper hand.

Yeah, I knew guns. I knew them well. Ever since my high school days at Valley Forge Military Academy. I shot them, cleaned them, took them apart and put them back together again. Even once while naked, blindfolded, and being blasted by a power washer during the school's version of Hell Week.

I *hated* guns.

"Call nine-one-one," I said with a quick glance at the guy who'd saved my life. Man, did he look young. He was practically a kid. Hell, he *was* a kid. He was also way ahead of me, his cell already in hand.

"On it," he said.

I could hear him perfectly amid the hush that had fallen over the terrace and the fountain. Never had so many New Yorkers been so quiet all at once. I could feel them, though, as they began peeking out from whatever they were ducking behind, at least those who didn't have the camera lenses from their cell phones trained on me. I was about to trend mightily on YouTube.

All the while, I kept my eyes fixed on the man on the ground, hoping he wouldn't even blink until the police arrived. Turned out, his gun wasn't the only thing that had gone flying when he was tackled. Gone, too, were his sunglasses. Good thing.

If he'd still had them on, I would never have known about his partner.

CHAPTER 24

IT WASN'T much of a poker face. In fact, if anything, I could've sworn he cracked the slightest of smiles the second he glanced over my shoulder.

Following his eyes, I quickly turned to see the only person in the crowd who was actually running *toward* us—a second guy in great shape sporting short-cropped hair and apparently the de rigueur wardrobe among the assassin set. Dark suit, white shirt, open collar . . . and a semiautomatic handgun.

So much for my having the upper hand.

He was racing down the farther of the two massive stair-cases that connected Bethesda Terrace to the Seventy-Second Street Cross Drive. Fifty yards away and gaining. Fast. He might as well have been Moses, the way people were parting for him. Wielding a deadly weapon has a funny way of doing that.

"C'mon, let's go!" said the kid.

The kid.

The way he'd said it, as if there weren't even a decision, it all clicked. He was Claire's source. He was the one at the Lucinda. He was what this was all about—even though I still had no idea what this was really all about. Except that this was him. The kid.

"C'mon," he repeated. *"Let's go!"*

He took off, hurdling the concrete bench where I'd been sitting. He was sprinting across the lawn, heading for the cover of the trees lining the Lake. I didn't need any more prompting to follow him, but it came anyway with the crack of a single shot splitting the air. People and pigeons were scattering all over again.

I might have been the only other one with a gun, but the bullet wasn't intended for me. Assassin #2 was aiming for the kid and nearly got him, the divot of grass flying up a mere foot to his left as he ran. There was a better-than-good chance the guy wasn't going to miss twice . . . unless I did something.

Hopping over the concrete bench, I didn't run right away. Instead, I spun around, crouched, and let go with a few rounds. Then a few more. Not at him, though.

You still smiling, buddy?

The guy on the ground had seemed all too pleased to stay there and watch me sweat, but as I sprayed a circle of bullets around him, he was quick to find the fetal position. Even quicker was his partner, who got the message. From a full sprint he stopped on a dime, lowering the gun to his side.

I was about to tell him to lay it on the ground and back away. Problem was, I didn't have much of a plan from there. I was just buying time, and only a few extra seconds at that. As soon as he stepped back, I was taking off, and then we'd see how fast we both could run.

That was when I glanced up and saw her.

There she was, the *Angel of the Waters*, perched high in the air and watching. *Now* she was looking out for me, and her plan was a hell of a lot better.

I jerked my head at the fountain. I didn't need to explain. In fact, I didn't say another word. All I did was keep aiming where I was aiming.

Maybe I have it in me to shoot your asshole partner, or maybe I don't. But do you really want to take the chance?

My two would-be killers exchanged glances, the one on the ground nodding somewhat helplessly at the one with the gun. He nodded back. Then—*plop!*—he tossed it into the fountain.

One Mississippi, two Mississippi, three...

I was waiting until the count was ten, long enough for the barrel to fill with water. Would it still fire? Sure. But first he'd have to fish it out and shake it dry, and even then the compression would be off. And as for me?

Eight Mississippi, nine Mississippi, ten...

I was off and running.

Sprinting for my life across the open stretch of grass, I could feel my lungs on fire. Only when I reached the trees did I look back for the first time, relieved as hell to see they weren't chasing after me.

Still, I kept running. Fear of the unknown, partly, and the rest hoping I could find the kid. But he was nowhere to be found. Until, that is, I felt the quick vibration of my phone again. It was another text from him.

Last 4 of ur SS#

I knew right away what he was doing—making sure it was really me who had my phone. He obviously hadn't hung around to see how things played out back at the fountain. Couldn't blame him. But I also couldn't figure out how he would know my Social Security number. Just add that to the litany of questions I had for him.

I texted back the last four digits, and within seconds he responded with a location where we should meet. Finally, I was going to get some answers.

Careful what you wish for . . .

CHAPTER 25

I DIDN'T look around the street before opening the door to the Oak Tavern on Seventy-Fourth off Broadway, but I knew he was watching me from behind some stoop or parked car, or more accurately, watching to see if anyone was following me. The kid wasn't dumb. That was why he was still alive. That was why we were both still alive.

So this guy walks into a bar with a Beretta M9 tucked under his shirt...

Most New Yorkers can tell you that last call in the city is 4 a.m. Far fewer of them can tell the flip side—first call, the time at which a bar can legally start serving. It's 8 a.m. I knew it only as trivia.

For sure, the four guys scattered along the stools, who didn't even bother to glance my way as I approached the bartender, knew it as a way of life.

"Double Johnnie Black, rocks," I ordered.

The fact that I was having whiskey for breakfast didn't seem nearly as relevant as my having just had a gun aimed at my head. Drinking to numb the pain of Claire's death was one thing; drinking to settle an entire body of frayed nerves was another.

The bartender, tall and thin and hunched with age, nodded, completely expressionless, before heading off to grab the bottle. He might as well have had a sign hanging around his neck that read NO JUDGMENTS.

Waiting for him to return, I looked around a bit. Fittingly, the Oak Tavern was a genuine throwback, not the kind of place that hung reproduction crap on the wall to imitate a time gone by.

Instead, what hung on the wall was actual crap and old as shit. Signed photos of D-list celebrities from the seventies. A painting of a horse that looked as if it had been bought at one of those hotel art fairs off the highway. And right next to it, a coatrack missing half its pegs.

Genuine as well was the musty smell of the place. I could practically feel the dust traveling up my nose with each breath.

"Five fifty," said the bartender, standing in front of me again and pouring.

I gave him seven, picked up my glass, and headed for the rear of the tavern and a row of booths. They were those classic highback ones, the crimson leather so worn and cracked it looked like a marbleized porterhouse. I slid into the last booth on the left, beyond the line of sight from the bar.

A few minutes later, the kid arrived.

As he walked toward me, I noticed that almost everything about him was a contradiction. He was skinny, with unusually broad shoulders. He had disheveled hair and slacker clothes and was staring ahead with the most focused eyes I'd ever seen. His gait was slow and deliberate, and yet his hands couldn't keep still. He was rubbing them together as if they were under some imaginary faucet.

The kid sat down across from me without saying a word. No introduction. No offer of a handshake, either, lest one of those hands of his might actually have to stop moving while waiting to grip mine. Finally, he spoke.

"Sorry for all this," he said.

That was the biggest contradiction of all, as far as I was concerned. "For what?" I asked. "You saved my life."

"I'm the only reason it was ever in danger, dude."

"We'll get to that in a moment," I said. "That, and whether I'm really going to let you call me *dude*. But speaking of names, what's yours? And don't say Winston Smith."

"It's Owen," he answered.

"And you already know mine, don't you? Among other things."

He nodded.

"Are you some kind of hacker?" I asked.

"It's not what I do for a living, if that's what you're wondering."

"Okay. What do you do for a living?"

But it was as if he hadn't heard me. Or, more likely, as if he needed to ask a few questions for himself before answering that one.

CHAPTER 26

"WHAT'S YOUR connection to Claire?"

"Close friend," I answered. It was a good enough explanation for the time being.

"Are you a reporter?"

"No."

"You don't work at the *Times*?"

"No."

He hesitated, reluctant to ask his next question. He needed to know, though, and I needed to tell him.

"She's dead, isn't she?" he asked.

"Yes," I answered.

I explained how it had happened. His head dropped. "It's my fault," he said. "Everything."

"Claire would've been the first to tell you that isn't true," I said. "And I'd be the second."

"How do you know?"

"Because I was with her before she went to meet you. This was her job, Owen. It's what she did."

"So you knew about me?"

I smiled. "No. Claire never discussed her sources. I don't even know how she found you."

"She didn't—I found her," he said. "I knew her work. That's why I called her."

"When was this?"

"She and I spoke two days ago," he said. "I was planning on coming up here next week."

"What changed?"

He reached into his pocket, taking out his iPhone. After a few taps, he handed it to me. On the screen was an obituary from the online edition of the *Sun Gazette* down in Virginia. "Dr. Stephen Hellerman, 48, Leading Neurologist," the headline read. A picture of a clean-cut, good-looking guy was underneath.

"Who's that?" I asked.

"My boss."

I leaned in, squinting to read the first few sentences. "'An early-morning home invasion'?"

"That's what it was made to look like. They shot him in the head. Then, last night, they almost got me, too."

"Who's *they*?"

"I'm not sure yet. I was hoping Claire could tell me."

Were we homing in, I wondered, or just going around in circles? "Why would she know?" I asked.

"The piece she wrote last year about the CIA black site in Poland."

I knew the article well, if only because Claire was in Warsaw for two weeks researching it, and missed my birthday. "The secret jail?"

"Yeah, in Stare Kiejkuty," he said with a perfect Polish accent. Impressive.

Stare Kiejkuty was a Polish intelligence-training site tucked away in a forest about two hours north of the capital. Claire got a guided tour of it from Polish officials, the key word being *guided*. As she described it, the whole purpose of the tour was to convince her the CIA wasn't using a spare room or two to interrogate suspected Muslim terrorists outside the reach of US legal protections.

"So you have actual proof that it's a CIA black site?" I asked.

The kid shook his head slowly. "No, what I have goes way beyond that," he said. *"Way beyond."*

CHAPTER 27

"DO YOU know the name Abdullah al-Hazim?" Owen asked.

"No," I said. "Should I?"

"He was thought to be the number two guy in Al Qaeda," he explained. "Of course, it's pretty silly how we imagine terrorist groups to be structured like our own government, with a neatly organized line of succession. Let's just say al-Hazim was one of the ringleaders based in Yemen."

"*Was?*"

"About a year ago, the State Department announced he'd been killed by a drone attack in the Shabwah province," Owen said. "If I'm not mistaken, the *Times* gave it two columns above the fold in the International section."

Two columns above the fold...

"You sound like Claire," I said. "There was the story, and then there was where the story was placed."

"In this case, though, the story was wrong."

"The guy's still alive?"

"No, al-Hazim is dead, all right. It just wasn't a drone attack that killed him."

With that, Owen slid out of the booth and joined me on my side. I didn't know what he was doing until he removed a small device from his pocket, attaching it to the Lightning dock on his iPhone. It was one of those tiny portable projectors. We were going to the movies.

The backrest of the bench where he'd been sitting became the screen. The video was black-and-white and as grainy as the leather of the booth, but it was clear enough to see what was happening…and to whom.

"That's al-Hazim in the chair," said Owen.

The Middle Eastern man was probably in his late thirties, with a short beard and rimless glasses. I was hardly an expert on body language, but this was an easy read. Al-Hazim was trying to act defiant but was clearly scared to death.

"This is from Stare Kiejkuty?" I asked.

"Yeah."

The room was average-sized and well lit, albeit with no windows I could see. The chair al-Hazim was shackled to—hands and feet—was the only furniture, at least in front of the camera. There were two male voices in the background speaking English, but I couldn't make out the conversation.

I turned to Owen. "What are they saying?"

"I haven't been able to make it out," he answered. "Keep watching, though."

I leaned forward for a quick peek toward the front of the tavern. I couldn't see anyone, and no one could see us; this was truly a private screening. If I hadn't been so intrigued, I would've been more aware of how surreal this all was, even by New York standards.

What the hell am I about to see? Torture? Some sort of confession? A combination of both? Or is it D, none of the above?

I kept watching. Seconds later, three men entered the picture. Two were in suits and ties, while the third was wearing a white medical smock. That man, presumably a doctor, was holding something as he approached al-Hazim.

"Is that a syringe?" I asked.

"Yes."

"He's not getting a flu shot, is he?"

Owen shook his head. "Nope."

CHAPTER 28

THE TWO men restrained al-Hazim, one of them gripping him in a headlock as the doctor swabbed the side of his neck with an alcohol pad. Quickly, the doctor injected the contents of the syringe into the carotid artery. All three then stepped out of frame.

As al-Hazim simply sat there as he had before, I was about to ask Owen what was going on. That was when I heard a man clearing his throat off camera. This sound, unlike the previous conversation, I could hear perfectly.

"What is your name?" the man asked.

Immediately, another voice off camera translated the question into Arabic. I hadn't suddenly learned the language—there were actually subtitles at the bottom of the frame. It was like a foreign film, albeit not the kind Claire and I would watch at the Angelika down in SoHo.

Al-Hazim didn't answer, and everything repeated itself. One voice asked the question again in English, the other translated it again in Arabic. And once again, al-Hazim didn't respond.

"Are you a member of Al Qaeda?" came the next question. The translation followed, along with the subtitles. Still, al-Hazim didn't say a word.

Then something strange started to happen. It was as if his chair had been electrified, although not with a sudden jolt. Rather, a slow build. His arms and legs began to shake, his face contorting. He was clearly feeling pain.

"Are you aware of any plans by Al Qaeda to kill American citizens?" came the third question, the interrogator's voice unchanged. It was calm, placid, even as al-Hazim began to shake uncontrollably as if he were having a violent seizure. He was in agony, and no one was laying a finger on him.

Meanwhile, the question was repeated—louder, finally, so as to be heard above the metal cuffs around his ankles and wrists, which were now clanking and rattling incessantly against the chair.

"Are you aware of any plans by Al Qaeda to kill American citizens?"

If he was, al-Hazim still wasn't saying. I wasn't sure he could even if he wanted to, at this point. His mouth was open as if to scream, but there was no sound coming out. His eyes rolled back. He looked possessed. There was no control, not anywhere. His jumpsuit darkened around his crotch and thighs. He was urinating on himself, if not defecating.

Suddenly, everything stopped. Like someone had pulled the plug. Al-Hazim collapsed in the chair, his body limp and lifeless.

The doctor in the white smock reappeared and placed two fingers on the neck, exactly where he'd administered the shot. He turned and shook his head to those behind the camera. His face was as expressionless as the bartender who had poured me my whiskey.

"Christ!" was all I could sputter at first. I was still staring at the opposite side of the booth and what was now just an empty white square being projected. It was all sinking in. Finally, I turned to Owen. "The syringe. Whatever was in it killed him, right?"

"Technically, no," he said.

"*Technically?*"

He folded his arms on the table. "What you just saw was actually a suicide."

CHAPTER 29

BEFORE I could ask what the hell that meant, Owen reached for his phone and began tapping the screen again. He was bringing up another video. It was a double feature.

"If this is the same thing with a different prisoner, I don't need to see it," I said.

"Just watch," said Owen.

He hit Play and positioned the phone again, the image beaming across the booth as it had before. Same room, same chair, different Middle Eastern man chained to it. His beard was slightly longer, and he didn't wear glasses.

The only other difference was that he filled out his jumpsuit more. He looked bloated, puffy where there might otherwise be edges.

Maybe for that reason alone, his blank stare didn't seem as determined.

The same three men entered the frame, the one in the white

smock administering the shot. As they retreated behind the camera, I was already bracing for what was to come.

It came. The man was asked his name in English, followed by Arabic, and he refused to answer, once and then twice. As with al-Hazim, the "symptoms" started.

"Are you a member of Al Qaeda?" came the next question, and again he refused to answer. But that was when things took a turn.

As his heavy body shook and convulsed, the man's face looked as if he were in a tug-of-war. He was trying to fight the pain, not give in to it, but as his teeth gnashed and the tendons in his neck stretched so tight I thought they would snap, he opened his mouth not to scream . . . but to talk.

"Yes," read the translation beneath him.

The voice of the interrogator resumed. So calmly, so eerily. "So you admit that you are a member of Al Qaeda?"

"Yes," the man repeated.

And no sooner had he done so than the shaking, the convulsing, the outright agony he was experiencing began to dissipate. Quickly, the interrogator followed up.

"Are you aware of any plans by Al Qaeda to kill American citizens?"

Seconds passed as the man remained silent—and motionless—in the chair. He was clearly deciding what to do, how to answer. His forehead was dripping sweat. He didn't have much time, and he knew it.

"No," he answered. "I don't know anything."

He tried to sell it, his eyes pleading desperately with everyone behind the camera to believe him. The room was silent for another few seconds . . . and then came the sound. The handcuffs, the ankle cuffs—they began to rattle against the chair. His faced seized up, his dark eyes practically popping out of his head. Everything was starting all over, only faster and more severe.

"Yes!" he screamed. In English, no less. "*Yes! Yes!* I know of plans..."

And for a second time, everything stopped. No more convulsing, no more pain. No more video, either. It ended abruptly.

Owen turned to me. "Go figure, huh? Of all things, it's the plans they didn't want recorded."

"How the hell did you get these?" I asked.

"It's a long story."

"I've got nothing but time."

"Yeah, that's what I used to think."

I got what he was saying. His life was never going to be the same. Maybe that was why he was eyeing my glass as I threw back the last of my whiskey.

"You want one?" I asked.

"No thanks," he said.

But it was the way he said it, like it wasn't even a possibility. "How old are you, by the way?"

"Nineteen."

"Are you in school?"

"No," he said. "I work."

"What do you do?"

"I design artificial neurological implants."

I stared at him blankly.

"Yeah, I know," he said. "But Subway wasn't hiring."

The kid definitely had a snarky streak. In a good way, though. Claire would've liked him.

He and I were all alone in the back of the Oak Tavern, everyone else out of earshot. Still, I couldn't help lowering my voice for what I was about to ask. It was just one of those kinds of questions. "Do you work for the CIA, Owen?"

He nodded at his phone. "Not anymore, I'm guessing."

"And those injections, what we just watched. Did you have something to do with that?"

"It depends."

"On what?"

"Whether you think the Wright Brothers had something to do with nine-eleven," he said. He slid out of my side of the booth and back into his before explaining. "I was working on artificial neurotransmitters for the human brain. I'm not a sap, I knew there were possible military applications. But I also knew that they were the cure for dozens of neurological diseases. Sometimes you just have to take the good with the bad."

"Until you saw the bad with your own eyes," I said.

"I was their missing link. They had isolated all the neurological changes, everything the brain does when we lie, but they didn't know how to manipulate it." He drew a deep breath, exhaling with regret well beyond his years. "I thought I was curing Alzheimer's."

The irony was inescapable. "They *lied* to you."

"No, not exactly," he said. "Those people in the recordings— the men in suits, the doctor—I don't even know who they are."

"But they know who you are, don't they? They know you wanted to go public, and now they want you dead and anyone else you might have told."

I leaned back, sinking into the booth as those last words of mine hung in the air for a few seconds. I'd said them thinking entirely about Claire.

That was when it dawned on me, the morning I'd had. I was leaving someone out of the proverbial risk pool. Me.

As if on cue, Owen tilted his head and, of all things, smiled. "Welcome to the club, dude."

BOOK TWO

STRANGER THAN FICTION

CHAPTER 30

BRETTON SAMUEL Morris, ten months into his first term as president of the United States, shook what remained of his bourbon and rocks, the springwater ice cubes rattling against the crystal of his favorite glass. *Tink-tinkity-tink.*

The glass, specially commissioned from Waterford and featuring an etched American flag on one side and a bald eagle on the other, had originally been a gift to Ronald Reagan from the president of Ireland, Patrick Hillery. In total, there were four glasses in the set, but after a visit to the White House by Boris Yeltsin a few years later, only three remained. The Russian leader notoriously couldn't hold his liquor, and since he was missing the thumb and forefinger on his left hand, he apparently couldn't hold the glass, either.

"What time is it?" asked the president, breaking the silence of the Oval Office. He was staring out the window by the east door, which led to the Rose Garden, his back turned to the only other people in the room, his two most trusted advisors.

Clay Dobson, the chief of staff, glanced at his watch. "It's approaching midnight, sir."

The president drew a deep breath and then exhaled. "Yeah, that figures...."

In less than twelve hours, the Senate confirmation hearing for Lawrence Bass to become the next director of Central Intelligence was scheduled to begin. With the extensive background check long since completed, confidence in the White House had been riding high. Since the days of George Tenet, no one dared use the phrase *slam dunk* anymore, but everyone was certainly thinking it.

Bass, the current director of intelligence programs with the NSC, did not keep highly classified information on his unsecured home computer; he did not belong to an all-white country club; he drank socially, and sparingly at that; he paid Social Security taxes for his Guatemalan housekeeper; he did not secretly like to dress up in women's clothing; and he did not have a thing for little girls. Or, for that matter, little boys. Lawrence Bass, the early-to-bed-early-to-rise ex-marine and Silver Star Medal recipient, had been vetted back to his diapers. Checked and rechecked. Everything had come up clean. Spic-and-span. Spotless.

The president turned from the window, facing the room. "Tell me this much, at least," he said. "Are you absolutely sure what you've got is true?"

"As sure as we can be," said Dobson, glancing down at the file in his hands. He then watched as the president nodded slowly.

"So, basically what you're saying is...we're screwed."

"That's one way to look at it, sir," said Ian Landry, sitting cross-legged on the far sofa. The White House press secretary then shifted to his bread and butter: the spin. "On the flip side, knowing there's a problem now sure beats the hell out of knowing it after the hearing tomorrow. At least tonight we have some options."

"Who do you guys have in mind?" asked the president.

Dobson didn't hesitate. "Karcher," he said.

"*Karcher?* He wasn't even on the short list."

"That's not what the *Times*, the *Post*, and *Politico* will be reporting in a couple of days," said Landry, all but bragging.

"And what about Bass?" asked the president. "What am I telling him?"

With a quick nod, Landry deferred to Dobson. Golden parachutes were strictly the chief of staff's domain.

"You simply tell Bass that his support collapsed in the wake of the assault-rifle ban bill, and that he's the sacrificial lamb for the Republicans on the committee looking for payback," said Dobson. "I'll take care of the rest. After three months, he'll land on K Street clearing a million five a year. Trust me, he'll play along. He'll have no choice."

Tink-tinkity-tink. The president rattled his glass again, his eyes narrowing in thought. Five seconds passed. Then ten.

"Okay," he said finally. "Wake the poor son of a bitch up."

Dobson and Landry both quickly assured their boss that he was doing the right thing. Then, even faster, they left the Oval Office before he could change his mind.

President Morris was prone to that sometimes. Uncertainty. As a Blue Dog Democrat from Iowa, he managed a straight-shooter persona in public, but behind closed doors, according to "unnamed sources," he had a tendency to agonize over decisions. His critics relentlessly seized upon this as the ultimate sign of weakness. A particularly scathing article in the *New York Observer* went so far as to attribute it to his height, or lack thereof. Only two presidents in the past century have measured under six feet tall, the article pointed out: Jimmy Carter and Bretton Morris.

But as he sat behind his desk and waited for Dobson to patch him in with Bass so he could break the bad news, President Morris felt something deep and strong in his gut. Something certain. That this night, of all nights, was going to haunt him for the rest of his life.

Clearly, Dobson hadn't shared the details of that file in his hands because what was in that file could embarrass the hell out of the administration, if not worse. Giving specifics to his boss meant knowing the truth, and knowing the truth meant accountability.

Rule #1: Presidents don't get impeached for the things they don't know.

So leave it at that, right? Lawrence Bass had been involved in something he shouldn't have been, and whatever it might be was enough to keep him from becoming the next director of Central Intelligence.

There was just one problem, one more thing the president didn't know. That file in Clay Dobson's hand?

There was nothing in it.

It was empty.

CHAPTER 31

"WHO IS he?" asked Dobson, pausing before a sip of coffee. At nine a.m. the following morning in his West Wing office, he was already on his third cup of the day. At least three additional cups, if not more, would follow before noon. Always black. Just black. No sugar.

"Maybe it's better if you don't know," replied Frank Karcher, sitting on the other side of Dobson's desk with his thick arms folded. The current National Clandestine Service chief of the CIA never drank coffee. Nor did he smoke or consume alcohol. From time to time, though, he did give orders to have people killed.

This was the first time the two were meeting publicly, as it were, in Dobson's office. For the past two years, they had met in secret, a routine that had been no small feat given that the beat bloggers working the nation's capital made Hollywood paparazzi look like agoraphobic slackers. The empty parking garages after midnight, the abandoned warehouse in

Ivy City—that part of their plan was over. It would now be *expected* that Karcher's name show up on the White House visitors' log.

Dobson forced a smile, an attempt at patience with his strangest of political bedfellows. "If I didn't need to know the guy's name, Frank, you wouldn't be sitting here," he said. *"Your mess is my mess."*

Karcher couldn't argue with that, choosing instead to simply scratch the back of his very large head before opening the file in his lap. This one wasn't empty. "His name is Trevor Mann," he began, summarizing in bullet-point fashion. "Former Manhattan ADA with an outstanding conviction rate...left to become general counsel for a hedge fund...apparently that didn't go too well."

"What happened?" asked Dobson.

"The firm was sued by one of its largest clients, the Police Pension Fund of New York City. This guy, Trevor Mann, discovered during the trial that the hedge fund managers were withholding evidence that should've been given to the prosecution. In short, the cops were getting screwed out of profits."

Karcher was about to continue when he glanced up at Dobson and suddenly stopped. There was something about Dobson's expression, although Karcher couldn't quite peg it. "What is it?" he asked.

"Nothing," Dobson lied. "Go on. Or better yet, let me guess. The lawyer grew a conscience and sold out the hedge fund managers."

"Something like that," said Karcher. "He ended up being disbarred. Now he's teaching at Columbia Law. Ethics, no less. Just finished his second year there."

Dobson took another sip of coffee, leaning back in his chair. He knew that Karcher, all six foot two and two hundred and forty pounds of him, could be a sick fuck with a short fuse, if provoked.

But Dobson also knew what they had in common, what had initially brought them together.

A complete and thorough understanding of leverage.

CHAPTER 32

"FRANK, DID you ever take Latin?"

Karcher, a bit wary of the lack of segue from Dobson, slowly shook that large head of his. When he first enlisted in the army over thirty years ago, they had to special-order his helmet. "I'm assuming you did?" he asked.

"Yeah, four years of it at Phillips Exeter Academy," said Dobson, fully aware of how pretentious that sounded. "And you know what the irony is? The only Latin expression that's ever had any meaning to me whatsoever in my job is one that most anybody would know without studying the language for a single goddamn day. *Quid pro quo.*"

Karcher was well acquainted with the expression. He also knew where Dobson was heading with it. But before he could even open his mouth to mount his defense, Dobson went right on talking.

"Last night, I convinced the president of the United States to make you the next director of the CIA. *You*, Frank. Not the half dozen or so more qualified men at the top of the intelligence world, but you. I did this because this was our agreement, what you got in return for helping me with my plan. And everything was going well with that plan, wasn't it?"

Dobson paused. It was a rhetorical question, but he still wanted at least a nod from Karcher, something that would make it all very clear. Not that Karcher agreed with him. Screw that. Rather, that Karcher understood just who exactly had the leverage.

So let's see it, big boy. Tilt that huge melon of yours up and down like a good soldier.

And there it was, right on cue. It was the slightest of nods but a nod just the same, and for a proud man like Karcher, easily more painful than passing a cactus-sized kidney stone.

Dobson continued. "So now you're here telling me that not only is the kid still alive up in New York, but there's also a new guy, the boyfriend of the reporter, who might know everything as well?"

"I'll take care of it," said Karcher.

"That sounds awfully familiar."

"Then what do you want me to say?"

"Nothing. I want you to *do*," said Dobson. "As in, whatever it takes to clean this up. Do you understand?"

"Yes."

"Quid pro quo, Frank."

"I got it."

The hell he did, thought Dobson. *"Quid pro quo!"* he shouted at the top of his lungs. *"I want my fucking quid pro quo!"*

Karcher didn't say another word. Not even good-bye. He stood up from his chair and walked out of Dobson's office.

Cave quid dicis, quando, et cui.

CHAPTER 33

PARANOIA, I was quickly discovering, has a sound all its own. *Loud.*

"Christ, do you hear that?" I asked as we walked south along Broadway after leaving the Oak Tavern.

Owen turned to me without breaking stride. "Hear what?"

"Everything," I said.

It was as if someone had grabbed a giant municipal dial with two hands and turned up the volume on the entire city. The clanking of a construction crane overhead, the idling engines of the bumper-to-bumper traffic, the back-and-forth chatter of the people we passed along the sidewalk—I could hear every single noise Manhattan had to offer, louder than ever before. And each one, I was convinced, wanted to kill me.

"It's actually pretty cool, if you think about it," said Owen.

That wasn't exactly the reaction I had in mind. *"Cool?"*

"Yeah. Three-point-eight billion years of evolution tucked

away in your DNA," he said. "Survival instincts. Hear better, live longer."

We came to a stop at a DON'T WALK sign at the corner of Fifty-Eighth Street. My neck was craning like Linda Blair's in *The Exorcist*. We were out in the open, two sitting ducks. "Are you sure it isn't *hide* better, live longer?"

"I know how it must seem," he said, "but we're actually fine for a bit."

"What makes you so sure?"

"The Achilles' heel of the intelligence community," he said. "They only act on intelligence."

"Meaning what, exactly?"

"Our two friends from the park are too busy right now turning your apartment upside down. They want to know what you know. They'll comb through every hard drive you have; they'll hack your phone records, bank and credit card accounts, anything and everything. Then they'll wait and hope."

"For what?"

"For us to do something foolish," he said. "That reminds me. Can I borrow your phone for a second?"

"Sure," I said, handing it to him. *"Hey! What the hell?"*

The kid promptly took my iPhone and dropped it down the sewer. *Plop.*

"*Now* we're fine for a bit," he said.

I got it. GPS. On or off, it's always on. In which case...

"What about your phone?" I asked. I knew he had one on him.

"Let's just say my phone's configured a little differently."

The WALK signal flashed. It might as well have been a starter's pistol. Owen immediately took off, crossing Broadway and heading east on Fifty-Seventh Street. I was struggling to keep up with him in every sense.

"Where are we going?" I called out.

"I told you," he said over his shoulder. "I need to make a stop. It's close by."

I jogged up alongside him. The kid was a workout. "Yeah, but you didn't say where."

"It's right up ahead."

As we walked another block, I couldn't help picturing the two guys ransacking my apartment. As unsettling as that was, though, the idea that they were there instead of getting ready to leap out from around the next corner with guns blazing managed to muffle the loudness between my ears. Still...

"If we're supposedly safe for a bit," I said, "why are you walking so damn fast?"

"Margin of error," he said, his shoulders lifting with a quick shrug. "There's always the chance I could be dead wrong."

And just like that, the city was screaming into my ears again, right up until the next corner, where Owen stopped on a dime and pointed.

"There," he said. "That's where we're going."

I followed the line of his finger across the street to a giant glass cube, at least three stories high and just as wide. If it had been shaped like a pyramid, we would've been in front of I. M. Pei's entrance to the Louvre in Paris.

Instead, it was the entrance to the Apple store beneath the concourse of the General Motors Building. *Is the kid buying me a new iPhone?*

"What do we need to do in there?" I asked.

"What they're hoping for," he said. "Something foolish."

CHAPTER 34

OWEN LOOKED as if he were casing the joint, but only to me. To the rest of the store he simply looked like another Apple fanboy browsing about the tables of iPads, iPods, and iPhones.

I was following closely behind him. "Are we waiting for something?" I finally asked. "Or someone?"

Owen stopped in front of a MacBook Pro, angling the screen toward him a bit before clicking on the icon for the Safari Web browser. I couldn't tell if he'd even heard me.

"McLean, Virginia," he said.

"Excuse me?"

"That's where the very first Apple store opened. It was in a mall called Tysons Corner Center in McLean, Virginia."

"I would've guessed somewhere near Cupertino," I said.

"Yeah, I would've guessed the same thing." He was typing a series of letters and numbers into the search bar. It looked like gibberish. "Instead, Steve Jobs opened the first store nearly three thousand miles away from his headquarters." Owen turned to me. "Interesting, huh?"

"I suppose."

"Of course, you know what's also in McLean?" he asked.

This much I did know. Or, at least, I was able to figure it out given the kid's résumé. "Langley," I answered.

He nodded. "Just saying."

With that, he punched the Enter button, the screen instantly going black as if he'd turned it off. Just as quick, it flashed back on with a burst of white and a loading icon I'd certainly never seen before on a Mac or any other computer, for that matter. We weren't in Kansas anymore.

"Any blue-shirts looking this way?" he asked, typing what looked to be a password.

I looked around. All the Apple store employees in their blue T-shirts were busy with other customers.

"All clear," I said. *For what, though? A Swiss bank account withdrawal? Rerouting planes over Kennedy?*

Owen pulled a flash drive from his pocket, sliding it into a USB port and pulling up a video file. Immediately, I recognized the image. The beige carpet, the beige walls, the seamless tunnel of blandness . . .

Once again, I was back at the Lucinda Hotel.

The angle of the video—looking down—was from the end of the hallway on the seventeenth floor. My first thought was that Owen had tapped into a feed from a surveillance camera, albeit a color one with a super-crisp picture. *Why would the Lucinda spring for that?* They wouldn't.

"I attached the camera above the exit sign by the stairs," said Owen, all but reading my mind. "It's wireless."

He interrupted the live feed to cue up the footage from the

beginning, back when he first checked into the hotel. *He had recorded everything.* Every second of every minute of every person who wanted to kill first him and then, later, me.

He was fast-forwarding through it all, but it was all right there, surreal as hell. Claire's killer arriving. Owen leaving. My showing up, followed by the duo from Bethesda Terrace, who, after wielding their magic pliers, indeed pulled double duty as the world's fastest cleanup crew, complete with removing Claire's killer wrapped in a blanket. Perhaps the most unsettling part about that detail was how nonchalant they were carrying a dead body toward the stairwell. Just another day at the office.

Next came the arrival of the police and me again. Or, at least, it would've been. Owen had paused the recording, rewinding slowly before stopping on a clean shot of one of our would-be assassins. With a crop, cut, and paste, Owen fed the image into what I gathered was some kind of restricted personnel file of the CIA. But nothing was happening.

"Shit," he muttered under his breath. "So much for the front door."

That was when things got a bit freaky.

Owen reached into his other pocket, pulling out a small contact lens case. Before I could even ask what the hell he was doing, he'd put a red-tinted lens in his left eye and stared directly into the tiny camera above the MacBook Pro's screen.

Now, suddenly—*open sesame*—everything was happening. Pixelated fragments of the guy's facial features were bouncing from one photo to the next at the speed of a strobe light while charts and graphs measured the similarities. Seizure alert. The screen looked like the love child of a PowerPoint presentation and a pinball machine on tilt.

"This might take a while to get a match," said Owen, removing the lens from his eye with a quick pinch.

"You just hacked your way into the CIA, didn't you?" I asked.

He looked at me and flashed the quickest—and guiltiest—of smiles. "*Hacked* is such an ugly word," he said.

CHAPTER 35

OWEN WATCHED the screen and waited. I waited and watched Owen. He was doing that thing again, washing his hands under an imaginary faucet.

And me? What was I doing?

From the get-go, the very beginning, I'd been playing catch-up. Who killed Claire? Who was the source she was going to see, and what did he know?

Now I knew. So what next?

It seemed pretty obvious to me. Of course, that should've been my first red flag.

"Owen?" I said.

"Yeah?"

His eyes remained locked on the screen. He was barely even blinking. That was fine. He didn't need to look at me so long as he listened.

"We need to go to the police," I said.

"Yeah, I know. That makes sense."

"Good."

"But we're not going to."

"Why not?"

"Because it doesn't work that way," he said. "They can't help us."

"They can at least protect us."

He threw me a look. "You really think so?"

It had occurred to me. Maybe I wasn't seeing the big picture, or at least how it looked from his point of view. "You want to go to another paper, is that what you're saying? Maybe a news network?" I asked.

Finally, he stopped rubbing his hands and turned to me. The words were calm and measured, but the meaning was anything but. *To hell with whistle-blowing.* This was no longer about going public. This was now personal.

"A decision was made to kill my boss...then Claire...then me...then you," he said. "And if you can make a decision like that, you're not worried about the law. You're above the law."

Attorneys, especially former prosecutors, generally bristle at the idea of anyone being above the law. Then again, I'd been disbarred.

"What exactly do you have in mind?" I asked.

"The only way to smoke them out is to remain their target," he said. "Think about it. As long as they're coming for us..."

"It's a path right back to them," I said.

Owen nodded—bingo—before glancing back at the screen. "Now we just need a little background information," he said. "Always get to know better the people who want you dead."

Words to live by.

So there you had it. Why we were standing in the middle of an Apple store playing match-dot-com with the personnel files of the CIA. Let them come after us, Owen was saying. *Let's be foolish.*

"Can I borrow your phone for a minute?" I asked. "I seem to have lost mine."

Owen ignored my sarcasm. "Who are you calling?"

"No one."

He still wasn't sure, but he handed it to me anyway. Then he watched as I made a beeline to the accessories section, pulling an i-FlashDrive off the shelf.

As I began to open the package, a female blue-shirt with a ponytail and geek-chic glasses came over in a panic. She looked as if I'd just defaced the Mona Lisa.

"Sir! You can't just—"

"How much is it?" I asked, reaching for my wallet.

She craned her neck to check the price. "Forty-four ninety-five," she said. "Plus tax."

I gave her fifty. Then, before she could tell me she needed to scan the bar code, I removed the drive and handed over the packaging. "I think I'll pass on the extended warranty," I said, walking away.

I returned to Owen while plugging the drive into his phone. "What are the file names of the two recordings you showed me at the Oak Tavern?" I asked.

He gave me the names and I transferred them to the drive. I handed him back his phone. "Thanks," I said.

He motioned to the drive as I put it in my pocket. "What's that for?"

"Just tell me where I can meet you in an hour," I said, taking a couple of steps back.

"Wait. Where are you going?"

I reached for my sunglasses, sliding them on. "Margin of error," I said. "Just in case you get us both killed."

CHAPTER 36

I QUICKLY wrote everything down on the only blank piece of paper I could get my hands on in the back of the cab taking me across town to Eighth Avenue. It was the flip side of a log sheet the driver was using to keep track of fares. He was fine letting me have it, although when I also asked for his pen and clipboard it was clear I was pushing my luck.

"You want to drive, too?" he asked.

After he dropped me off in front of the New York Times Building, it dawned on me how long it had been since I'd last set foot in Claire's office. One reason was that she didn't actually have an office, just a desk out in the open in the very crowded national affairs section. Visiting Claire was like being on the wrong side of the bars at the zoo. No privacy. You were essentially on display.

The other reason was the guy sitting twenty feet from her desk who actually did have an office, a Brit by the name of Sebastian Cole. Before I first met Claire, she and Sebastian had a brief, hush-hush office romance that, according to Claire, "was the second-best-kept secret after Deep Throat."

"You might want to go with a different analogy," I suggested after she told me that, on one of our early dates. "At least for my benefit."

I remembered we both cracked up over that.

Anyway, as Claire described it, she was young and he was her boss, a surefire way to jeopardize your career even before you really have one. After four months, she ended it.

In the grand tradition of the British stiff upper lip, Sebastian handled her breaking up with him with aplomb, sparing her any retaliation such as reassigning her to the obituary department. Good for him. Even better for Claire. As for me, that was a different story.

The true extent of Sebastian's coping abilities was put to the test a couple of years later at cocktail party thrown by another editor in national affairs. The test consisted of seven simple words spoken by Claire. *Sebastian, I'd like you to meet Trevor...*

So much for the British stiff upper lip. Instead, I got the stink eye along with all the bloody attitude that an Oxford-educated, bow-tie-wearing chap hailing from Stoke d'Abernon could throw my way. Sebastian hated American lawyers and hated even more the idea that Claire would be with one. At least, that was how she explained it later. I was more partial to the adage that guys will be guys, especially when it comes to girls. Jealousy rules the day, and at the end of it we're all just a lyric in a Joe Jackson song. *Is she really going out with him?*

But that was then. This was now. Claire was suddenly gone, and neither of us would ever be with her again. That was certainly the subtext as I sat down with Sebastian. Let bygones be bygones.

"I'm in shock," he said from behind his desk, slowly twisting a paper clip in his hands. I could tell he'd been crying, as had everyone else I'd passed en route to his office.

"*Shock* is a good word," I said.

We discussed the details of how he'd heard the news, an early-morning phone call at home from the executive editor.

"Where was she going?" Sebastian asked.

"Seeing a source," I said.

I watched his face carefully, looking for a tell. If he knew anything about Owen and his recordings, he'd never admit it. Not verbally. While I was 99.9 percent sure Claire hadn't said anything to him or anyone else at the paper yet, the .1 percent chance that she had would certainly grow with a slight twitch or flinch from Sebastian. But there was nothing.

Nor, I was sure, would there be anything to be found on the computer at her desk. Ever since some Chinese hackers infiltrated the Gray Lady's computer systems back in the fall of 2012, Claire kept all her sensitive files on her personal laptop and nowhere else.

Of course, maybe those "Chinese hackers" were really just Owen showing off from an Apple store in Beijing. Anything was possible at this point, I figured. . . .

"I don't mean to be rude," Sebastian said finally after an awkward silence. We were simply staring at each other across his desk. "But I'm fairly certain you didn't come here just to commiserate with me, Trevor."

"You're right," I said. "I need to ask you to do something."

"You mean, like a favor?"

"Sort of. Although depending how things play out, I might actually be the one doing you a favor," I said. "Confused yet?"

"Intrigued is more like it."

"That's good," I said. "Now tell me, on a scale of one to ten, how strong is your willpower?"

"*My willpower?* Is this a trick question?"

"No, I'm simply looking for the truth."

"In that case . . . nine-point-five," he answered. "How's that?"

"I'm not sure," I said.

"Why? What number were you looking for?"

I folded my arms. "On a scale of one to ten? *Eleven.*"

CHAPTER 37

I'D PIQUED his interest. Sebastian was a newsman, after all. He was actually leaning in a bit over his desk, waiting for me to explain.

"First, can I borrow an envelope and a pen for a moment?" I asked.

"What for?"

I cocked an eyebrow. *"Really?"* The cabdriver on the way over here—a complete stranger—had given me less of a hard time.

Sebastian relented, reaching behind him to grab an envelope from his credenza before scooping up a red felt-tip pen next to his keyboard. "Here you go," he said.

He couldn't see what I began to write in my lap. That was on purpose. What I did want him to see, however, was the i-FlashDrive I took out of my pocket when I was finished.

After I placed it in front of me on the edge of his desk, it immediately became all he could look at. Even more so when I sealed it in the envelope along with the note I'd written in the cab on the ride over.

I handed him back the pen. Then the envelope. "It's all yours," I said.

Sebastian adjusted his horn-rimmed glasses as he read the front of the envelope. He looked at me, then at the envelope, and then back at me again.

"You're kidding, right?" he asked.

"Unfortunately, no," I said.

"What's this all about?"

"It's all in the note and on the flash drive."

"No, I mean the instructions."

He flipped the front of the envelope around to me, but of course I knew what I'd written. *Only open in the event of Trevor Mann's death.*

Admittedly, it was a bit melodramatic as far as instructions went, but I couldn't have been more concise or direct.

"And I mean it, too," I said. "The only way you open that envelope is if I'm dead."

"This has to do with Claire, doesn't it?"

"Of course."

"Why can't you share it me while you're alive?"

"Good question," I said. "But that's a flash drive for another day."

I watched as Sebastian looked at the envelope again, staring at it now. He knew exactly what was in his hands. A major story. Front page, far right column, above the fold.

"Why would you trust me?" he asked.

"Because you were the one who taught Claire," I said. "'Never burn a source.'"

In that moment, the way Sebastian nodded while choking back a tear, it was as if Claire were suddenly in the room.

Although for the very first time, she was no longer standing between us.

"You're an idiot," he said. "You realize that, don't you?"

"Yes."

"She loved you."

"I know," I said.

"I mean, she really loved you."

"I know."

The rest didn't need to be said. I had loved Claire just as much as she had loved me—that wasn't why I was an idiot.

I was an idiot because I hadn't done anything about it.

Standing, I thanked Sebastian for his time and, yes, his trust. "Keep it in a safe place," I half joked, referring to the envelope. He smiled, although I could tell there was something else on his mind.

He hesitated, falling silent. "Trevor, maybe you should sit down again," he said.

Slowly, I did. "What is it?" I asked.

"I wasn't going to tell you," he began to explain, almost as if he were disappointed in himself. "Now I realize that would be wrong."

CHAPTER 38

THERE WASN'T a cloud in the sky when I walked out of the Times building, but I was in a complete fog. Dense. Thick. Furious.

All I could see was the next step in front of me, nothing more. I knew where I was ultimately heading, except I couldn't remember making the decision to go there. Or, for that matter, either of the two stops beforehand. It was a bit like sleepwalking. *In the middle of my worst possible nightmare.*

"Can I help you find something?" asked the sales clerk at the Innovation Luggage store at the intersection of Sixth Avenue and Fifty-Seventh Street. He was a blur standing right in front of me. His voice sounded like a distant radio station.

"I need a small duffel bag that comes with a lock," I said.

"A lock, huh?" he repeated, tapping his chin in thought. "Combination or key?"

"It doesn't matter."

"Will you be flying with it? The TSA folks can—"

129

"Really," I said. *"It doesn't matter."*

He led me over to a wall display of cubbyholes that looked like a tic-tac-toe board. Before he could even make a suggestion, I saw what I needed.

"The one in the middle," I said.

He took down the bag and I gave it a quick once-over. It was black, medium-sized, with a small padlock—the key for it, along with a spare, hanging from a zip tie around one of the handles.

"Yeah, I'll take it," I said.

"Do you want it in its box or would you like this one?" the clerk asked. By this point, it was abundantly clear that what I really wanted was to get the hell out of there.

"This one's fine," I said, already reaching for my wallet.

He spun the price tag around. "You're in luck. It's on sale."

"Good," I grunted, or something to that effect, as I pulled out my Amex.

I didn't care about the price. I also didn't care about using a credit card. The charge—and my location—could be traced in an instant. Even quicker than an instant. It would be like drawing a straight line to me, then lighting it like a fuse.

So be it.

Trevor, maybe you should sit down again. There's something you need to know . . .

"Are you all right?" asked the clerk. He certainly didn't think so. It was bad enough that I had all the charm and charisma of a cinder block. Now I was standing there frozen like one.

"Sorry," I said, handing over my credit card. He ran it and I signed. As he handed me back the receipt, I nodded at the zip tie holding the keys. "Do you have any scissors?"

He glanced around under the counter, finding a pair. "Here, let me," he said, cutting the tie. Then he leaned in as if he were about to whisper some nuclear codes. "Just so you know, that lock really doesn't offer much protection. It's super-easy to open without the key."

"Not if you're a cop," I said.

"Excuse me?"

But I was already halfway out the door. Me and the Fourth Amendment.

Without just cause and a warrant, my new duffel bag might as well have been Fort Knox with two side pockets and a shoulder strap.

Good thing.

Because I wasn't about to fill that duffel bag with jelly beans.

CHAPTER 39

WALKING INTO a bar with a gun tucked under your shirt is one thing. Doing it in a bank?

One block shy of my Chase branch on the Upper West Side, I dumped the Beretta M9 in a trash can. I didn't need it. Trust me.

"Do you have your key?" asked the safe-deposit box attendant on the lower level.

Maybe the woman picked up on my vibe, or maybe this was how she acted with everyone who came through the bank, but her monotone delivery was music to my ears. There would be no polite chitchat. No delay. In fact, she even had her guard key raised in her hand, ready to go.

Quickly, I reached for my key—sandwiched between the one for my apartment and the one for my office up at Columbia Law—and showed it to her. The irony. I never used to keep it on my key chain. Then, one day, I'd asked Claire about a certain key on hers.

"This way I don't have to remember where I put it," she'd told me.

I never knew what Claire kept in her safe-deposit box. I never asked. That was because I didn't want her asking what I kept in mine.

She hated those "damn things" even more than I did.

Standing alone in the small viewing room with nothing but white walls and a shelf, I opened the lid and removed an original SIG Sauer P210. Steel frame, wood grip, locked breech. Old school. And, in the right hands, still the most accurate semiautomatic pistol in the world.

Then out came my Glock 34 with a GTL 22 attachment giving it a dimmable xenon white light with a red laser sight. As a weapons instructor during my first year at Valley Forge once declared with the kind of sandpaper voice that only a lifetime of smoking unfiltered Lucky Strikes will give you, "Sometimes shit happens in the dark."

Both guns went into the duffel along with four boxes of ammo, one shoulder holster, and one shin holster, the latter being custom-made to accommodate the light and laser sight on the Glock 34.

Like I said, I didn't need the Beretta M9.

Finally, there were some paper goods. Two wrapped stacks of hundreds totaling ten grand. Cash for a rainy day. Or, in this case, when it was pouring.

And that was that. Everything I'd come for, everything I needed. Before zipping the duffel closed, I took one last look inside it. Then I took one last look inside the safe-deposit box.

If only I hadn't.

Sticking out from underneath my birth certificate was a 1951 Bowman Mickey Mantle rookie card. My father had given it to me after my very first Little League game. "Take good care of it," he told me. *It's your turn.*

The card was far from mint condition. One of the corners was dog-eared, and there were a couple of creases along the side. But it had been given to me by my father, who had gotten it from his father, and that made it absolutely perfect.

I picked up the card, staring at it in my hands, and suddenly it weighed a million pounds. My knees buckled and my legs gave out. I fell back against the wall, sliding slowly down to the floor. I couldn't stand up. I couldn't breathe. I could only cry.

"*The autopsy…*" Sebastian had begun.

Claire was an organ donor, so it had already been performed. He'd seen the results. He'd had to. Leave it to the *Times* to need a corroborating source before reporting the cause of death of one of its own.

"What?" I asked. "*What is it?*"

Sebastian hesitated, his eyes avoiding mine. But it was too late for second thoughts; he had to tell me.

"Claire was pregnant," he said.

CHAPTER 40

READY OR not, you sons of bitches, here I come…

I took the stairs, walking the six flights up to my apartment on the top floor. The SIG Sauer was in my hand, my hand was hidden in the duffel, and the duffel was hanging off my shoulder.

Fog or no fog, there was a small part of my brain that knew exactly how stupid I was being. Whatever fine line existed between risky and crazy, I was nowhere near it. What I was doing bordered on insane. I was a walking death wish, and if it hadn't been for the rest of my brain, I would've surely turned around and hightailed it out of my building.

But the rest of my brain was consumed by one thing, and one thing only. *Love of justice perverted to revenge and spite.* That was how Dante defined it during his tour through Hell.

Vengeance.

I shared the sixth floor with only one other tenant, a trader at Morgan Stanley who left each morning at the crack of dawn.

His apartment faced the back of the building; mine faced the front. I got the natural light, he got the quiet.

Fittingly, there was nothing but silence as I passed his door, heading toward mine at the opposite end of the hall.

Out came the SIG Sauer from the duffel, leading the way. All the while, I kept waiting for a sound, a noise, something up ahead to let me know I had company. But that would be too easy, I thought.

Sometimes you just have a feeling you're about to catch a break. This wasn't one of those times.

Which was all the more reason why I wasn't expecting the door to my apartment to be wide open, or kicked down, or hanging off its hinges like some giant calling card. And sure enough, it wasn't.

The door was closed. Locked, too. Easing my back against the wall and out of the line of fire, I reached over for the knob. It barely budged. Maybe the whiz kid, Owen, was wrong. They never came. They weren't inside.

Maybe.

I took out my key—everything was one key or another now—and unlocked the door as quietly as possible. It was a losing battle. There was simply no preventing the audible snap of the dead bolt retreating. In the silence of the hallway, the way the sound echoed, it might as well have been a giant gong announcing my arrival.

I waited for a moment, trying to listen again into my apartment while staying clear of the door. I could hear every beat of my heart, every swallow, every breath I was taking—but nothing more. Each second passing was all the more reason to believe no one was waiting for me on the other side.

Still, that didn't stop me from putting the duffel down on the floor and pulling out the Glock to go with my SIG Sauer. I was like the title of a badass wannabe country song. "Double-Fisted with Pistols."

I peeled my back off the wall, my shirt damp with sweat and sticking to my body. *Damn, it's hot.*

Whether I was steeling my nerve or just stalling, I suddenly found myself counting back from ten. That, and thinking of Dante once again and the final line of the inscription he encountered on the Gates of Hell.

Abandon all hope, ye who enter here.

CHAPTER 41

I STEPPED back, raised my right foot, and let it fly, my heel hitting the door dead center with a deafening *bam!* The door flew open and my duffel bag quickly followed as I kicked it into the foyer to draw their fire. But the only noise I heard was the bag sliding across my hardwood floors.

My turn.

Crouched low with both guns drawn, I angled around the door frame, my eyes darting left, right, and everywhere. Nothing moved. No one was there.

Correction. No one was *still* there.

Creepy isn't bursting into your apartment to see it ransacked. It's bursting into your apartment to see everything as you left it . . . and still knowing someone's been there.

Owen wasn't wrong; I'd had company. The vibe was immediate. The proof came soon after.

I'd already done a quick sweep of every room to ensure I was truly alone when I circled back to my foyer and tried to think how *they* would think. Owen had summed it up. They'd want to know as much about me—and what I knew—as they could.

I started in my library and the easiest egg in the hunt, my laptop on my desk. *Gone.*

Next was the fruit bowl in my kitchen, where my mail piled up instead of fruit. All the mail was there, but at the bottom of the bowl was where I kept a spare key to the apartment, as well as one for my car and my office at Columbia.

All three keys? *Gone.*

By then, the old yew-wood chest in my bedroom was a foregone conclusion. I pulled open the top drawer on the right, which held my passport along with the lone weapon I kept in the apartment for protection, a 9mm Parabellum.

Gone and gone.

They had my hard drive. They had access to my home, my office, my car. They had one of my guns and the only way I could leave the country. Maybe they'd taken a few other things, but by that point I'd stopped looking.

Then I just stopped.

I froze in the middle of my bedroom, trying to listen. I'd heard something. The sound was faint but definitely there, or at least somewhere. I couldn't tell where it was coming from.

There it was again.

I took a few wrong steps toward the door out to the living room, only to turn around when I heard it yet again. The sound was coming from my bathroom. I was positive I'd already looked in there. *It wouldn't hurt to check again, would it?*

I sure as hell hope not.

Guns up and elbows locked, I put one foot in front of the other and moved toward the bathroom. After a few steps, I had the sound pegged. It was water. Not running, but dripping.

There was no need to channel Chuck Norris again. The door

to my bathroom was wide open. The only kick I needed was one to my pants.

After a few deep breaths, I slowly peered around the hinges...and saw everything I'd seen the first time. My sink. My toilet. My shower. Nothing and no one else.

Ker-plop.

Immediately, my eyes went to the shower. The sliding doors were two-thirds closed. I could see enough through the frosted glass to know the boogeyman wasn't standing behind them. I simply hadn't turned off the water all the way after showering that morning.

I should've known, though. The déjà vu alone was enough of a tip-off. *Those motherfuckers...*

After a few steps forward to reach for the knob, I took one giant jump back. I wasn't surprised about anything they'd taken from my apartment, not at all.

It was what they'd left behind.

CHAPTER 42

"DETECTIVE LAMONT, please," I said, although the "please" was hardly polite. It sounded more like *Right away, dammit!* I couldn't help it.

Not that it changed the officer's answer on the other end of the phone. "He's off duty, do you want his voice mail?"

No, I want his actual voice. I stared down again at the business card Lamont had given me, even flipping it over twice, as if somehow that would make his cell phone number magically appear. It wasn't printed on the card.

"Is there a way you can reach him for me?" I asked. "It's important."

"Oh, wait a minute," said the officer, his voice trailing off as if he were reaching for something. "There's a note here. Are you Trevor Mann?"

"Yes."

"Hold on a second."

It was more like thirty seconds, but I hardly cared so long as the next voice I heard was Lamont's. On second thought...

"What the hell were you thinking?" he immediately barked, skipping right past any pleasantries. The way he said "hell," it pretty much rhymed with "truck." He was pissed.

I knew he was referring to Bethesda Terrace. There were a few ways he could've found out already, but I wasn't interested in asking. I had my own line of questioning, beginning with "Where are you?"

"At home," he answered. "They patched the call from the precinct. Where are you?"

"At home as well."

"I tried calling."

"I just got here," I said. "More importantly, how fast can you get here?"

"Why?"

"Because you're not going to believe this."

"You might be surprised," he said.

"Not as much as I was. *Claire's killer is in my bathtub.*"

I was expecting any number of responses from Lamont, all of them falling under the heading of disbelief. Instead, I got sarcasm.

"Is the guy still dead or is he doing the backstroke now?" he asked.

"You think this is funny?"

"Do you hear me laughing?"

No, I didn't. This was about more than Bethesda Terrace. I was missing something.

"They must have put him there," I said. "They're trying to frame me."

"*They*, as in the two federal agents who just left my apartment twenty minutes ago?" he asked. "The ones you shot at in Central Park?"

"They were there to kill me. Christ, what the hell did they tell you?"

"I think you're going to need a lawyer, Mr. Mann."

"I am a lawyer, Detective Lamont."

"You know what I mean," he said. "We're going to need a formal statement from you regarding Claire Parker's murder."

"Are you saying I'm a suspect?"

"More like a person of interest," he said. "And I'm hopeful you'll cooperate with us."

"This is crazy."

"With all due respect, Mr. Mann, I'm not the one with a dead guy in my bathtub."

"But I can prove—"

He shut me down so fast I was actually startled. "You'll have your chance, I assure you," he said.

I was back to my original question. "Fine. Then when can I expect you here?"

"You can't," he said. "It's not my shift. Detectives Charrington and Goldstein will be there soon. We've got to do things by the book, Mr. Mann." He paused. "Do you understand?"

"Yes," I answered. I finally did understand. Or, at least, I was pretty sure I did. A lot of years had passed since I'd read the book he was referring to. It was the one we had in common.

Lamont wasn't ticked off. He was tipping me off. The faster I got off that phone . . .

The better my chances of staying alive.

CHAPTER 43

"*STUPID, STUPID, stupid…*" I muttered, berating myself as I quickly hung up the phone.

In the heat of the moment, at the shock of seeing Claire's killer in my own bathtub, I'd gotten sloppy. Leave it to Lamont to catch my mistake.

He was now the official study guide—the human SparkNotes—for *1984*. The two detectives he told me were coming to my apartment instead of him had the names of two other characters from the novel. Had he said one without the other, I probably never would've made the connection. But the two together? *Charrington and Goldstein?*

By the time he tacked on, "We've got to do things by the book," I knew what Lamont was trying to tell me, the clever to my stupid. Big Brother was most likely listening in. My phone line was tapped.

So now they knew where I was. *Where are they?*

I dashed from the phone to my living room window, which

faced the street below, pressing my nose against the glass. There was a windowless white van double-parked directly in front of the building. They hadn't exactly spray-painted BAD GUYS on the hood, but I just had a feeling. This wasn't the dry cleaners or a florist making a delivery. Nor was it the cable guy.

Time to pare down.

I kicked off my shoes, threw them in the duffel along with one of the guns—the Glock—and bolted from my apartment. Once in the stairwell, I silently stepped along the concrete in my socks for a peek over the railing, five flights down. One of the two guys from Bethesda Terrace was turning the corner to the second floor. It was only a glimpse, but that was all I needed.

Where's the other one?

I ducked back into the hallway, eyeing the elevator. The floor light moved from 2 to 3, and it wasn't stopping. There was my answer.

The options were shrinking fast as I ruled out the roof. The closest I'd ever gotten to jumping from one building to another was watching a Nike parkour commercial. With the alleyways on both sides of me measuring at least ten feet wide, this was no time for a crash course, emphasis on crash.

The only remaining option seemed to be standing my ground and letting the bullets fly. It was two against one—not the best odds—but probably my best chance.

Unless.

I made my way over to the middle of the hallway. There were only two apartments on the sixth floor, but there were three doors. As fast as you can say Monty Hall, I was opening door number three.

Like a moment straight out of *This Is Your Life*, I was flashing back to one of my earliest cases as a prosecutor with the Manhattan DA's office. A sicko had killed his wife in their Upper East Side apartment and almost got away with it, thanks to the way he disposed of her body. He literally threw her away like yesterday's trash.

Of course, he denied it, so one of the things I had to prove during the trial was that a 5-foot-7-inch woman weighing 145 pounds could indeed make it all the way down a garbage chute. I came up with the idea to film a crash test dummy with the same dimensions and show it to the jury. Worked like a charm.

But what about a 6-foot-1-inch man weighing 190 pounds?

I pulled open the chute with my free hand, looking into a black rectangle that might as well have been a black hole.

There was only one way to find out.

CHAPTER 44

ZIP-ZIP.

I quickly put the SIG back in the duffel with the Glock. Tossing the bag ahead of me, I listened for the sound it made on impact. A hollow, echoing, bone-crushing *BANG!* would spell certain doom.

Instead, what came back to my ears was more of a muffled thud, and with it the decent chance that there was enough trash in the Dumpster below to break my fall. Call it only *possible* doom.

I jumped up, grabbing the exposed pipe running parallel to the wall, and swung my legs into the chute. Cirque du Soleil wouldn't be calling me anytime soon, but it got the job done. I was in.

Gravity took over as I began to free-fall, as did the panic of not being able to slow myself down. My hands kept slipping against the metal lining of the chute, which felt like it had been coated with grease or whatever god-awful slime had built up after years and years of funneling garbage. If the fall didn't kill me, maybe the stench would. But so far, the smart money was on the fall.

I was dropping too fast—my hands were useless. So were my feet, the soles of my sneakers sliding like ice skates. *Shit, this is going to hurt....*

Plunging into the Dumpster, I felt my right knee buckle, followed by a sharp, stabbing pain in my left thigh. There was plenty of garbage to break my fall, all right, but none of my neighbors were throwing out their old pillows.

For a few seconds, I simply lay there sprawled like a frozen snow angel, catching my breath while taking a quick inventory of all my moving parts. Nothing seemed broken, but I could already feel the bruises forming. I wanted to scream out in pain. Instead, I settled for a slight moan. I had to stay quiet and listen. *Did they hear me?*

With any luck, the two guys were back in my apartment searching for me top to bottom in every room. I'd now have plenty of time to slip out the basement door near the storage lockers.

So much for luck, though.

I heard the sound the second I turned to look for the duffel amid the other bags of garbage. It was the creaking of hinges, one of the doors to the chute somewhere high above me. *Damn.*

There was nothing to see but darkness as I looked up into the chute. Still, I could picture one of them peering down, trying to tell if indeed I'd been crazy enough to jump.

I wanted to move out of the way, hug the side of the Dumpster, but even more than that, I wanted to stay absolutely, positively quiet. I didn't move.

Ten seconds passed. Twenty. Everything around me...everything above me...was silent. I kept waiting for the sound of those hinges again, the door closing as one of them maybe convinced the other. *Nah, there's no way he jumped. He's not that crazy....*

If only.

Finally, it came. The sound I wanted. Unfortunately, it was preceded by the sound I'd never imagined.

Crazy? We'll show you crazy....

CHAPTER 45

LIKE A missile, he shot into the Dumpster headfirst, his hands outstretched. Had I been standing a few inches to the left, he would've crushed me for sure. I suppose I should've felt lucky about that, but I was too busy falling back on my ass from the force of his impact to give it much thought.

Get up! Those were the only two words I was telling myself. If I didn't, I was a dead man. *Get up! Get up! Get up!*

I pushed off whatever I could, trying to stand. He was doing the same, although I could tell he was feeling the pain of his landing. He was hobbled, favoring his right leg. But his right arm was working just fine as he dug his hand into his jacket. He wasn't reaching for his business card.

Besides, we'd already met back at Bethesda Terrace. He'd been a split second away from killing me until Owen intervened. But Owen wasn't here to tackle him. It was up to me.

I lunged for him. It was like trying to dive in one of those birthday bouncy houses, my feet all but giving out underneath me. The best I could do was wrap up his legs and send him top-pling over, but his hand was still on his holster.

My guns were in my duffel somewhere. His gun was at his fingertips.

Blindly, I reached for the nearest trash bag, swinging it across my body into his as hard as I could. The gun went flying as he fell back into the pile of garbage, his head banging against the steel wall of the Dumpster with a horrific *crack!* He should've been knocked out cold.

Instead, he was just getting warmed up.

Screw the gun, said his grin. He'd find it later after he beat me to death with his bare hands.

I didn't even see the first punch, a lightning-fast roundhouse. He hit me high up on the jaw, a bull's-eye to the molars. The only thing that kept me upright was the second punch, a roundhouse to the other side of my head. That one split my lip, the blood spraying everywhere like an exploding packet of ketchup.

His smile grew wider as I fell to my knees. I was practically teed up for him, about to be lights-out. We both knew it. The only thing delaying the inevitable was the one thing he wanted to know. He dangled the question as if it were my salvation, the only way he'd spare me.

"Where is he?" he asked. "Where's the kid?"

I was dizzy, nauseous. My vision was quickly narrowing, blurred and fuzzy around the perimeter. That was why I didn't see it at first, even though it was only a few feet to the left. My duffel.

The chain of the zipper was catching just enough light from the naked bulb overhead. The pull tab was on the near side, within arm's reach. *How fast do I need to be? Can I distract him?*

The answer came suddenly with the piercing hiss of hydraulic pistons as the trash began to rumble all around us. It wasn't exactly divine intervention, but I wasn't complaining. This wasn't your ordinary Dumpster. It was also a compactor—clearly triggered by weight—and it was about to do its job.

For one second, he took his eyes off me. It was like a reflex hammer to the knee. He couldn't help it. He had to see what the hell was happening... that yes, the wall was closing in behind him.

And that was all I needed. Just one quick second.

Zip.

CHAPTER 46

MY HAND dove into the duffel, feeling for the first piece of metal I could find. I pulled out the Glock as he turned back around.

Surprise, buddy. The wall's closing in from this side, too.

I squeezed off two rounds right to his chest, his body thrashing as if he'd just been jolted with electric paddles.

He wasn't the only one shaking, though. I'd never shot anyone before. The feeling was otherworldly, and not in the good way.

Trying to hold it together, I stood over him. His eyes were closed, his body motionless. The only thing missing was the coffin.

Still, something wasn't right. *There's something else missing.*

There should've been blood—lots and lots of it—staining his white shirt. The moment he opened his eyes was the moment I realized why there wasn't any. He was wearing a vest.

The shots were still echoing in the Dumpster as the hydraulics of the compactor suddenly hissed to a stop. Another sound, someone's voice, immediately filled the silence.

"Gordon!"

He now had a name. We both looked up at the chute. Gordon's partner was calling down to him. He'd undoubtedly heard the gunfire.

With my Glock pointed at Gordon's head, I raised a finger to my lips. *Don't answer.* I needed a moment to think, not that I really had one.

"Gordon!" came the voice again, even louder.

The only thing I knew for sure was that I didn't want his partner coming down for a visit.

"Tell him you'll be right up," I said.

Just in case Gordon had thoughts of his own, I tightened my grip on the Glock. As nervous as I must have looked, I'd already pulled the trigger twice.

What Gordon wouldn't have given to know where he'd dropped his gun.

He coughed, his face contorting with pain. The vest had stopped the shots, but the wind had been knocked clear out of him. He was struggling to catch his breath.

"All good," he finally yelled. "I'll be up in a minute."

I didn't look away, not for a second, as I leaned down to pick up the duffel with my free hand.

"You have a badge?" I asked, only to see him shake his head. "How about a wallet?"

"No."

Strange thing was, I believed him. In his line of work you don't really carry ID around with you. In any event, I wasn't about to risk searching him.

"I should kill you," I said.

"But you won't."

He was right. Shooting a man in self-defense was one thing. Shooting him in cold blood was something else entirely. Something I wasn't.

"Who's behind all this?" I asked. "Who wants the kid dead?"

He just stared at me. If he knew, he wasn't telling. Where had I seen that before?

Would I really be bothered by the moral implications of an injection that could make him tell me what I wanted to know? Nothing is ever black and white.

Not even the truth.

CHAPTER 47

"REAL SLOWLY," I said, "I want you to pull up your right pant leg."

If I was ever going to leave that Dumpster alive, I couldn't risk his having a second gun. He pulled up his pant leg to show me there was no shin holster.

"Now your left one," I said.

No shin holster there, either.

"Satisfied?" he asked.

"Not yet," I said. "I want you to tie your shoelaces together."

I was expecting him to give me a look that said *You've got to be kidding me.* Instead he just said no.

"*No?*"

"That's right," he said. "No."

But it was the way he said it. Cocksure. As if he'd suddenly regained all the leverage. *Really?*

I knew exactly what he was thinking. Forget the shoelaces,

if I couldn't kill him, the only things about to be tied were my hands.

"Fine," I said.

But it was the way I said it. And had he been paying a bit more attention, he would've stopped smiling well before I lowered my aim and fired one shot into his right foot.

"Motherfucker!" he screamed as the dime-sized hole in his black wing tip gurgled blood like a garden hose.

He grabbed his foot and I grabbed the side of the Dumpster, climbing out with my duffel. I walked straight out the basement door to the back of my building, through the alley, and onto the sidewalk. As soon as I turned the corner, I hailed a cab.

Only after telling the driver the address did I lean back in the seat and think about what I'd done, or more to the point, how I hadn't thought twice about doing it.

Most people will live their entire lives believing they know exactly who they are and what they're capable of. But that's only because most people will never have to find out for real.

I ran my tongue over my split lip, tasting the warmth and slight saltiness of my own blood.

This was for real, all right. As real as it gets.

CHAPTER 48

"JESUS CHRIST, what happened?" asked Owen as he opened the door.

"Oh, nothing really," I said. "I just beat up a fist with my face, that's all."

He leaned toward me for a closer look. The closer he got, the more he winced. "I'll go get some ice."

He backtracked to grab the ice bucket near the television and headed off down the hallway while I put down my duffel and made a quick turn into the bathroom. I opened one eye slowly to the mirror. The other eye was already swollen shut. *Cut me, Mick....*

I washed off all the blood and gave the hand towels a proper burial in the garbage pail below the sink. Housekeeping could put them on our tab, because there wasn't enough bleach in the world to bring those puppies back to white.

That got me wondering as Owen returned with a full ice bucket. I just wanted to make sure.

"You didn't check in under Winston Smith again, did you?"

"Of course not," he said. "Care to guess, though?"

I wasn't really in the mood. Then again, I was the one who'd brought it up. "Fine," I said. "I'll take Fake Names for five hundred."

Turns out, the kid did a pretty decent impression of Alex Trebek. "Eric Arthur Blair," he said.

I stared at him blankly with my one good eye. I had no clue.

"What is George Orwell's real name?" he answered.

Of course. The kid was as consistent as he was clever. That might have explained why he'd chosen to hide out in another hotel, this time in two adjoining rooms at the Stonington down in Chelsea. Frankly, though, I didn't know which genius to believe.

On the one hand was Albert Einstein's definition of insanity: doing the same thing over and over and expecting a different result.

On the other hand was Owen channeling the Fodor's travel guide to Manhattan. "There are over two hundred fifty hotels in this city, totaling over seventy thousand rooms," he informed me. "As long as you weren't followed here, I think we're good."

He looked at me, cocking an eyebrow. That was my cue to assure him that no, I hadn't been followed to the hotel.

"Besides," he added, "we're both in desperate need of some sleep, as well as showers." He sniffed the air around me. "And one of us is a little more desperate for that shower than the other, if you don't mind me saying. *Where the hell were you?*"

After fashioning an ice pack from the liner bag in the ice bucket, I filled Owen in on where I'd been. The Times Building. The luggage store and the bank. (Hence the duffel and its contents.) Then my apartment and . . . oh, yeah, did I mention the Dumpster?

I would've preferred to leave out the part about Claire being pregnant, but that would've left unanswered the only question

Owen could've had for me when I was done explaining. Particularly about the trip to my apartment. *Are you freakin' nuts?*

Maybe I was. But at least he now knew why.

"I'm very sorry," he said.

"Thank you."

He was staring at the carpet, a fresh wave of guilt over Claire's death crashing down on him. "I just feel so—"

"I know you do," I said. "But don't. I told you, this will never be your fault."

"It's not fair, though," he said. *"It's not fair."*

I looked at him, with his shaggy hair and baggy jeans, forgetting for a second the incredible intellect he possessed. He truly was just a kid, wasn't he? Never more so than in that moment.

For everything he knew about the world, Owen was still learning the greatest lesson of them all. Life.

"Your turn," I said. "Any luck at the Apple store?"

Owen's update was a lot shorter, as he'd had no luck identifying the two guys who wanted us dead. The fact that I'd learned the first name of one of them didn't really change anything. But I had an idea what could.

"I need to get ahold of Detective Lamont again," I said.

"Where is he?"

"Hopefully still at home. His precinct patched me in last time." I took a step toward the hotel phone before stopping. Thoughts of my home line being tapped had jumped squarely in the way. "Is there any chance they would've bugged Lamont's phone, too?"

Owen didn't answer. He was suddenly glued to the television. I hadn't even realized it was on; the sound was down.

"What's up?" I asked, pulling up alongside him. I literally had to nudge him to respond. "What are you watching?"

"Something pretty strange," he said.

CHAPTER 49

NEXT TO the CNN logo were the two favorite words of any news network. BREAKING NEWS.

Above those words was Wolf Blitzer, presumably elaborating on the other two words filling the screen next to him. BASS OUT.

Owen quickly grabbed the clicker, turning up the volume. No sooner could we actually hear the Blitzmeister, as Claire got such a kick out of calling him, did the scene cut to the East Room of the White House.

The name Bass didn't register with me at first, but as soon as I saw him standing at the podium, I put it together. Lawrence Bass was supposed to be the next director of the CIA. Now here he was—flanked by the president on one side, his family on the other—announcing that he was withdrawing his name from consideration.

"Wasn't his confirmation hearing coming up pretty soon?" I asked.

"That depends," said Owen.

"On what?"

"If you think this morning qualifies as pretty soon."

Owen had pegged it, all right. That was pretty strange. On the flip side, Bass's rationale couldn't have been more common. Not only was he turning down the CIA director's post, he said he was leaving his current position as director of intelligence programs with the National Security Council. Why?

To spend more time with his family.

"Turn it up more," I said.

Owen ramped the volume on the remote as we both sat down on the edge of the bed to watch.

"Some decisions are easy, others are hard," Bass explained, his hands tightly gripping the podium. "And then there are the ones that are both."

He turned to glance at his wife, who was corralling their young twin daughters, an arm draped over each of their shoulders. The girls, who looked to be around seven or eight, were smiling, almost preening for the host of photographers before them. As for the wife, she was wiping away a tear.

"As honored as I was to be chosen by President Morris to lead the Central Intelligence Agency, I couldn't ignore the sacrifice it would require of my family," Bass continued. "All my life, I've known only one way to approach a job—and that's with everything I have. That's what I would've brought to my job as CIA director, just as I did at the NSC. But in the end, there's an even more important job for me, and I already have it. That's to be the very best father and husband I can be. So as much as this was a hard decision for me, in some ways—three very beautiful ways, to be exact—it was an easy one."

With that, he let go of the podium, stepped back, and hugged his wife and daughters—one, two, three. The sound of cameras clicking away was nearly deafening, even through the television.

"Very touching," said Owen as the screen switched back to Wolf Blitzer. He was introducing some pundit for comment.

"Yes, it was," I said.

Owen turned to me. Each of us knew what the other was thinking. "For a minute there, I almost believed him."

"Yeah, me, too," I said.

CHAPTER 50

A HOT shower and some sleep used to do wonders for me. I'd wake up with that can-do attitude straight out of a breakfast cereal commercial trumpeting all those essential vitamins and nutrients.

Now I was just wondering if I'd live to see another breakfast.

Not to say there weren't any saving graces.

For instance, watching Owen hack one of those disgusting websites selling personal information about people was the best irony I'd seen in a long time. It looked simple, too. That is, until I asked Owen what he was actually doing.

"It's called a Structured Query Language injection," he explained. "SQL for short. I trick the website into incorrectly filtering for string literal escape characters."

String literal escape characters? Structured Query Language injection?

Carry on, I told him.

The upshot was that we weren't taking any chances in communicating with Detective Lamont. That resulted in the second-best irony I'd seen in a long time. We were evading the prospect of the highest of high-tech surveillance by going seriously old school.

"How did you know I had a fax machine at home?" asked Lamont the moment we stepped into the backseat of his car that night outside what used to be the Juliet SupperClub near Twenty-First Street and Tenth Avenue. Given how many people had been either stabbed or shot at coming out of the place, I figured he'd know it well.

"I'll let Owen tell you," I said, making the introduction. Nothing in my fax had mentioned I was bringing someone along, and certainly not someone so young.

"How old are you?" asked Lamont. He was squinting. Partly because there was barely any light in the car, but mostly due to disbelief.

"Nineteen," answered Owen.

Lamont turned to me. "My car's older than him."

I glanced around the interior of his Buick LeSabre, my eyes moving from the crank handles for the windows to the ashtray below the radio. *An ashtray.*

"Your car's older than everybody," I said.

With that, the headlights of an oncoming car lit my banged-up face. We were still parked along the curb.

"Shit," said Lamont. "How did that happen?"

I told him the story. It also gave me a chance to thank him for tipping me off about my phone line.

"Call it a hunch," said Lamont. "The two guys who paid me a visit were CIA."

Owen chimed in. "Special Activities Division, right?"

"How did you know?" asked Lamont.

"Let's just say we share the same company health plan."

Lamont shot me another look. *He's nineteen* and *he works for the CIA?* "What other surprises do you have?" he asked.

Lamont had helped me up until this point based on little more than his gut. The time had come to prove his instincts right. I asked Owen to take out his phone and show Lamont some highlights from the hallway of the Lucinda Hotel.

"How's that for a special activity?" I said as we watched the body of Claire's killer being removed from the room.

Then came the main attraction. The big picture, if you will.

Owen showed Lamont the two recordings he'd played for me at the Oak Tavern. Even having seen them already, I got the same anxious, uneasy, pit-in-my-stomach feeling I'd had the first time. All of it was so painful to watch. And yet that was all I could do. I couldn't take my eyes off the screen.

As for Lamont, he remained completely silent. In fact, he barely even moved. I tried to imagine all the things he'd seen as a New York City detective. Much of that, I was sure, was far more unsettling from a blood and guts standpoint.

But this was different. This had *implications*. The likes of which he most definitely hadn't seen before.

"We need a favor," I said as soon as the second recording was finished.

I half expected Lamont to shoot back, "No, what you need is a federal grand jury." This was the guy, after all, who had warned me about trying to do other people's jobs.

But that seemed like a very long time ago. A lot had changed. Including Lamont.

"Let me guess," he offered, nodding at Owen's phone. "You have faces but no names."

"Exactly," I said.

Lamont looked at me and nodded again. Sometimes a man's

character reveals itself slowly. Over months, maybe even years. Other times, all it takes is a New York minute.

"Yeah, I can help you," he said.

As he threw the car into drive and pulled away from the curb, he began to whistle. It was the first few bars of "Take Me Out to the Ball Game."

Buy me some peanuts and what?

CHAPTER 51

LAMONT REACHED for his cell, tapping a speed dial number as we stopped at a red light at the corner of Tenth Avenue. He waited a few seconds while the line rang. We all waited.

After a couple more rings, someone picked up. It was a guy's voice. I could just make it out. "Hey," the guy said. "Where are you?"

"You're about to get an e-mail from someone you don't know," Lamont said into the phone. "I need you to do me a favor."

"Go ahead."

Hearing the voice for the second time, I recognized it. Lamont was talking to his partner, Detective McGeary.

"There'll be three videos attached," Lamont continued. "Load them into CrackerJack and run that ID filter thingamajiggy."

I could hear McGeary chuckle. "You mean the ISOPREP for facial recognition?"

"Yeah, that's the one."

"What am I looking at?" McGeary asked.

"That's the thing," said Lamont. "You can't look at them, not even a glance. At least, not yet."

"You're joking, right?"

"Just trust me on this, okay?"

The line was silent for a few seconds. "Yeah, sure," McGeary said finally. "Whatever."

"Thanks, partner," said Lamont. "I'll see you shortly."

He hung up, turning to us in the backseat. Owen's fingers were already hovering over his phone, ready to type in McGeary's e-mail address. Lamont gave it to him.

"I need to send the files one at a time," said Owen. "They're too big as a group."

"Whatever it takes," said Lamont. "As you could tell, I'm not the most tech-savvy guy in the world. All I know is that prepping files on that damn machine takes a while. This way, we've got a head start."

"Is he really not going to watch them?" I asked, incredulous. "That was like putting a biscuit on a dog's nose."

"Yeah, I know," said Lamont.

"Are you trying to protect him?"

"I'm trying to give him the option. I'll explain it to him at the precinct, and he'll make the decision. That way, he owns it," Lamont said. "You can't unwatch what you just showed me."

"Done," said Owen, looking up from his phone. "All three sent."

"Good, thanks," said Lamont as the light turned green.

He turned left onto Tenth Avenue, heading the only way you can, which is north. The traffic was one-way.

Apparently, though, someone didn't get the memo.

"Jesus, look at this asshole," said Lamont, pointing up ahead.

Amid all the taillights was a pair of headlights, right smack in the middle of the street and coming right toward us. Fast. The guy was either drunk or a tourist or both.

Lamont flashed his high beams as drivers began leaning on their horns left and right. A taxi fifty feet ahead of us missed getting hit by inches as the oncoming car swerved around it at the last possible moment.

Whoever it was wasn't stopping. If anything, he was picking up speed.

"Get over!" I yelled at Lamont.

But to his credit, he wasn't thinking only about us. Every car around us was in danger.

Lamont jammed the brakes and reached down by the shotgun seat, grabbing a cherry top. There was no time to throw it up on the roof of his car. He quickly plunked it on the dash, flipping it on.

I shielded my eyes as best I could to the blinding flashes of red and blue filling Lamont's car. Even more blinding was the white of the two headlights getting closer and closer. The car was right in our lane and there was nothing between us.

What the hell is happening?

"Hold on!" said Lamont.

CHAPTER 52

I BRACED for the collision. My arms outstretched, the palms of my hands pressed hard against the back of the front seat. Owen was doing the same.

Lamont, white-knuckled, had the steering wheel gripped at ten and two. He was bound to get the worst of it. *Is this LeSabre so old it doesn't even have airbags?*

I could already hear the crash in my head, the horrible crunch of metal against metal, of glass shattering, of Newton's First Law being proven at 120 decibels.

But those sounds never came. It was an entirely different one we heard, albeit just as loud.

At the last possible second, the oncoming car came to a halt mere inches from our front grille, the tires screeching as if they were being ripped from their rims. I couldn't just smell the burnt rubber; I could taste it.

"Son of a bitch!" shouted Lamont.

Whatever relief came from not being hit was quickly overtaken by his anger. He couldn't unbuckle his seat belt fast enough to get out of the car and tear this driver a new one.

With the cherry still spinning on the dash, he was barely more than a silhouette as he opened the door and swung his legs out all in one move. The moment his heels reached the asphalt, I could hear a door opening on the other car. Someone was getting out, another silhouette.

But I still recognized him. So did Lamont.

Just not fast enough.

Before Lamont could even reach for his gun, the sound of shots split the air. There were four of them right in a row. *Pop! Pop! Pop! Pop!*

Instinctively, I ducked, but not before seeing Lamont drop to the ground, his hands clutching his chest. He was gasping, wheezing, trying to catch his breath. It was the sound of a man dying.

All at once, I wanted to puke, to mourn him, to click my heels three times and wake up safe in my bed next to Claire. But all I could see was Owen right beside me, completely frozen. He couldn't have been more exposed if he'd had a neon target on his face.

"Get down!" I screamed, grabbing his shoulders.

As I pulled him flat against the backseat, the second wave came, as I'd known it would. There were so many shots I couldn't keep count, one after another riddling the windshield. I'd expected the sound of shattering glass, but not like this. Not with bullets flying over us.

Damn, my kingdom for my duffel . . .

I'd left the bag back at the hotel, not wanting to bring what amounted to a small arsenal into Lamont's precinct. Call me crazy.

But I wasn't *that* crazy.

I reached down, grabbing the Glock strapped to my right shin. With that and two extra clips, I had just enough for one plan.

"Get ready," I said.

"For what?" asked Owen.

I flipped the safety. "We're getting out of here."

CHAPTER 53

ALL I knew was that my ears would have to be my eyes.

That flashing cherry meant I couldn't see out of the car, but it also meant he couldn't see in—he being Gordon's partner. It was him, all right. The gamble was whether it was only him.

That was what I was hearing, though. Shots from only one gun. One gun, which he was currently reloading. The slide and click were unmistakable.

I could almost hear his thoughts, too. He knew I had a weapon. His buddy, Gordon, had a hole in his foot that proved it. *Sitting this one out, Gordo?*

I sure as hell hoped so.

There was no time for any countdown or a moment to steel my nerve. My window was now, and it looked a lot like the space between the front and back seats. The car was in park and idling, but not for long....

GO!

I popped up like a deranged, gun-toting Whac-A-Mole, firing

blindly through the windshield and into the other car. As I unloaded half my clip, the only thing I was aiming for was to send Gordon's partner scrambling for cover.

GO!

I lunged over the seat, shifting into reverse with my gun hand while punching the gas with the other. Steering wasn't exactly a high priority as we took off backward with Owen sneaking peeks out the back window.

"Clear!" he shouted, while I remained on the floor of the front seat.

All the surrounding traffic had backed the hell away as soon as they heard the gunfire, more of which was now spraying through what remained of the windshield. Suffice it to say, Gordon's partner didn't particularly like this latest development. Meanwhile...

"Thirty feet!" shouted Owen with the update, the distance before we'd hit another car. Or anything else, for that matter.

By now it had stopped raining shards of glass over my head. We were out of range. Time to get a better view.

I pulled myself up by the steering wheel, immediately spinning us into a one-eighty that nearly flipped us over and had Owen practically doing a somersault across the backseat.

"Jesus!" he yelled.

"Sorry!" I yelled back.

The second we were on all four tires again, I grabbed the rearview mirror, twisting it into my eye line to see what Gordon's partner was doing behind us. Instead, I should've been looking straight ahead.

"Car!" said Owen. *"Car!"*

I looked just in time to see a white BMW swerving up on the curb to avoid us. So did the taxi behind it. Now *we* were the asshole who didn't get the memo. We were going the wrong way.

The chorus of horns kicked in, but the only car that really mattered was still behind us. Glancing into the rearview mirror again, I could just make out Gordon's partner getting back behind the wheel. For the first time, I could see what he was driving. A Jeep Wrangler.

I killed the cherry and made the first turn possible, onto Twenty-First Street. We were finally going the right way, but it was clear we were about to have company.

Just how fast can a Buick LeSabre from the early eighties go?

CHAPTER 54

MY RIGHT foot was like a cinder block on the gas, while my head was like a bobble doll, bouncing all around as I tried to see through the shot-up windshield. There were so many cracks and jagged edges, I might as well have been looking through a prism.

I blew through one red light and then another without a scratch, a double dose of lucky on our way to the West Side Highway. More lanes, less traffic, better chance of losing him. Or so I was thinking.

"He's gaining," said Owen, looking out the back while I frantically weaved in and out of the cars around us.

"How many behind?" I asked.

"Five cars," he said. "Shit, make that four."

We were a block away from the highway, but suddenly that idea wasn't looking so good. I couldn't shake him. Four cars back would become three and then two and then one, and he'd be right on my tail, shooting out my tires.

I glanced back at Owen. "Time for plan B," I said.

"I didn't know we had a plan A."

"Good, then you won't fight me on this."

He fought me anyway.

"Hell, no," he said after I told him what I wanted him to do. "It's two against one."

"Yeah, but we've got only one gun," I said. "That makes it one against one."

"Then I'll be the decoy," he said. "I'll distract him."

"Yeah, right before he puts four bullets in your chest."

It wasn't just what I said, it was the way I said it. Angry. Pissed.

Guilty.

All I could see was Lamont falling to the ground. It was playing in my head over and over, a vicious loop.

And as Owen went silent, it was as if he knew exactly how I felt. He'd felt the same thing with Claire.

I need you to run with this story, kid. Literally…

"Okay," he said, relenting. "But you better know what you're doing."

"I do," I assured him. And with any luck, that wouldn't be a lie.

Flipping the cherry back on, I looked up ahead to the end of the block about fifty yards away. I was straddling both lanes as parked cars dotted each side of the street like Morse code. What I needed was two cars lined up opposite each other like gateposts. Because I was about to close the gate.

The sound of my jamming the brakes was immediately drowned out by everyone else's brakes behind me. Not only was I stopping on a dime, I was stopping on an angle to block both lanes. Instant chaos.

No one was going anywhere…except Owen.

"Now!" I told him.

He hesitated for a split second, but that was it. He burst out of the backseat, dashing around the corner and out of sight as fast—and as low—as he could.

Now it was my turn.

Only, I was heading in the opposite direction. Suddenly, my life had become an existential fortune cookie.

Man chased too long must find new path.

CHAPTER 55

WITH THE cherry still flashing on the dash, there came an eerie silence as I all but crawled out of the front seat on my hands and knees to avoid being seen.

New York drivers have a well-earned rep for impatience, but even they know when to lay off their horns. You honk at a cop and you're likely to see some *real* impatience, and that old Buick LeSabre blocking traffic was an unmarked police car, as far as everyone could tell.

Everyone, that is, except the guy at the wheel four cars back who wanted me dead.

Quickly, I made my way behind a Prius parked along the curb. The angle was wrong, though. I couldn't see well enough up the street.

So much for the gift of silence, too. The line of cars now stretched all the way down the block, well beyond sight of the flashing red and blue. Any driver bringing up the rear had no idea why he was stopped. The horns began kicking in, one louder than the last.

Fine by me. I was banking on the confusion.

As fast as I got to the curb was how slowly I began moving alongside the parked cars, peering over the hoods until I had a clean line. But it wasn't happening. The headrest of a seat, a side-view mirror—something was always in the way.

I should've been able to spot him by now.

Finally, there came a good angle. I was maybe twenty feet away, sidled up next to the back tire of a MINI Cooper. Looking through the glass of the rear hatch, I had the perfect view.

Of nothing.

I could see the Jeep, but the driver's seat was empty. The engine was running, and I couldn't suppress the immediate thought that maybe I should've been, too.

Gripping my pistol with both hands, I was whipping it around like a pointer. *Where are you? Over here? Over there?*

I didn't know whether to move or stay put. People were starting to get out of their cars. Some were yelling, others walking ahead for a closer look. No one knew what was happening. Including me.

Then, with one glance to the left, I saw him.

He poked his head out from behind the Prius back where I'd started. I'd gone to him; he'd come to me. We'd missed each other. He had no intention of letting that happen again.

Like a bull out of the gate he came at me, running with his arm raised. His first shot caromed off the sidewalk mere inches to my left, the sound setting off screams up and down the block. People were scattering everywhere as I bolted around the next car at the curb, just barely eluding the second shot. Had the MINI Cooper been any less mini, I would've been nailed in the back for sure.

Three-point-eight billion years of evolution tucked away in your DNA…

Immediately, I spun around with my arms locked, the inside of my index finger flush against the trigger. Once again, I had the perfect view.

And once again, it was of nothing.

The sidewalk was empty. He wasn't there.

But he was far from gone.

CHAPTER 56

I'VE NEVER cracked the cover of Sun Tzu's *The Art of War.* It's never even made the to-read pile next to my bed. But I had to believe that somewhere buried in the book was a rule that said if the enemy knows where you are but you don't know where the enemy is . . . *move.*

As fast and low as I could, I zigzagged across the street, stopping only when I saw some bald guy in a suit halfway out of his shiny red Cadillac. He was crouched, looking through the window with his entire head exposed as if he'd somehow missed that physics class in high school explaining the effect of a speeding bullet on a piece of glass. *This just in, pal, the bullet wins. . . .*

"Hey," I tried whispering, which was pretty much a lost cause given the cacophony of horns still blaring. The entire street had become a parking lot, an exceedingly angry one at that.

"Hey!" I tried again, louder.

Finally, he turned around and I motioned with both hands for him to get down. That immediately got me a look suggesting

I should mind my own effin' business. Then he saw the gun in my right hand. That did the trick. He ducked back into his seat so fast he literally banged his bald head on the top of the car.

Any other time, any other place, that would've been funny.

I wasn't laughing.

All I could do was keep looking left and right as I approached the other sidewalk, my head on a swivel. Forget my trigger finger, the slightest movement anywhere in front of me had my entire body twitching. Throw in some self-doubt, and I was close to drowning in my own sweat. Did I really need to go after a trained CIA field agent head-on?

Too late.

It was like lightning before the thunder. I first saw a flash in the corner of my eye. I turned quickly to look, squinting for focus, and heard a booming voice right behind it.

The voice was saying something. *He* was saying something. But he was too far away; I couldn't make out the words.

The voice, though... I knew the voice. It was familiar.

It was Owen.

He was sprinting toward me on the sidewalk, his cell phone lit up with one of those flashlight apps. Damn, those things are bright. He was close enough now, the words beginning to come together.

"You!" he was screaming. "Find you!"

Find me? No.

Behind me!

I spun around, hands out front, my eyes blowing up wide with panic as I looked out over the barrel of my pistol to see another gun already lined up with my chest. Somehow he'd gotten behind me.

Now he was right in front of me, dead center. All Gordon's partner had to do was pull the trigger. But he suddenly had a problem...

He couldn't see me.

The light from Owen's phone hit his face so fast I could practically see his pupils snap shut. He raised his arm to shield his eyes, but it was the other arm I was watching. The one with the gun. He was swinging it right at Owen.

There was no thought, no planning, no decision. Just instinct. And maybe a little trace memory thrown in for good measure in case he was wearing a bulletproof vest.

In other words, I aimed a little bit higher.

I got off two shots. I couldn't tell if the first one hit him, but there was no doubt about the second. Let's just say it was going to be a closed-casket funeral, and leave it at that.

"C'mon," said Owen. "Let's go."

That was all he said. Or maybe that was all I heard.

For sure, it was more than I was able to say, which was nothing. I could barely breathe, let alone talk. But I was keenly aware. *The kid came back for me.*

Later, I would thank him. The heart rate would slow; the thoughts and words would come. I'd point out that this was the second time he'd saved my life. I'd even crack that I'd never been so happy to have someone ignore what I asked him to do. If Owen had fled back to the hotel from Lamont's car as I'd asked—as he'd told me he would—I would've been the one lying on the pavement in a pool of blood.

But he hadn't. So I wasn't.

Yes. Later, I would do all this. When there was time to think and sort things out. But the moment after I pulled the trigger was no different than the moment right before.

No thought, no planning, no decision. Just instinct. The same instinct Owen had.

Let's go.

CHAPTER 57

I WENT to sleep having killed a man. I woke up thinking I'd at least find out who he was.

It didn't matter if he wasn't carrying ID. There were other ways. So many other ways. Fingerprints. Dental records. Facial recognition software. If ever there was a job for CrackerJack...

"What time is it?" I asked Owen with my one good eye open off the pillow. My head was killing me. The rest of me wasn't faring much better.

Owen was sitting on the edge of the other queen bed in our two-room bunker at the Stonington staring intently at the television and the start of the local morning news. He could've been a statue if it hadn't been for his hands. They were doing that dry wash thing again. *What's the deal with that?*

"It's six," he answered.

That explained the hint of daylight along the perimeter of the drawn curtains, not to mention why I still felt so tired. It was barely dawn, and I'd only been asleep for a couple of hours. Longer than Owen, though, apparently.

There's one exception to the age-old maxim about news reporting—if it bleeds, it leads—and that's the early-morning broadcast. At the start of the day, one thing trumps everything else. The weather. Short of an apocalypse, that's what people want to hear about first. The eternal question? It's not the meaning of life. It's *Will I need an umbrella?*

According to the far-too-chipper weatherman pointing out some incoming clouds on the Doppler radar, the answer was a definite maybe. There was a forty percent chance of showers in the afternoon.

Of course, there was a hundred percent chance of two shooting deaths overnight in the Chelsea section of Manhattan.

The weatherman, still grinning, sent it back to the anchor, who did her best to segue into a more somber tone as the words DETECTIVE DEATH appeared on-screen. Next to them was a picture of Lamont. He must have fallen to the ground a thousand times in my mind before I'd finally been able to drift off to sleep.

Now tell us who the goddamn son of a bitch was who killed him. Tell us about "Gordon's partner."

As if he could read my mind, Owen stopped rubbing his hands and glanced back over his shoulder at me.

"They're not going to know," he said softly.

The second he said it, I knew he was right. Even if the police did know, they wouldn't be quick to release the name to the press. It would raise more questions than answers.

"At this time, the identity of the second victim, who is believed to be the man responsible for Detective Lamont's murder, is unknown," said the anchor, so keyed to her teleprompter that she didn't seem to even grasp how twisted that sounded.

Even more so because there wasn't even a mention of the other triggerman. Me.

Was there really no one who saw me shoot him?

The anchor moved on to a fire in a Queens tenement building, prompting Owen to shut off the television. As soon as he turned to me, I knew the question coming, and it certainly wasn't about how I'd slept.

"How do you want to do this?" he asked.

That was the part we hadn't discussed after returning to the hotel. The *how*. Our focus had been the what, as in *What do we do now?* The night had changed everything.

Detective Lamont was dead, and we knew why. We owed it to him, his family, and everyone he worked with to come forward. Maybe Owen was right. Maybe justice wouldn't be served in the end. But it no longer seemed like our call to make.

"Lamont's precinct," I said. "I think that's where we begin."

Owen nodded. "Do you want to call ahead?"

"No. Let's just show—"

Before I could get the word *up* out of my mouth, Owen's phone lit up on top of his backpack by the TV. I thought it was an incoming call at first, but there was no ring, no buzzing or vibrating.

"That's strange," said Owen, going over to check it.

"What is?" I asked.

"It's an e-mail."

"So?"

"I shouldn't be getting any," he said. "The account uses an entity authentication mechanism I designed myself. It's way beyond the X.509 system."

I stared at him blankly. "Okay, now in English," I said.

"It means that for me to get an e-mail it has to be piggybacked on one I already sent. But I only set up the account yesterday. I haven't sent an e-mail to anyone."

No sooner did he say it than we both realized he was wrong. He had sent an e-mail to someone. From Lamont's car.

"What's it say?" I asked, watching him read.

Owen tossed me the phone so I could see for myself. It was more than an e-mail. It was hope.

Underneath a screen grab from one of the interrogation videos were a name and an address in Washington, DC. Georgetown, to be exact.

My partner always believed in what he was doing, McGeary added. I hope you do, too.

BOOK THREE

TRUST NO ONE, NOT EVEN YOURSELF

CHAPTER 58

IT DOESN'T matter if you don't know a door card from a river card or whether a full house beats a flush, anyone old enough to see the inside of a Las Vegas casino can walk right into the poker room at the Bellagio.

Walking into Bobby's Room is a different story.

Bobby's Room—named after Bobby Baldwin, the 1978 World Series of Poker champion—is the poker room *inside* the poker room at the Bellagio. It features two high-stakes tables that are completely walled off from the other forty some-odd tables, complete with a polished-looking host, a maître d' of sorts, who stands guard at the door to make sure none of the riffraff ever make it in. Minimum buy-in is twenty grand. The games being played, however, almost always require a much bigger bankroll. *Much* bigger.

On the one hand, Bobby's Room caters to a very privileged clientele. On the other hand, there remains a certain egalitarian element. Especially if that other hand is clutching a boatload of money. Better yet, a yachtload.

Truth is, almost any Tom, Dick, or Harry flashing a lot of cash is more than welcome to play in Bobby's Room.

That goes for any Valerie, too.

Valerie Jensen, dressed in a leather Chanel skirt, a silk Valentino blouse, and a pair of red Christian Louboutin Lady Peeps, handed the host at the door a house marker for two hundred thousand dollars with the carefree ease of someone who had plenty more where that came from. The fact that she didn't was the first lesson her father, a professional gambler, had taught her when she was a little girl back in Somers, New York.

Poker is a game of lies. If you want to tell the truth, go to confession....

"Gentlemen, I'd like you to meet Beverly Sands," announced the host as he pulled out the lone empty chair at the table for Valerie. It was the "three seat," three spots to the left of the dealer.

Valerie, aka Beverly Sands, sat down amid the polite nods from the other players. Save one, they were all pros. She looked around the table; she'd seen them numerous times before on TV, playing tournaments. And more times than not, they were winning those tournaments.

But as attractive as Valerie was—stunning, really—not a single pro allowed himself the slightest gawk or ogle. That would be a sign of weakness.

Never show weakness at the poker table.

That was the second lesson Valerie's father had taught her. This one doubled as a life lesson, his mantra all during the battle with the lung cancer that ultimately took his life but never his spirit. *Never show weakness...period.*

"Two," said the host, giving the dealer what would've been

the peace sign anywhere else. In Bobby's Room, it meant give the lady two hundred thousand dollars in chips, which was what the dealer promptly did after gathering up the pile of cards in front of him. A hand had just finished.

The game was No-Limit Texas Hold'em. Two cards facedown to each player, followed by five share cards in the middle. Best five from the seven wins. Simple as that.

Of course, if it were really that simple, there wouldn't be nearly a thousand books out there dedicated to explaining how the game should be played.

Given the high stakes, there were no blinds to jump-start the betting. Instead, every player had a five-hundred-dollar ante. This meant Valerie wouldn't have to wait for the dealer button to come around her way. She could be dealt in immediately.

With the speed of a robotic arm on a Detroit assembly line, the dealer placed the cards from the last hand in the automatic shuffler to his right and pulled out the second of the two decks used in the game. After a quick cut, he began to deal, giving Valerie a few seconds to look around the table again. Her father's voice was so clear in her head, it was as if he were back from the grave, sitting right there next to her.

There's a fish in every poker game. That's the player who's in way over his head. If you look around the table and can't spot him, get the hell up immediately. Because you're the fish.

Valerie smiled to herself. She wasn't going anywhere.

Her fish was seated directly across the table in the eighth seat. He was the only other nonpro at the table, but everyone knew who he was. That's just the way it is with multimillionaires. When you land in Vegas in your own Gulfstream G650, it's tough to fly under the radar.

Shahid Al Dossari was a Saudi Arabian banker who was purportedly an advisor to the Saudi royal family, among other things. He was handsome, he was charismatic, and he was currently under investigation for money laundering by the US Government.

Including Special Agent Valerie Jensen.

"It's your action, Ms. Sands," said the dealer with a slight nod. The betting had been checked around to her.

Valerie reached for the sunglasses that had been resting in her blond hair, dropping them down across her blue eyes. Slowly, she lifted up her two hole cards on their edges, pulling them toward her across the felt as if she were giving the table a shave. Game on.

This one's for you, Dad....

CHAPTER 59

VALERIE WASN'T sure when the exact moment would come. Only that it was coming.

It could take an hour. Maybe upward of three or four. Or maybe only twenty minutes, over and done lickety-split. The cards had to cooperate, of course. But so did Al Dossari. And so far, he was.

Educated in the States—Yale undergrad, Wharton MBA—Al Dossari was as Americanized as a Saudi could ever be. He loved Tennessee whiskey, New York Fashion Week, and shoot-'em-up Hollywood movies, but most of all, what he loved was women. He worshipped them. Never mind that they were treated like second-class citizens back in his homeland. That was there. He was here. America. Where women had all the power. *Just so long as they were pretty.*

While the pros at the table maintained their well-trained discipline, paying far more attention to the action in the middle of the table than to the eye candy seated at one end of it, Shahid

Al Dossari was a man distracted. Never a good thing in a high-stakes poker game.

In fact, forty-five minutes after sitting down, Valerie was fairly convinced that the only reason he flat-called her raise from out of position was so he would have an excuse to introduce himself. Maybe even flirt a little.

The moment had come.

Valerie had raised the initial bet of twenty-five hundred dollars, making it ten thousand. Al Dossari called quickly, while the remaining players all folded, including the initial bettor.

That left just Valerie and Al Dossari in the hand. Heads-up action, as the saying goes.

The dealer promptly buried a card and proceeded to turn up three cards in front of him, otherwise known as the flop.

7♣ 9♥ 8♥

It wasn't just any flop; it was an action flop. There were straight possibilities. Flush possibilities. In fact, with two cards still to come, there were very few hands that *weren't* a possibility at this point.

The betting was on Al Dossari, who promptly checked with a silent tap of the felt. Valerie had been the one who'd raised preflop, so this was hardly a surprise move. She had control of the hand, but the only way to keep it that way was for her to increase the pot. A "continuation bet."

"Twenty thousand," she said, reaching for her chips.

Behind her sunglasses, though, she wasn't looking at her chips. Her eyes were focused on Al Dossari, hoping to see a reaction of some kind—a tell—that would give away the strength of his hand.

But he barely blinked. Instead, he snap-called her, tossing two ten-thousand-dollar chips into the pot.

So much for the easy way, thought Valerie. Besides, easy was boring....

Again, the dealer buried a card before flipping over the "turn"—the fourth card—faceup next to the other three. It was the ace of diamonds.

The betting opened with Al Dossari, who checked as he'd done before. As much as he was staring at Valerie, he still hadn't said anything. At least, not out loud. The fact that he'd called her last two bets, though, was definitely telling her something. It was time to find out more.

"You wouldn't happen to be stringing me along, would you?" asked Valerie, flashing the most disarming smile she could muster.

Al Dossari kept his stare, and for a moment or two remained silent. But it was no use. Beverly Sands, the buxom blonde dressed to the nines, was exactly his type. She was his Miss America.

"I was actually thinking the same thing myself, that you were stringing me along," he said, smiling back with perfect teeth. "I've been known to have a weakness for women."

That got a few knowing chuckles from around the table. Al Dossari's reputation preceded him.

"So that ace of diamonds on the turn didn't help you?" asked Valerie.

Al Dossari dropped a forearm on the padded rail of the table, leaning forward over his stack of chips. "Who said I needed help?"

And there it was, an absolute rarity at the poker table. Someone telling the truth. Al Dossari had a made hand. Valerie was sure of it. Because that's what men do when they're trying to impress a woman. *They talk too much.*

"In that case, I'll check as well," she said.

With a simple tap on the felt, Valerie surrendered any leverage she had in the hand. But leverage can be a tricky thing.

And there was still one more card to be played.

CHAPTER 60

THE DEALER tapped the table with a closed fist, the deck cradled tightly in the palm of his left hand. He peeled off the burn card before turning over the final card, the "river." It was a jack of spades. The board was now complete.

7♣ 9♥ 8♥ A♦ J♠

Gone was the chance of a flush or anything higher on the pecking order of poker hands. Still, there remained a lot of possibilities. A pair. Two pair. Three of a kind. A straight. And, of course, nothing at all—which on paper would be the worst hand you can have.

But poker isn't played on paper.

For those with the balls to bluff, the worst hand can easily turn into the winning hand. Those same balls are what usually separate the pro from the amateur. Or the sharks from the fish.

Al Dossari, however, wasn't bluffing when he reached for his chips to open the final round of betting. Valerie had already seen the way he glanced at her stack to see how much she had left. Bet-sizing was as much a part of No-Limit Hold'em as anything else.

"Twenty-five thousand," he said, slowly sliding the chips out in front of him.

The amount was a little less than half the pot, not exactly small but hardly big enough to force Valerie off a decent hand. Al Dossari was making the classic "value bet." He wanted her to call.

But Valerie had no intention of calling.

"Raise," she announced.

She made a move for her chips and then stopped, instead resting her forearms against the railing. It looked like indecision. Maybe even nerves. At the very least, Valerie wanted it to appear as if she were thinking, doing the math in her head and then doing it again while trying to calculate the right amount to come over the top of Al Dossari and get him to fold.

Once again, my darling daughter, poker is a game of lies....

There was no more thinking to be done. No more math, either. Valerie already knew there was no chance that Al Dossari was going to fold.

Finally, she lifted her hands, gathering them behind her entire stack of chips. That motion meant the same thing at every poker table in every language, but it wouldn't be gambling— or any damn fun, for that matter—if you didn't say the three words out loud in crystal-clear English.

"I'm all in," she declared.

Al Dossari didn't ask the dealer for a count of how much he now needed to match her bet. Nor did he give it much thought. He simply continued staring at Valerie for another few seconds, oblivious to the other woman who'd just sidled up next to her. Lady Luck.

"I call," he said.

Valerie was supposed to show her cards first, but Al Dossari couldn't wait. If he wasn't about to win the hand outright, he thought for sure it would be a chopped pot—that they would both have the same straight.

Confidently, he turned over his two hole cards. "I flopped it," he said.

Valerie, along with the rest of the table, looked at his 6♣ and 10♣. Sure enough, the first three cards on the board of 7♣ 9♥ 8♥ A♦ J♠ had given him a ten-high straight. It was a made hand, and the best hand, even after the ace of diamonds on the turn. But then came the river.

Saying nothing, Valerie reached for her cards. Everyone else at the table—all the pros—knew what she was about to turn over. She was no fish, and neither were they.

Al Dossari looked across the felt to see the 10♦ and Q♦ staring back at him. Valerie had a queen-high straight. It was the nuts, the best hand possible.

The pot? Over four hundred thousand dollars.

Al Dossari's expression? Priceless.

But not because he was upset. He couldn't care less about the money. Nor did he care about losing to a woman.

In fact, it was quite the opposite. And exactly what Valerie was betting on.

Al Dossari was more than intrigued. *He was aroused.* The fish was on the hook, all right.

Now it was time to reel him in.

CHAPTER 61

"DEALER, WHERE would I find the ladies' room?" asked Valerie, calmly raking in the pot.

The question wasn't exactly the prototypical reaction after winning a big hand. In fact, a few of the pros around the table even let go with wry smiles. *All in a day's work, right, lady?*

If they only knew. Poker pros were awfully good at reading people. Not that good, though.

Valerie knew exactly where to find the ladies' room. She simply wanted to make sure the Saudi knew where he was going. After stacking her chips, she stood up from the table and walked away, not once looking back at Al Dossari to make sure he was watching. Hell, that would've been redundant.

Right on cue, he was waiting for Valerie when she stepped out of the ladies' room a couple of minutes later. He was pretending to be finishing a call on his cell. She was pretending to be surprised to see him.

"Well played," he said.

"The right card fell for me, that's all," she answered. "But thank you."

He took a step toward her, extending his hand. "My name's Shahid, by the way."

Valerie extended her hand in return, smiling when he held on to it for a split second longer after she let go. "I'm Beverly."

His black suit was clearly custom-made. The white shirt was silk, and the open collar showcased a gold chain that was gaudy but not quite rap star–esque. *Some men will never learn that outside of a wedding band, jewelry is best left to the women.*

"Where are you from, Beverly? I'm assuming not from here."

"Back east," she said. "DC."

"I know the town well. I actually do a little business there."

More than a little, Valerie was thinking. *None of it legal, either.* This charade, the entire operation, was all about proving it.

"And what about here?" she asked. "Is Vegas business, too?"

"Sometimes it is, yes," he said. "This particular trip, though, is simply for pleasure."

"I hope I didn't just ruin it for you."

He smiled. "That depends."

"On what?"

"On whether or not I can buy you a drink."

"If I'm not mistaken, we're in a casino, Shahid," she said. "The drinks are free."

His smile widened. "In that case, I'll buy you two."

Valerie inched closer to him. It was subtle but unmistakable. "You're quite the charmer, aren't you?"

"Is that bad?" he asked, playing along.

"It may not be good."

"According to Oscar Wilde, it doesn't matter," said Al Dossari, flashing his Ivy League education. "It is absurd to divide people into good or bad. People are either charming or tedious."

Valerie tried to bite her tongue. The trickiest part of any undercover operation was forgetting who you were in light of who you were supposed to be.

She knew the quote. She even knew the Oscar Wilde play it came from, *Lady Windermere's Fan*. But between her and Beverly Sands, only one of them had been a drama major at Northwestern.

Still, she couldn't help herself. Besides, the goal was to beguile Al Dossari, wasn't it?

Valerie took another step toward him, this one far less subtle. They were close now, very close. Had it been a Catholic school dance, the nuns would've surely separated them. *"We are all in the gutter,"* she whispered. *"But some of us are looking at the stars."*

Immediately, Al Dossari took a step back. He was genuinely surprised. "You're familiar with the play?"

Considering she'd just quoted another line from it, it was a rhetorical question. But Valerie wasn't about to point that out. Neither was Beverly Sands.

"The girl can do more than just play poker," she quipped.

He stepped toward her again, his crocodile loafers barely touching the ground. "I'd like to learn more about you, Beverly."

Valerie smiled, the kind of smile that suggested the feeling was mutual. She'd practiced it many times in front of a mirror.

I want to learn more about you, too, Shahid. And I intend to. Far more than you could ever imagine, far more than you ever thought possible....

CHAPTER 62

IT WAS more like a pit in the brain, as opposed to the stomach. *I'm going to miss Claire's funeral.*

The thought had been lodged in the back of my head, if only because the rest of me was still grappling with the fact that there was going to be a funeral in the first place.

Maybe, just maybe, I'd thought, the fact that I couldn't be there—or even, for the time being, explain why to her sister—would get easier to bear as the days pressed on. Instead, it was only getting more difficult. Especially after Owen and I left the city.

Every man has his price. For the driver of the livery cab who took Owen and me all the way from Manhattan to Washington, DC, it was nine hundred dollars. The guy made a big stink about having to get it all in cash. Little did he know that was the only way we could pay him.

Our credit cards, each and every one, had been canceled before we even crossed the George Washington Bridge into Jersey.

A few attempts at some online purchases in an open Wi-Fi hot spot were all it took to find out. Presumably, our ATM cards were shut down, too.

So that was the game now. They—whoever "they" were—knew there was no point trying to find us courtesy of Amex, Visa, or MasterCard, or any bank withdrawal. That left the flip side, cutting off our funding and hoping it would limit our options travel-wise. It's always harder to hit a moving target.

All the more reason why Owen and I were on the move.

Our first stop after the five-and-half-hour drive was the part of DC you never see in the brochure. It was a used-car dealership on the Anacostia side of the city in the Southeast quadrant. The owner, who looked like a walking mug shot, didn't have a showroom. He didn't even have an office. It was basically a dirt lot behind an abandoned warehouse with about a dozen beat-up cars, half of which had had their VIN numbers altered or filed away altogether.

"How the hell did you know about this place?" I asked Owen.

"I overheard some Georgetown frat boys talking about it in a Dean & Deluca," he said. "Apparently, driving Daddy's Mercedes around campus has fallen out of vogue. Junk is the new black."

In that case, Owen and I were now the trendiest guys around. We drove away in an old Toyota Corolla that was dinged up so much you would've thought it had been parked out in the middle of a golf driving range. But it ran okay and came with plates, our two requirements.

As for the paperwork, that consisted only of the money that changed hands. Seven hundred dollars, cash. Needless to say, we didn't ask to see the CARFAX.

"What a steal," said Owen.

"Yeah, that's because it probably was," I said. "Stolen."

From Anacostia we drove into Georgetown, heading straight to Biltmore Street and the town house of Dr. Douglas Wittmer, last seen—on camera, at least—deep inside the CIA black site at Stare Kiejkuty outside Warsaw. *That was one hell of a house call, Doc. Care to tell us who hired you? Yes? No?*

According to Google, Wittmer had been a thoracic surgeon at Lenox Hill Hospital in Manhattan for eleven years, followed by a four-year stint at Cedars-Sinai Medical Center in Los Angeles. Then he apparently quit the operating room, joining a medical research company, BioNext Laboratories, in Bethesda, Maryland, as its CEO. That was five years ago.

The website for BioNext looked legit, although that wasn't really saying much. A tenth grader these days can build a believable website in less time than it takes to watch a rerun of *The Simpsons*. So, too, can the CIA.

"Do you think it's a front?" I asked Owen.

"It doesn't have to be," he said. "The guy might simply be pulling double duty. It's more common than you'd think among certain doctors, whether it be for the FBI or the CIA."

For a few moments, I thought about my primary care physician back in New York, who once dropped my urine sample all over his suede shoes. Great guy and a good doctor, but somehow I just couldn't picture him doing a secret gig for the government.

Dr. Douglas Wittmer was a different story, and as Owen and I walked up the steps of his faded brick town house, we couldn't wait to hear it.

But that was exactly what we had to do. Wait.

We rang the bell, knocked on the door, and even peeked through the windows. No one was home. Wittmer's phone number was unlisted, and for all we knew, he could've been back in Poland or at any one of a number of other black sites.

Seeing the day's mail waiting for him in his mailbox, however, gave us some hope.

Now all we could do was park our shiny new Corolla a little way down the street and keep watch. If only we'd known.

We were being watched as well.

CHAPTER 63

"GO AHEAD and ask," said Owen.

"Ask what?"

He looked at me across the front seat like I was an idiot for trying to play dumb. "You want to know why I keep doing this thing with my hands, right?"

We'd been waiting for Wittmer for close to an hour, and half the time the kid was doing his dry wash routine.

"Sort of hard not to notice," I said.

"You can blame my aunt Eleanor." He rested both palms on his knees and explained. "My parents, both professors, weren't terribly religious, but they thought it was important for me at a young age to experience church. So my aunt Eleanor was enlisted one Sunday to bring me to a service. I was five and doing complex algebra, but I also still believed in Santa Claus and the tooth fairy. So the minister is giving this sermon about temptation and sin and he's all fired up, and I'm sitting there in the pew listening and hanging on his every word. And that's when he quotes an old proverb, only I don't know it's a proverb; I take it literally. *Idle hands are the devil's workshop.*"

"You're kidding me."

"Nope. That's how it started," he said. "Problem is, I haven't been able to stop ever since." He laughed. "You know, I've never told anyone that before."

"Trust me," I said. "You've got far bigger secrets these days."

As if on cue, a black Jaguar XK Coupe pulled into the short driveway at the base of Wittmer's town house. It had to be him. The wait was over.

Quickly, Owen and I stepped out of our slightly less expensive Corolla and approached him as he was getting his mail. By the time he looked up and saw us, we were practically in his face. No exaggeration, he must have jumped back at least three feet. We'd scared the shit out of him. Good.

Next up, with any luck, was getting the truth out of him.

"Dr. Wittmer?" I asked.

He was still catching his breath. *Who the hell wants to know?* said his look. But no normal person outside the Bronx actually says that in real life, and Douglas Wittmer appeared as normal as they come. With his glasses and neatly trimmed dark hair that was gray around the temples, he was a doctor who looked like the stock photo of a doctor.

"Yes, that's me," he said finally.

I introduced myself and was about to introduce Owen when I saw Wittmer's eyes beat me to it with a squint of recognition. His jaw then literally dropped.

"Jesus...you're the kid, aren't you?" he asked.

"Alive and in the flesh," said Owen. "Of course, you probably thought I'd be dead by now."

Wittmer nodded almost sheepishly.

"Rest assured, it hasn't been for lack of trying." Owen turned to me and my beat-up face, the bruises just beginning to settle into a nice shade of eggplant. "And that's to put it mildly."

"Wait, what's going on?" I asked. "How does he know who you are?"

To say the kid was quick on the uptake didn't do him justice. "Because he's been shown a picture of me," said Owen. "And if I were ever to pay him a visit, he was supposed to let them know."

"I wouldn't, though," said Wittmer. "I mean, I won't."

"Of course you won't," said Owen facetiously. "What possible motivation could you have?"

Now I was all caught up. If these weren't their exact words, they had to be damn close. *Help us find the kid before he brings us all down, Dr. Wittmer...including you.*

"I don't care that I'm in the recordings," said Wittmer. "It was a mistake, and I can live with the consequences."

"Actually, I don't care that you're in the recordings, either," said Owen. "All I care about is who put you there. That's what we need to know."

Wittmer's eyes shifted between Owen and me for a few moments, the latest issue of *Car and Driver* and the rest of his mail pressed hard against his chest.

It was one thing for him not to rat us out. It was another for him to rat out whomever he was working for. There would need to be a reason. A damn good one.

Wittmer looked up at the sky. We all did. The sun was beginning to set behind a mass of charcoal-colored clouds that seemed to have arrived out of nowhere. Much like Owen and me.

"I think we should go inside," said the doctor. "It looks like rain."

CHAPTER 64

IT WAS a home for a guy who basically wasn't home all that much. That, or he just didn't care.

Not to say it was messy. Rather, it was sparse. In the few rooms we walked past before settling in the kitchen, the furnishings consisted of the bare minimum, or in the case of the empty dining room, even less.

I wasn't much for metaphors, but Claire always was. For her, this would've been a lay-up. Dr. Douglas Wittmer clearly had money, but to see where he lived—*how* he lived—was to see a man defined by what he didn't have. There were things missing in his life.

"You want coffee?" he asked, pointing to the Keurig machine on the counter near the stove.

Owen and I both declined. We were anxious enough as it was.

The three of us headed over to a small cherrywood table in the corner underneath a small clock, the kind you'd more likely see hanging in an office or waiting room. After we all sat down, Wittmer immediately stood up to remove his blue blazer, hanging it on the back of his chair. He wasn't stalling, but he wasn't exactly rushing, either.

Finally, after sitting down again, he took a deep breath and began.

"I was targeted," he said, his tone straight as a ruler. To his credit, there wasn't a hint of his trying to make an excuse for himself. He was stating the facts, or really just one fact. "They knew my wife was on Flight Ninety-Three."

Owen and I both dropped our heads a bit. It spoke volumes about the events of 9/11 that a particular flight number could be so ingrained in the collective memory of a nation.

"I'm sorry," said Owen.

"Yes," I said. "I'm sorry."

"The thing is," Wittmer continued, "grief and anger can help you rationalize almost any behavior in the name of revenge. I know that's what he was banking on with me."

It was so clear what we were witnessing. This was a man who needed to explain himself. Bare his soul a little, if not a lot. I was sure that Owen, even at his relatively young age, was thinking the same thing.

Perhaps it was that same youth, though, that had Owen wishing the doctor would explain things just a tad bit faster. Fittingly, the only sound in the kitchen other than us was the measured *tick…tick…tick* of the wall clock above us.

"He?" Owen asked impatiently. In other words, *Please, for the love of Pete, start naming names. . . .*

"I don't know if he's the only ringmaster, but it's certainly his circus," said Wittmer. He drew another deep breath. "Frank Karcher is the one who first approached me."

I didn't recognize the name, nor, apparently, was I supposed to, given the way Wittmer was looking directly at Owen. And given the way Owen was nodding back at him, I guess it made sense. "The kid" absolutely recognized the name.

"Frank Karcher is the National Clandestine Service chief of the CIA," said Owen, turning to me. "Basically, we're talking the kind of guy who likes to kick puppies."

"So human torture wasn't much of a leap," I said.

It was a quip, completely off the cuff. Still, the second the words left my mouth, I regretted them. I didn't know Karcher, but I did know that Wittmer was sitting right in front of me. He was also on the recordings. At best, the doctor was an accomplice. At worst? That was between him and his God.

And that was the point. Owen and I were there in his kitchen to get information, not to pass judgment on him. And I just had. A bit unfairly, no less. I wasn't the one who'd lost his wife on 9/11.

"I apologize," I said to Wittmer. "I didn't mean to—"

"That's all right," he said. He drew another deep breath. "At the beginning, I knew exactly what I was doing and why. Those recordings you have? As bad as they may look to a whole lot of people, there are just as many people these days—the Machiavellians in our so-called war on terror—who would believe the end justifies the means."

"I'm confused, then," I said. "What changed? Why would you be talking to us?"

Wittmer leaned in, pressing his palms down on that cherrywood table with what might as well have been the weight of the world. "Because those recordings you have don't tell the whole story," he said. "But mine do."

CHAPTER 65

WITTMER PUSHED back his chair and disappeared from the kitchen, returning about a half minute later with an old Dell laptop. While he was gone, Owen and I didn't utter a single word to each other. Really, what was there to say? The doctor had basically just promised to blow our minds. The only thing to do was shut up and wait for it.

Another half minute passed while Wittmer's laptop booted up. Given the anticipation, it felt like an eternity. Finally, he clicked on a file and pressed Play, angling the screen in front of us so we all had a good view. It was showtime.

"This is from the same black site outside of Warsaw during the same time period," he explained.

Indeed, from the get-go everything about the recording looked familiar. The windowless room shot in black-and-white. The lone metal chair with a Middle Eastern man shackled to it, followed by the two men in suits who restrained him while he received the shot to his carotid artery.

Of course, the doctor wielding the syringe looked familiar as well. We were in his kitchen.

"What is your name?" asked the voice off camera.

Immediately, a second voice translated the question into Arabic, and as with Owen's recordings, the Arabic was translated back into English via subtitles. Everything was the same.

Except, in this case, the prisoner's response.

"I speak English," he said softly.

The two voices from behind the camera could be heard conversing, but even with the volume maxed out on Wittmer's laptop, we couldn't understand what they were saying. I assumed it was about the way they wanted to proceed, although you wouldn't know it given how the first voice repeated the question—"What is your name?"—as if he were some automated prompt.

"My name is Makin Pabalan," answered the prisoner.

Hearing him speak again, it was clear that he was fluent in English. His accent notwithstanding, there was no hitch from his having to translate in his head from Arabic. If I had to guess, I'd say he'd been educated at some point in the US.

Again, there was more talking behind the camera. We still couldn't make it out. Whatever was said, though, it resulted in a deviation from the script.

"We'll proceed in English only," came the voice. "Do you understand? The questions now will only be in English."

"Yes," said the prisoner. "I understand."

"And you will only answer in English. Is that understood as well?"

"Yes."

"Please state your name again."

"My name is Makin Pabalan."

"Are you a member of Al Qaeda?"

"No," said the prisoner.

"Are you aware of any plans by Al Qaeda to kill American citizens?"

"No."

"Are you a member of any organization that considers the United States of America an enemy?"

"No."

"Are you aware of any organization that is planning to bring harm to any American citizens anywhere in the world?"

"No."

There wasn't the slightest hesitation from the man in the chair as he answered each question. He looked nervous, but not to the point of fear. Nor was there any anger in his eyes. If I had been cross-examining him in a courtroom, he would've qualified as a cooperating witness.

More importantly, there wasn't the slightest physical change in him. His jaw didn't clench, the chair didn't begin to rattle. There was no downward spiral of pain followed by even more pain. No sign of *lie and you die*.

He was telling the truth.

Owen and I exchanged glances, the thought being that the doctor had it wrong. This wasn't the whole story, it was the *same* story.

In unison, we turned to Wittmer. *What gives?*

But he was still staring at the screen, a subtle but unmistakable cue that we should be doing the same.

The doctor knew exactly what he was talking about.

CHAPTER 66

IT HAPPENED so damn and scary fast.

One second, the prisoner was fine. The next, he wasn't. Only this was different from Owen's recordings. So very, very different. This began in an instant and barely lasted much longer. It was a flash. No, it was a detonation.

It was as if the man's brain had actually exploded inside his head.

I watched as his eyes rolled back, his face convulsing like it was lodged in a paint mixer at Home Depot. The force was so strong it literally lifted the man off the ground, chair included. By the time gravity fought back, he and the chair were tipped over on the floor, motionless.

"Christ..." Owen muttered, his voice trailing off.

Wittmer reached out and hit the space bar on the keyboard, pausing the recording. It was right then that the thought occurred to me. As quickly as all hell broke loose in that interrogation room, it wasn't as if the doctor couldn't have tried to intervene.

But he was nowhere in the frame. *Why not?*

"That might have been the sickest part of all," Wittmer said as if reading my mind. "The second I tried to help, I was literally held back. They didn't want the guy saved. They wanted him *documented*. Like a lab rat."

He hit the space bar again to resume the recording. True to his word, Wittmer finally sprang into the frame as if he'd just broken free from the two other guys behind the camera. Within seconds of his kneeling down and placing two fingers on the prisoner's neck, he shook his head slowly. The man was dead.

"Was there an autopsy performed?" asked Owen.

"Yes. It was an aneurysmal subarachnoid hemorrhage," said Wittmer. *"Each and every time."*

Boom.

"Wait...*what?*" I asked. But I'd heard him perfectly. So had Owen.

"It happened seven other times out of twenty trials," said Wittmer. "At least, the twenty trials I was overseeing."

Owen shook his head in disbelief. "A forty percent fail rate," he said. "Was the prisoner cooperating each time?"

The doctor nodded, his gaze retreating. It was as if he had nowhere to look. "Karcher just calls it collateral damage," he said, disgusted. "I call it murder."

There was no pushing that last line aside, no ignoring its implications. The words simply hung there at the table, filling the silence. If I hadn't known better, I would've sworn the clock above us had stopped as well. I couldn't hear it tick.

Eventually, Owen spoke up. "Does Karcher know you have this recording?" he asked.

"If he did, I'd probably be dead right now," said Wittmer.

It was hard to argue with that. Owen and I were living proof.

Immediately, all I could picture in my head was this guy, Karcher, arranging for Claire's death. Then Owen's. Then mine.

Sometimes the only thing more dangerous than a man with nothing to lose is a man with everything to lose.

Frank Karcher was every bit that man.

"What we need now is the link," said Owen. "Proof that the serum exists, that it was used, and that Karcher's fingerprints are all over it."

Am I missing something? "Don't we already have an entire film festival that proves the first two?" I asked.

"The recordings prove a lot of things," said Owen. "Without the person responsible, though, it's just an embarrassing home movie for the entire country."

"Fine. So commence with the congressional hearings," I said.

Owen turned to Wittmer with an air of certitude that people only grant you when you can back it up. "Excuse the assumption," he said, "but you didn't actually develop the serum, did you? Nor do you know the name of the person who did, using my research, right?"

"I was never told," said the doctor.

Owen turned back to me, continuing. "And the two henchmen in the recording, the ones restraining the prisoner and ultimately restraining Dr. Wittmer? They're undercover agents. So making the recording, any of the recordings, public would expose their identities. That's never going to happen."

"In other words," I said, "what we need is proof that can go public."

"Exactly," said Owen.

Without a word, Wittmer pushed back his chair once more and left the kitchen. To quote Yogi Berra, it was déjà vu all over again. Owen and I simply looked at each other with nothing to say.

Until the doctor returned.

He placed what was in his hand on the table. "This might be your answer," he said.

"Is that what I think it is?" asked Owen.

"Yes," said Wittmer. He folded his arms. "But let's be very clear about one thing. You didn't get it from me."

CHAPTER 67

THE SMALL white stucco building with only a number next to the door and no other signage wasn't quite hiding in plain sight in the heart of Georgetown. But it wasn't exactly off the beaten path, either. From where Owen and I parked, we could look over our shoulders and see the back entrance to a Starbucks out on M Street.

That just made this whole thing feel even weirder. *Is that even the right word? Bizarre... surreal... unnerving? Break out the thesaurus....*

Behind us were cappuccinos, Frappuccinos, and chai mocha lattes with pumps of gooey, sweet syrup. In front of us? A top secret CIA lab producing a lethal truth serum that skirts the US Constitution and the right of due process to the extent that the state of Kansas skirts the Atlantic and Pacific Oceans.

"What are the odds someone's inside?" I asked, turning off the engine. We were an hour past sunset, a lone floodlight overhead providing what little view we had of the one-story building. There were no windows in front.

Owen shrugged his broad shoulders. Wittmer hadn't been able to guarantee the place would be empty. "No clue," he said.

It was the way he said it, though, as if those words were a bit new to him. I couldn't help a slight smile. "That doesn't happen to you a lot, does it?"

"What's that?"

"Being clueless about something."

He returned the smile, all modesty aside. "Nope."

I reached into the backseat, grabbing my duffel, which was sitting next to his backpack. The kid had his bag of tricks; I had mine. "What about guns?" I asked. "Ever fire one?"

The look he gave me was the polar opposite of clueless. "I grew up in New Hampshire," he answered.

Enough said.

I pulled out the semiautomatic SIG Sauer P210, checked the magazine, and handed it over. *Live free or die....*

"You ready?" I asked.

Owen unbuckled his seat belt, flipped the safety alongside the trigger, and with a blind hand hooked an arm through one of the straps of his backpack. "Ready."

The walk from the car to the building's entrance was no more than ten yards, albeit a zigzag given all the potholes filled with water from the earlier downpour.

I led the way with my Glock, never more thankful for its xenon light and red laser sight. With every measured step I took toward the entrance, that former weapons instructor of mine back at Valley Forge, the one with the sandpaper voice, was all but echoing between my ears. A prick and a prophet all at once.

Sometimes shit happens in the dark....

CHAPTER 68

"ONE MORE for luck," I whispered to Owen, reaching out with my arm. I was making a fist so tight every fingernail was digging deep into my palm.

We'd stationed ourselves on either side of the windowless door, bags at our feet and our backs pressed hard against the stucco. I'd already knocked once. The second knock got the same result. Either the place was empty or whoever was inside wasn't answering.

"My turn," Owen whispered back.

In the age of retinal scanners, digital thumbprint readers, and whatever other paranoid-inspired gizmos exist that make sure only certain people get into certain places, Wittmer had given us a little piece of irony. A simple key.

Actually, it made complete sense. Banks need vaults and guards and security cameras because people *know* that's where they keep the money. This, on the other hand, was four walls and a roof barely bigger than a shack tucked behind an alley with all the foot traffic of a Vineyard Vines store in Newark. In other words...

Just make sure you lock the door behind you, Doc.

Still, Owen and I couldn't help wondering the same thing. Hoping, really. That we could trust Wittmer.

In a way, he was merely a middleman. The crucial part of his job was picking up the serum and transporting it overseas, an MD as human mule. Possessing all the requisite paperwork for an international humanitarian mission, he was above suspicion. Barely an eyebrow raised through international customs.

So much better than swallowing two dozen little balloons and a postflight meal of Ex-Lax.

"Okay," I whispered to Owen.

He was holding up the key, his answer to the question that it would've been redundant of me to ask aloud. *What now?*

Slowly, Owen reached out, slid in the key, and gave it a twist.

We braced for everything. An alarm. An attack dog. The night cleaning crew. *Everything.*

Instead, pushing the door open, we got exactly what we desperately wanted. Nothing.

Just silence. And darkness.

I motioned for Owen to stay put, peering around the hinges like some guy who'd seen too many cop shows. Before turning on any lights, I wanted to shine my gun around a bit, as it were. The good news about that xenon light attachment was that being on the other side of it was like looking into the high beams of an oncoming car. The flashlight app on Owen's phone times ten.

Basically, I was a walking one-way mirror.

The first surprise was that there was no reception area, just a short hallway. After a small kitchen to the left and an even smaller bathroom directly opposite on the right, everything was right there in front of me, and it was pretty much as advertised by Wittmer. "The facility," he called it.

I stared through the blast of white light funneling out from my Glock, the red streak from the laser sight moving with my hands from one corner of the room to the next. Only the far wall had windows, three across with horizontal slat blinds that were drawn and closed tight.

What I was looking at was somewhere between a high school chemistry classroom and a meth lab, not that I'd personally seen a lot of meth labs. Truth be told, everything I knew about them—as well as pedophiles, runaway brides, high school teachers who sleep with their students, and people who try to hire hit men to kill their spouses—I owed to a guilty-pleasure habit of watching *Dateline NBC*.

Even in the moment, the thought was all but inescapable. *This would make one hell of an episode....*

The room was messy. Almost chaotic, even in its stillness. There were things everywhere on the large island in the center. Vials and beakers. A couple of Bunsen burners. A centrifuge, as well as a few other bulky machines that were a combination of glass and stainless steel, including one that was connected to a large ventilating air duct that shot up straight through the ceiling. There was also a red binder stuffed thick with papers.

What there wasn't, though, was another surprise. We were alone.

I looked back over my shoulder, Owen's silhouette peeking out from behind the doorway.

"No one home," I said.

And technically, that was the truth.

CHAPTER 69

THE SMARTEST thing I could do was get out of his way.

Owen stepped into the room, flipped on the lights, and closed the door behind him so fast I was out of breath just watching him. The kid was on a mission.

At first, I didn't quite understand the rush. Sure, we didn't want to loiter, but it wasn't like there was a shot clock ticking away in the corner. We had time.

Then I saw him reach for it. The *way* he reached for it.

Sidling up to the island in the middle of the room, he had over a dozen things to choose from, including what appeared to be the serum itself, contained in a rack of vials. He barely even noticed them, though. It was as if there was only one item he cared about, and that was when I understood.

With both hands, he pulled the red binder toward him.

Of all the base emotions that must have been kicking around in his head over the past few days—anger, fear, guilt, to name a few—they were still no match for what makes a genius a genius. *Curiosity*.

Someone had piggybacked on his brain and taken his work into uncharted territory. It might have been seriously misguided and ultimately doomed, but it was also something else, the one thing in common with anything that pushes the boundaries of innovation. It was bold.

And damn if Owen didn't want to see the blueprint.

Silently, I watched him make his way through the pages in the binder, one after another after another, his index finger tracing the words and formulas like he was in one of those old Evelyn Wood speed-reading commercials.

I kept waiting for him to take some sort of mental breather, at the very least a simple pause. Scratch his chin. Shift his weight from one leg to the other. Instead, he kept plowing his way through, barely even taking the time to blink.

Then, suddenly, he froze. I took that as my cue, if there was ever going to be one.

"What is it?" I asked.

Silly me, thinking I was about to get an answer. I was pretty sure Owen didn't even hear me. He was too busy now looking around the rest of the room, his eyes pinballing from one item to the next. Whatever he was searching for, though, he couldn't find it.

That was when his head snapped back with an idea.

He spun on his heels, disappearing into the small kitchen by the door. I could hear the refrigerator open, followed by the shifting and rattling of metal and glassware. Again, it was like someone had a stopwatch on him.

"You okay?" I called out.

Owen reappeared, clutching a large Styrofoam cup. He was staring down into it. I couldn't see from where I was standing, but I was guessing it wasn't coffee.

"N-stoff," he said, finally.

N-stoff? I looked at him blankly. It certainly wasn't my first blank look since we'd been together. "Excuse me?"

"That was the code name of chlorine trifluoride at the Kaiser Wilhelm Institute in Nazi Germany."

Great. More Jeopardy! *I'll take Random Trivia When You Least Expect It for six hundred, Alex....*

At my continued blank stare, Owen went on. "The Nazis experimented with chlorine trifluoride as a combined incendiary weapon and poison gas. What a big surprise, right? Thing is, though, it was too volatile. It would literally explode in their faces."

"And that's what you're holding in your hand?" I asked. *"Three feet away from me?"*

Owen tilted the cup so I could see the slightly green-and-yellowish liquid inside it. "It doesn't react with closed-cell extruded polystyrene foam," he said.

I shot him a deadpan look. "You mean Styrofoam?"

"Yeah, sorry," he said. "Of course, if this were most any metal, like an aluminum can, for instance...then *boom.*"

I swallowed hard. "Then thank God for Styrofoam," I said. "But what does chlorinated—"

"Chlorine trifluoride," he said. "CTF."

"Yeah, what does CTF have to do with the serum?" I asked.

"I'm not sure it has anything to do with the serum."

"Why are you holding it, then?" It seemed like the obvious question, as did my follow-up. "How did you even know it was here?"

"It's listed in the binder," he said.

"Under what?"

"Inventory."

How neat and organized of them. "So they needed it for something, right? If not the serum, then what?"

I watched Owen. He was thinking. At least, that was what I thought. His head was cocked to the side, his eyes narrowed to a squint.

Of all things, he began removing his sneakers. *Huh?* I then watched as he tiptoed past me oh-so-quietly in his bare feet— he wasn't wearing socks—and carefully placed the Styrofoam cup on the center island in the room before picking up my SIG, which he'd set down. *What's going on?*

I was about to ask that very question when his index finger shot up in the air, stopping me. Right then I knew. He wasn't thinking; he was listening.

He'd heard something.

And the next second, I heard it, too.

CHAPTER 70

IT WAS the sound of someone trying not to make a sound, an otherwise quiet set of footsteps betrayed by the wet pavement outside the building.

My guess was running shoes, maybe cross-trainers. Something with a soft and forgiving sole, perfect for sneaking around.

Unless, of course, it happened to be after a rainstorm. Rubber and water don't play quietly together.

I looked at Owen. He looked at me. We both looked at the light switch by the door. If those footsteps were coming for us, they already knew we were inside. No point making it any easier to be seen.

Owen grabbed the binder, stuffing it in his backpack before killing the lights. He settled in the doorway of the kitchen area by the entrance while I slipped off my Pumas and quietly lifted my duffel over to the doorway of the bathroom opposite him.

With our shoes off and bags in tow, we looked like we

were about to go through airport security. Of course, what we wouldn't have given for an X-ray machine to see through the door outside.

No one could blame us for being paranoid, and hopefully that was all we were being. But better to be safe than dead.

We had the door covered. Our shoes were back on our feet. I was on one knee with my Glock raised, the xenon light turned off and the laser sight aimed waist high.

Next to me, Owen was standing with his strong-side leg slightly back like a boxer and his elbows bent just a little. The Weaver position, as it's commonly called among police and military. Smaller profile, greater stability.

Somewhere in his nineteen years, someone had clearly taught him that. Not surprisingly, the kid had paid attention.

A minute passed with Owen and me having an entire conversation without words. Just nods, shrugs, and prolonged stares.

Neither of us could hear what we'd first heard. In a glass-half-full world, that meant it was just some passerby. A random. Maybe some Starbucks employee—excuse me, *barista*—taking the back way into work.

Of course, in the glass-half-empty world...

We kept listening, our eyes now trained on the door. I could feel the sweat forming in my palms, my right calf cramping, the strain building in my left shoulder from trying to hold my gun steady. It was like a thousand needle jabs.

But all in all, the feeling was relief. The longer we went without hearing anything, the better. Way better.

Isn't that right, Owen?

I glanced over at him, just a quick snapshot as I'd done before. It was so fast my eyes were already turning back to the door without really focusing on what I was seeing.

After all, I already knew what I was seeing. It was Owen in the same stance he'd had from the get-go.

We were maybe four feet from each other, give or take an inch or two. Of course, sometimes that's the difference between life and death, isn't it?

An inch or two.

CHAPTER 71

MY HEAD swiveled back to Owen so fast I could literally feel a breeze in my left ear.

He had moved ever so slightly to his right, just enough that his head—barely half of it, really—was now peeking out from the doorway of the kitchen area. Exposed.

And just like that, the red dot at the end of the laser sight from my Glock was trained on the back of his skull.

Only it wasn't my gun. It was someone else's.

"Down!" I yelled, diving across the hallway.

The sounds of the shot fired, the broken glass, and my shoulder barreling into Owen's rib cage all rolled into one piercing *crack!* as a second breeze hit my left ear, this one courtesy of the bullet that had just barely missed me.

By an inch or two.

Owen and I crash-landed on the linoleum floor of the kitchen. Immediately, he had it figured out—the mistake we'd made ignoring the windows. Just because the blinds were closed didn't mean the shooter was blind.

Two words. "Thermal imaging," he said.

The next sound was the blinds being violently yanked down, followed by more glass breaking. We scrambled to our feet.

"He's coming in," I said.

"No, but something else is. In five seconds, it's going to get real smoky in here."

Actually, it was more like two seconds.

The canister landed with a thud, the sound of it rolling to a stop quickly overtaken by the hissing of the tear gas. I couldn't help stating the obvious.

"We've got to get out of here," I said.

"Not quite yet," said Owen.

Not quite yet?

The gas was pushing toward us, filling the hallway. Our eyes and throats were about to get scorched. All I knew was that staying put gave us no chance. The fact that we were armed gave us at least a fighting chance.

But Owen didn't even look at the SIG I'd given him, still gripped in his right hand. In fact, he put it down.

"What are you doing?" I asked.

But he was too busy doing it to answer. He was searching the cabinets above the counter, opening one door after another.

Until he found it.

Owen turned back to me, holding another large Styrofoam cup, this one empty. I had no idea what he was thinking.

"Please tell me that cup has something to do with our getting out of here," I said.

Owen nodded. "It does," he answered. "Now take off your socks."

My socks?

CHAPTER 72

THERE WAS no time to ask why, not with my eyes feeling the first sting from the tear gas filtering into the kitchen. The first cough couldn't be too far behind.

I quickly took off my socks and gave them to him. Hell, if he had asked me to stand on one leg and clap like a seal, I probably would've done that, too. Anything to speed things along.

"Now I need some cover," he said.

But Owen didn't pick up his backpack as if we were leaving. And when he stopped just shy of the doorway, waiting for me to line up behind him with my Glock, he wasn't looking left toward the door. He was looking right. As in, right into the line of fire.

That was when I knew. He was getting that chlorine stuff, the CTF.

Not that either of us could actually see it by this point. He'd left it on the island in the middle of the room, but the cup hold-

237

ing it—along with the island itself—had disappeared in the cloud above the canister.

Owen lifted the neck of his T-shirt over his nose for a makeshift mask. Clearly, I'd picked the wrong day to wear a button-down.

"Go!" I said.

I squeezed off a few rounds through the shattered windows as Owen flung himself toward the island. For better or worse, whoever was out there, singular or plural, knew we were armed.

But there was no red stream of light aimed our way, no return fire.

Meanwhile, the coughing officially kicked in. Owen was doing the same. On the plus side, it was the only way I could get a read on where he was.

I was waiting for his signal so I could spray a few more bullets as he came back. He didn't bother, though. Next thing I knew, he was crawling into the kitchen on his hands and knees.

Or, at least, one hand. In his other were my two socks. I didn't need to ask what was inside them; Owen had put a cup containing some of the CTF in each one.

In fact, I was pretty sure I had it nailed, especially when the first thing he did was grab a lighter from his backpack. What he'd created was akin to a couple of Molotov cocktails straight out of the *MacGyver* school of impromptu weaponry. Light the fuse, aka my dirty socks, and let her rip.

Turns out, I just got the chemistry backward.

I knelt down with Owen, the only breathing room left being a foot off the floor. We were coughing up our lungs now, our throats burning. Tears were streaming down our cheeks.

Which made the question he managed to get out all the more bizarre.

"You ever play cornhole?" he asked.

Once, at a tailgate party before a Yankees game. Though I never could bring myself to call it that. It was beanbag toss, as far as I was concerned.

I nodded. "Yes."

"Good. Because it's not the fire, it's the water," he said. "Fire's just the accelerator."

"What do you mean?"

"I mean you've got to hit a puddle and you've only got one shot."

Cornhole.

"Okay," I said.

What the hell else could I say? It wasn't exactly the best time to raise my hand and question how water could turn this liquid into a small bomb. Sometimes you've just got to go with the flow.

We grabbed our bags.

"Maybe there's only one guy out there, but I'm guessing more. We draw their fire, and we fire back," he said. "You throw left, I throw right, and then we both run straight as fast as we possibly can."

"What about the car?" I asked.

Owen looked at me, and of all things cracked a smile. We were at death's door—quite literally—and yet somehow he managed to seem more excited than scared, like a mad scientist about to flip the switch.

"*Dude,*" he said. "If this works . . . there won't be a car."

CHAPTER 73

HERE GOES everything...

I yanked open the door, barely jumping back into the bathroom in time to evade the barrage of bullets littering the hallway.

Owen had it pegged; there was definitely more than one shooter. The crisscrossing of all the red laser sights looked like a Pink Floyd concert, complete with the tear gas as smoke.

It was *Us and Them*, all right. They had a small army and automatic weapons. We had pistols.

Oh, yeah. And socks.

The split second the first wave ended, I crouched low and peeked outside with the xenon light, squeezing off shots while looking for the nearest potholes filled with water.

Not too near, though. Collateral damage is no way to die.

I jumped back as the second wave came; this one was even more furious than the first. The drywall was literally disintegrating all around us, every bullet launching a bit of white chalk through the air. Mixed with the tear gas, it was like we were in a snow globe from Hell.

"Where?" yelled Owen.

"Fifteen feet at ten o'clock," I yelled back.

"And yours?"

"Twenty feet at two."

He lit the bottom of his sock and tossed me the lighter. "I'll throw first, then you," he said.

"Fine. Age before beauty, *dude.*"

I flicked my thumb. The sock caught fire immediately. I'd say the feeling was like holding a live grenade, but it wasn't like that. It *was* that.

Spinning around again, I sprayed bullets back and forth like a windshield wiper before stepping aside so Owen could throw. I was giving him light from my Glock the best I could. As soon as he released his sock, he unloaded the rest of his magazine and peeled to the side.

My turn.

There was no time to aim, but there was also no time to think about it and choke. I just let it fly.

It was the second little fireball tossed through the air. Who knows what they must have thought? Maybe nothing at all. They were too busy trying to gun us down as we dove back out of the doorway.

I tossed another magazine to Owen, who quickly reloaded. There was one thing he'd forgotten to mention. *When this CTF stuff mixes with water, how long does it take before—*

BOOM!

The explosion shook and shattered everything around us. Every wall, every nearby window. Suffice it to say, anyone standing outside was no longer on their feet. The proverbial rug not just yanked out from beneath them, but incinerated.

But how long until one of them got back up? Good question. *Run! Right now!*

Owen and I did our best Butch and Sundance, launching out of the building with guns blaring. We were sprinting as fast as we could, hoping against hope that we'd bought ourselves enough time. That made for an even better question.

Was that boom the result of one sock or two?

That was when I saw him. Looking over my shoulder—it was one of the shooters. A clone of the two guys up in New York. Was there a factory somewhere?

Dazed but clearly determined, he was staggering to his feet with his arm raised, and it wasn't to wave hello.

Thank God it was only one sock.

BOOM!

Owen and I caught the edge of the second blast; it seared our backs and sent us hurtling forward across the pavement for the Evel Knievel of road rashes. It hurt like a son of a bitch, like I was being skinned alive.

And I'd never felt luckier in my life.

As we helped each other up, we looked back to see we were the only ones still standing. Not that we were about to linger.

"I'd high-five you, but I have no skin left on my palms," said Owen.

"Me, neither," I said. "C'mon, I know a doctor we should see."

CHAPTER 74

THERE'S ANGRY. Then there's smoldering. And then there's literally smoldering.

"What's that smell?" asked the cabdriver. "It's like something's burning."

"It's just our clothes," I said matter-of-factly. The smell was also our singed flesh, but I didn't feel the need to mention that.

Either way, that little tree-shaped air freshener hanging from the guy's rearview mirror didn't stand a chance.

We'd been burned, all right. Set up big-time.

And now it was time for a little follow-up visit with Dr. Douglas Wittmer. No appointment necessary.

He was so convincing in his kitchen. Of course he was. He was telling us the truth. The only lie was his allegiance. Who the hell did he call after we left him?

We had the taxi drop us off one block down from his town house. There was no telling if Wittmer was still alone, but first we had to see if he was there at all.

243

Maybe he'd gone to church for confession.

If he had, he'd walked. His black Jaguar was still there, parked in the driveway as when we'd first approached him.

Too bad he hadn't given us a second key, the one to his front door.

"How soon before a neighbor calls nine-one-one?" I whispered to Owen, only half joking as I peered inside one of the windows.

With our tattered, bloodstained clothes and shredded hands, knees, and elbows, the two of us looked like we'd just wandered off the set of *The Walking Dead*. At best, we were a couple of burglars. At worst, it was the zombie apocalypse.

I turned back to Owen when he didn't respond. He'd been right behind me.

Now he wasn't anywhere.

Finally, I found him back down by the street. He was staring up at a telephone pole.

"What are you doing?" I asked.

"Looking for the camera."

"What camera?"

"They were watching from either inside or outside. Actually, probably both," he said. "Inside, though, gave them audio."

I stood there trying to reverse engineer what he was saying. If we were being watched when we first showed up to see Wittmer, then that meant...

"Jesus, why didn't you say anything?" I asked. "We were coming here to confront him; he ratted us out."

"I never said that."

"You didn't have to. It was a given," I said. At least, I thought it was. "You mean, he didn't tip them off?"

"Highly unlikely."

"Then why are we even here?"

Owen was still staring up at the pole. "To search for more evidence," he said. "Stuff he didn't share with us."

"What, you think he's going to let us just waltz right in and take what we want?"

Finally, Owen turned to me. "We're hardly going to need his permission," he said.

Before I could ask why not, he was already halfway back to Wittmer's town house, heading up the steps.

Once again, the best I could do was try to keep up with him.

CHAPTER 75

THERE WAS zero hesitation, none whatsoever.

In fact, Owen had already taken off his T-shirt—what was left of it—and wrapped it around his hand by the time he reached the top step. I was only a few feet behind him, but I could see what was coming next a mile away.

What's a little breaking and entering among friends?

With a quick right jab, the window to the left of Wittmer's front door all but disappeared. Working clockwise, Owen knocked away the few holdout shards until we could both climb through without donating any more blood for the evening.

Just a guess, but being two pints down on a cavernously empty stomach is probably not recommended by the American Medical Association.

Owen put his T-shirt back on, entering first. I followed. And at no time did I bother asking him what he wasn't telling me. I figured I'd know soon enough.

Even sooner, as it turned out, when our arrival in Wittmer's foyer was greeted with nothing and no one. Just a dead silence.

The proverbial "bad feeling about this" was suddenly spreading fast from my gut.

"Upstairs," said Owen.

He might have just been talking to himself. I couldn't tell. Either way, there was no sign of the doctor on the first floor.

If "sparsely furnished" was the polite way of describing the downstairs of Wittmer's home, the upstairs made the first floor look like an episode of *Hoarders*. Of the first three bedrooms we looked into, only one actually had a bed. And by bed, I mean a queen-sized mattress on top of a box spring on top of a Harvard frame. No sheets. No pillows.

And still no Wittmer.

Which only made it worse, that feeling of dread. The tightening of the chest muscles. The extra pull on the lungs with each breath.

The inescapable truth of something inevitable.

Because at no time—not for one fraction of a second—did I think there was a chance that Wittmer wasn't there in his home. The only question was where.

"Here," said Owen.

This time, he was definitely talking to me. Pointing, too. He'd turned the corner into the master bedroom.

Two steps past the doorway, I saw him. Wittmer, wearing the same clothes as when we'd left him, was lying in the bed on his back. If I hadn't known better, I'd have said he was simply asleep.

But I did know better, if only because Owen knew better.

Wittmer was never waking up.

CHAPTER 76

MEANS AND motivation. The whole story was right there in front of us, exactly as intended. Although it wasn't intended for us.

On the bed next to Wittmer, where the ghost of his wife surely slept, was a large photo album opened to a spread filled with happy, loving pictures of the two of them in Paris. They were kissing in front of the Eiffel Tower, arm in arm beneath the external Habitrail-like piping of the Centre Pompidou in Beaubourg, and playfully leaning against Louis Derbré's *Le Prophète* in the Jardin du Luxembourg, the golden head of the statue—and their faces—beaming in the sunshine.

Claire and I used to talk about going to Paris together. But life is ninety percent talk, isn't it?

As if connecting the dots, my eyes moved from the photo album over to the empty pill bottle, the orange-brownish variety you get from your local pharmacy. Only, there was no label on it, no indication of a prescription.

Ironically, that made the story even more convincing. Wittmer was a doctor, after all. What pills *wouldn't* he have access to?

It all made so much sense. Of course, that was why it was all bullshit.

I was catching on quick, all right. Certainly faster than the police would, if at all. Odds were they never would.

This was no suicide.

"Temazepam, if I had to guess," said Owen with a nod to the empty pill bottle. "Very effective for insomnia, Michael Jackson notwithstanding. One injection, probably to the carotid artery, and the coroner would never know the drug wasn't swallowed."

The image of Wittmer giving injections to the prisoners in Stare Kiejkuty flashed through my mind. *Oh, the irony...*

Without even thinking, I leaned in, looking at Wittmer's neck for a needle mark. I didn't know why, I just did. I felt sorry for him. He'd made his choices, but he didn't deserve this.

"Christ, we can't even call the police," I said.

Wittmer lived alone. There was no telling how long it would be before his body was discovered. The same could be said for the guy in my bathtub back in Manhattan, but I couldn't give a rat's ass about him. This was different.

"Maybe we could somehow leave an anonymous tip," I said. "What do you think?"

I was still staring at Wittmer's neck, waiting for Owen to answer. When he didn't, I turned around. Again, he was gone. I called out to him.

"In here," he responded.

I followed his voice to the only room left on the second floor we hadn't searched. Wittmer's office.

Unlike every other room, though, this one looked the part. A large, messy desk, stacked bookcases, and a well-worn leather armchair with an ottoman. There was even a rug—a faded crimson and gold Persian with tassels, some of them frayed, some of them missing altogether.

To call it a lived-in look would be an understatement. In fact, what it really was, was depressing.

This wasn't Wittmer's office. This was Wittmer. Period. In the wake of his wife's death, his life had become defined by his work. This was all he'd had.

"What are you looking at?" I asked.

"Something I shouldn't be," said Owen. "Not if they're trying to cover their tracks."

CHAPTER 77

HE WAS standing by one of the bookcases, staring long and hard at a picture in a dust-covered silver frame. It was an old photograph of Wittmer from his undergrad days at Princeton, a group shot of some members of the Cap and Gown eating club.

Of course, if it hadn't been for the engraving at the bottom of the frame saying as much, I never would've known that.

So why is Owen staring at it so intently?

I leaned in close, focusing on Wittmer. He looked so young. Happy. Alive. "What am I not seeing?" I asked.

"The whole picture," Owen said.

If I'd somehow lost the forest for the trees, there was still no finding it as I canvassed the other half dozen faces staring back at me in the photo. Owen all but expected as much, giving me a hint.

"He had a lot more hair back then," he said.

With that, he reached out with his index finger, tracing a line from Wittmer to the guy on the end, who was lanky and, yes, had only a hint of a receding hairline.

But now I could picture him bald, and in doing so, all I could see—and recognize—was the same smirk masquerading as a smile that he always flashed in interviews as if there weren't a question in the world that could ever trip him up.

Of course, that was according to Claire, who had, in fact, interviewed him for the *Times*. She said he reeked of coffee and cockiness.

"Clay Dobson?"

"Exactly," said Owen.

"Okay, so Wittmer went to school with the president's chief of staff," I said. "What are you suggesting?"

"A connection."

"Or maybe it's just a coincidence."

"Yeah, except for one thing," he said. "There are no coincidences in politics."

That sounded a lot like an Aaron Sorkin line, but I wasn't about to debate it. "What kind of connection?" I asked. "Do you mean, like, *orchestrated*?"

"Of course not," said Owen, as facetious as I was incredulous. "Nothing illegal ever happens in the White House."

Point taken. Multiple points, actually. *Arms for hostages…sex with an intern and then lying about it under oath…a certain botched burglary at a hotel only a handful of miles from where Owen and I were standing?*

Suddenly, the only thing I could hear in my head was the voice of then-senator Howard Baker during the Watergate hearings, asking one of the most famous—if not *the* most famous—political questions of all time.

What did the president know and when did he know it?

Then again, maybe we were getting a wee bit ahead of ourselves.

I leaned in again, staring at the images of Wittmer and Dobson. "It's still only a picture," I said.

"You're right," Owen replied. "It's possible that it's nothing. Of course, it's also possible that Lawrence Bass really did want to spend more time with his family instead of running the CIA."

I'd forgotten about that. Owen hadn't. We'd watched the announcement Bass had made with his wife and two young daughters in the East Room of the White House. The guy had been the president's pick to become the next director of the CIA. Not only was he passing that up, he was resigning from the National Security Council.

Still. Forget Aaron Sorkin. This was starting to feel more like an Oliver Stone fever dream.

"So, now . . . what? Bass is somehow connected, too?" I asked.

Only, this time, I could hear it in my own voice. That incredulous tone was missing. Owen could hear it, too.

"Just for the sake of argument," he said, "what if there really was a path to the White House? *How would we follow it?*"

Between the two of us, I was the only one with a law degree, but you could've fooled me, the way he asked that question. Because lawyers—the good ones, at least—never ask a question they don't already know the answer to.

I wasn't the only one with Watergate on the brain.

"For the record, you don't look anything like Dustin Hoffman," I said.

Owen gave me a quick head-to-toe. He smiled. "Yeah, and you wish you looked like Robert Redford."

BOOK FOUR

PANTS ON FIRE, EVERYTHING ON FIRE

CHAPTER 78

CLAY DOBSON gazed across the clutter of his large oak desk, locking eyes with his 9 a.m. appointment while doing everything he could not to break into a shit-eating grin.

It wasn't easy.

The morning had already brought the good news from Frank Karcher that their little problem in New York had been taken care of—right here in their own backyard, no less. The kid and the reporter's boyfriend were both dead.

Of course, so was his old college chum, Wittmer, but there was a reason Dobson had had cameras placed inside and outside Wittmer's home. He'd never fully trusted the guy. Wittmer was weak.

So, too, was Lawrence Bass.

That was what made this meeting with him such a lay-up, thought Dobson, the former small forward for the Princeton Tigers basketball team. Dare he think it, a *slam dunk*.

After all, Bass hadn't bum-rushed him out on Pennsylvania

Avenue or cornered him with a clenched fist in the men's room at the Blue Duck Tavern, where all the political heavyweights fed both their stomachs and their egos.

Instead, he'd made an appointment. *An appointment?* That was like knocking on a door instead of kicking it down. Total milquetoast. No balls.

"I'd like an explanation, Clay," said Bass, sitting with legs crossed on the other side of the desk.

Even that was weak, thought Dobson. He'd *like* an explanation? No, you dolt, you *demand* an explanation!

Yeah, the decision to sandbag Bass, the former director of intelligence programs with the NSC, was looking better by the second. He would've made a lousy head of the CIA, not that he ever really had a shot at the gig. Bass was simply a decoy, the fall guy who would pave the way for Frank Karcher.

"Trust me," said Dobson, folding his arms. "Karch is not the loose cannon you think he is."

"So it's really going to be him?" asked Bass. "The rumor's true?"

"This is Washington, Larry. What rumor isn't?"

Bass let go with a defeated sigh, slouching a bit. Dobson was happy to have him vent a little, but they both knew Bass had no recourse. He was a good soldier, and good soldiers fall in line.

As if having just reminded himself of that, Bass straightened up in his chair. The air returned to his lungs, his chest expanding.

"I serve or don't serve at the pleasure of the president," he said. "I understand the politics in play, and I appreciate your wanting to look out for me and my family."

"You have my word," said Dobson. "In a few months, you'll have your pick of jobs and complete financial security."

Bass nodded. "I know, and like I said, I appreciate that. It's just that...Karcher? *Really?*"

"Listen, I understand your frustration, I really do," said Dobson, rising from his chair. He walked over to the credenza and poured himself more coffee. It was his third refill of the morning. "Oh, I'm sorry," he said, turning back to Bass. "Do you want a cup?"

"Actually, I do," Bass said. "Thank you."

Dobson cocked an eyebrow, surprised. The coffee offer was merely out of politeness. A perfunctory gesture. Everyone and their mother knew that Bass abstained not only from alcohol, but also from caffeine. It was the one and only thing he and Karcher had in common.

For a devout Catholic, Bass was more Mormon than most Mormons.

Was this the first loose thread, wondered Dobson? The beginning of the complete unraveling of Larry "Halo Head" Bass?

Coffee...then a little whiskey in the coffee...then hold the coffee, just give me the whiskey?

In the meantime, "How do you take it?" asked Dobson. "Cream?"

"No, but three sugars," Bass said.

Dobson turned his back, reaching for the sugar bowl and spoon on the credenza. He began scooping. "You like it sweet, huh?"

"Yes," said Bass. "Sweet."

Like revenge.

CHAPTER 79

THERE WERE two things on Frank Karcher's to-do list that morning. Both bordered on a death wish.

The first was lying to Clay Dobson. Bright and early, at oh-seven-hundred hours, he told the president's chief of staff that the kid and the former lawyer were eliminated, their bodies disposed of so thoroughly that even God himself didn't know where they were.

How much time this would buy Karcher, he didn't know. But there was only so much bad news and perceived incompetence he could dump in Dobson's lap, and that quota had already been met in spades.

So it was time for plan B. As in, bullshit. He'd played the game inside the Beltway long enough to know how things really worked. *When the truth doesn't cooperate, stop telling it.*

Sure enough, Dobson was so relieved to think the kid was no longer a threat that the collateral damage—the stuff that actually was true—was taken in stride. When he was told about

Wittmer, as well as about having to shut down the now bullet-ridden lab behind M Street, Dobson's only response, after a pregnant pause, was "So the kid is definitely gone, right?"

Of course, the fact that the kid actually wasn't gone was merely semantics, a minor detail, as far as Karcher was concerned. Sometimes a lie is just the truth that hasn't happened yet.

Or so he'd convinced himself as he made his way to the outskirts of McLean and the off-site training gym of the CIA's Special Activities Division, the same division he'd headed up years ago before moving up the ladder to become the National Clandestine Service chief.

The reason the gym was off-site was because it "officially" didn't exist. Nor was it open to all the agents-in-training of the Special Activities Division. Only a select group was invited to join, the CIA's equivalent of Green Berets.

Accordingly, hanging a sign out front that read MEN ONLY would've been redundant.

Paying a visit to the gym was the second item on Karcher's to-do list. It promised to be one the young agents would never forget, although that was precisely what they were required to do.

Nothing "officially" happens in a place that doesn't officially exist.

Barging through the door, his heels stomping the cement floor with each and every step, Karcher marched straight across the middle of the windowless gym toward an old-school boom box on a milk crate that was pumping out Metallica's "For Whom the Bell Tolls."

Without breaking stride, he grabbed a twenty-five-pound barbell off a rack and heaved it dead center into the boom box, a perfect strike that shattered the cheap molded plastic into a hundred pieces. The gym immediately fell silent, save for the lingering echo of Lars Ulrich's drumbeats.

Then, as patiently as possible for a man desperate to save his career, Karcher waited until every set of eyes was looking directly at him. He scratched the chin underneath his oversized head before folding his arms, his deep voice filling the room until there was no escape, not for anyone.

"Okay, he barked. *"Who's the toughest motherfucker here?"*

CHAPTER 80

THERE WERE no takers, no volunteers.

This, despite the fact that membership in this particular gym was predicated on being a badass, and being proud of it.

A *smart* badass, though. Someone not prone to unnecessary risk or exposure, or, at the very least, someone who knew a trick question when he heard one.

Karcher glanced around amid the deafening silence, making sure to lock eyes with the dozen or so men in the room. He was giving each and every one of them his live-grenade look, the full-on crazy, the kind of batshit stare that could make Charles Manson himself step back and say, "Hey, man, whoa...*chill out.*"

But Karcher was only getting started.

Slowly now, he made his way over to the largest agent in the room, a brick wall with a buzz cut who was sitting on the bench press between sets. The veins rippling up and down each arm looked like maps of the DC Metrorail.

"Do you know who I am?" Karcher asked, almost politely.

The young agent nodded. "Yes."

Karcher's face immediately soured. So much for polite. *"Then stand the fuck up when I'm talking to you."*

The agent stood. He had four inches on Karcher, easy. But right then, right there, he hardly seemed taller.

"What's your name?" asked Karcher.

"Evans, sir."

"Was I ever here today, Evans?"

"No, sir."

"Were any of us here today?"

"No, sir."

"So none of it ever happened, right?"

The agent, Evans, blinked a few times. Confusion in his eyes. *None of what? What's about to happen?*

Regardless, his answer wasn't about to change. "No, sir," he said. "It never happened."

Karcher leaned in, his big head getting right in Evans's grill. "I'll tell you what definitely did happen," he said. "The three-some I had with your mother and another whore last night."

Evans cracked a slight smile. He'd hardly be in the CIA, let alone the Special Activities Division, if he'd taken the bait.

But this heap of chum was pushing things.

"Your mom's quite the moaner," Karcher continued. "You want to hear what she sounds like? Do you? *Do you?*"

Evans dropped the smile, his jaw tightening, his fists balling. He shifted his feet, if only to give himself something else to do besides decking Karcher, who was far from finished.

"You're just going to stand there and take it, Evans? Huh? Like your mother did on her hands and knees? What kind of a pussy are you, Evans? You don't want to take a swing at me? C'mon, boy, take a swing at me!"

As if that invitation weren't open enough, Karcher stuck out his chin. He waited . . . waited . . . waited . . . before finally shaking his head in disgust.

"Yeah, I didn't think so," he said.

Neither did anyone else in the gym. A couple of the other guys even let out audible sighs of relief as Karcher turned to walk away. Only, he wasn't walking away.

He was winding up.

Karcher spun around and threw his first punch like he was throwing a javelin, thrusting the flat of his knuckles square into Evans's solar plexus. The bigger they are . . .

The young agent fell to his knees, immediately gasping for air that he no longer had. He was defenseless and teed up like a Titleist as Karcher began swinging, hitting him over and over and over in the face, the blood rupturing from his nose and mouth.

C'mon, you idiots, what are you waiting for? Stop watching me and do something. Get in here!

The group inertia from the initial shock wore off, the other agents collapsing on Karcher to pull him away from Evans. Karcher feigned a struggle, trying to break free from all the sets of hands holding him back.

But he wasn't looking for peacemakers.

"That's right, protect your boy, Evans!" Karcher shouted. "You probably all wipe each other's asses, too. In fact, I wouldn't be surprised if—"

Pow!

The punch came out of nowhere, as did the guy who threw it—a Hispanic agent with a shaved head who couldn't have been more than five-eight while standing on his toes.

"Martinez, no!" someone shouted.

A couple of the other agents let go of Karcher so they could hold back Martinez, or try to. Martinez pushed them away, one after the other, and resumed going after Karcher, unleashing a barrage of right jabs until the skull-and-bones tattoo on the inside of his wrist became a blur.

Everyone backed away now. There was no stopping Martinez. Karcher fell to one knee and then both, his head whipping back and forth with each punch until finally he collapsed, his blood-soaked face hitting the ground with a nauseating *squish*.

Martinez loomed over him, like Ali over Liston, daring him to get up for more. But Karcher had no such plans. He'd gotten what he'd come for.

Martinez had just owned him in a fight. But now he owned Martinez forever.

Winner, winner, chicken dinner . . .

CHAPTER 81

"MY NAME'S Trevor Mann," I told the guy in the black suit who opened the front door. He looked far more bodyguard than butler. "I believe Mr. Brennan is expecting me."

"He is," I was told with a nod that somehow managed to be both deferential and disinterested at the same time. "He's out back. I'll take you."

Great, you do that. Just so long as you don't frisk me first.

As much as I didn't really think that was a possibility, I wasn't a hundred percent sure of anything. The guy's boss, Josiah Brennan, didn't head up one of the most powerful—and profitable—law firms in DC based on his good looks and Southern charm alone, although those certainly didn't hurt his cause.

To read anything about this self-described "good ol' boy from Tennessee" was to know that when he was done slapping your back, he was just as capable of putting a knife in it. And not just figuratively speaking.

Which pretty much explained the Glock in my shin holster.

Had Brennan already been tipped off? Did he know the truth about me? Or did he buy the lie?

I walked behind his henchman—all six foot six of him, if I had to guess—through the front-to-back foyer the size of a cathedral. Along the way, I did my best to get the lay of the land without being too obvious. A quick peek down a hallway here, a slight crane of the neck there. When the moment was right, I could ill afford to be wasting time in the wrong rooms.

"Very cozy," I joked, my voice practically echoing.

Mr. Henchman smirked, opening a pair of oversized French doors to the backyard. "This way," he said. "Follow me."

Trust me, Lurch, I was following you before I even knew who you were....

For the past seventy-two hours, tucked away in the Comforter Motel near Arcola with $9.95-a-day Wi-Fi, Owen and I had done our best Woodward and Bernstein, taking Deep Throat's advice from the moment we'd left the late Dr. Wittmer's house.

Follow the money.

Not that the trail was easy. Tracing the title of the lab where Wittmer picked up the serum required a little more than a field trip to public records at city hall.

Whoever owned it didn't want anyone to know. Check that...they *really* didn't want anyone to know. The tangled web of trusts and LLCs was chock-full of misdirection and red herrings, not to mention the kind of firewalls designed to keep the most serious hackers on the sidelines.

Of course, there's serious...and then there's Owen. After a while, I simply stopped asking *"How did you do that?"*

From Georgetown to Delaware to the Channel Islands to a different bank in the Channel Islands and then back to

Delaware, the money moved like a carousel, around and around.

But one thing stayed the same. Brennan's law firm.

What was more, Brennan had personally drafted all the LLC agreements, including all filings with the state, the most boilerplate of legal documents. That was like hiring Mario Batali to heat up some Chef Boyardee spaghetti and meatballs for you. In a word, overkill.

Or maybe for a White House chief of staff taking no chances, just the right amount of kill.

Problem was, we were still missing that proverbial smoking gun: something that directly linked Brennan to Clay Dobson or whoever else owned that lab behind M Street.

Owen had hacked Brennan's law firm's network to no avail. Now the question was whether Brennan had a personal computer at home.

Good thing my face had healed, because it was time for my close-up.

I was on.

CHAPTER 82

HEY, ROOKIE, look out for the left hook!

During my first year with the Manhattan DA's office, when I was as green as a plate of peas, the chief assistant district attorney—a former Golden Gloves welterweight champion from Jersey City—used to put up his fists and bark that at me before the start of every trial. In other words... *expect the unexpected.*

"Watch your step," warned Mr. Henchman.

"I'm sorry, what?"

The guy pointed to the ground as we walked through the French doors. "The drop-off," he explained.

"Oh," I said. *That's what you meant.*

And with that, I stepped down onto a massive patio of blue slate with grass edgings, immediately wondering if I'd perhaps stumbled upon the set of a Ralph Lauren ad.

There were about fifty people, evenly split between genders. The men were all in blue blazers with Popsicle-colored slacks—cherry, orange, and lemon. On the women were sleeveless sundresses exposing tanned and toned arms.

Suddenly, I was keenly aware of the fact that I'd been wearing the same pair of brown chinos for the past three days. At least the sport coat and white button-down were new, purchased just for this occasion.

"He's over here," said Mr. Henchman with a glance back over his shoulder at me.

After another twenty feet, he peeled off at the exact moment that Brennan turned around to face me as if he had eyes in the back of his head.

"I know everyone else here, so you must be Trevor Mann," he said, flashing a near-blinding grin. He promptly extended his hand. It was hard not to notice that in his other hand was a double-barreled shotgun.

At least it wasn't pointed at me. Not yet.

No sooner did Brennan shake my hand than he practically spun me around so he could introduce me not just to the two couples he was talking to but to the entire guest list.

"Ladies and gentlemen," he began, playing up what remained of his Southern drawl after decades in DC, as well as a few years in Manhattan. "I think it was Will Rogers who famously said that you never get a second chance to make a good first impression. With that in mind, I have a favor to ask you all."

He promptly put his arm around me as if he'd known me for years.

"This here is Mr. Trevor Mann," he continued. "He's an esteemed professor up north with the Columbia Law School, which, much to the chagrin of my Confederate flag–waving father, happens to be my alma mater. Mr. Mann called me two nights ago because he's also a freelance writer for the *New York Times* and they're looking to do a profile on me for their

Sunday magazine. So the favor is this: Should Mr. Mann corner one of you at any point this afternoon and ask for your opinion about me, here's what I need you to do. *Lie with impunity.*"

Everyone laughed, except for the Jessica Lange look-alike who weaved her way toward me, rolling her eyes.

"You'll have to forgive my husband, there's nothing he likes more than the sound of his own voice," she said.

"Mr. Mann, may I present my beautiful and brutally honest wife, Abigail," said Brennan.

The polite smile she gave me soured quickly as she caught sight of the shotgun in her husband's hand. "Josiah, you promised," she said.

He turned to me with no admission of guilt. "Have you ever done any skeet shooting, Mr. Mann?"

"No, I never have," I said.

"Terrific sport, but the wife hates it, I'm afraid."

"What the wife hates is having pieces of clay birds scattered all over her lawn," said Abigail.

"They're called pigeons, darling. Though would you rather I shoot at real birds instead?"

Abigail linked her arm in mine. It was flirtatious, but it was also an act. If I had to bet, I'd wager she was even smarter than her husband. "Have you ever noticed that, Mr. Mann?" she asked me. "The way lawyers have a comeback for everything?"

"I think that's what makes them lawyers," I said.

Brennan liked that answer. "Did you know that Mr. Mann here used to be quite the practicing attorney himself?"

"*Used* to be?" asked Abigail.

"Mr. Mann made a principled stand in a rather noteworthy trial up in New York," said Brennan.

"Some say principled, others say boneheaded," I pointed out.

"Indeed," he said. "That's the dilemma of a man's integrity, isn't it? One way or the other, there always seems to be a price to pay." Brennan held my stare for a few moments before flashing that blinding grin again. "Now, c'mon, let's go dirty up my wife's lawn."

CHAPTER 83

SOCIAL ETIQUETTE may vary from country to country, but in the good old USA, when the host of a party asks his guests if they'd like to watch him show off, there's really only one answer.

Looking like a preppy parade, everyone followed Brennan off the patio to a long stretch of grass that was somewhere between a six and a seven iron. Off to either side were the small houses—or traps, as they're also called—for launching the clay pigeons. One trap releases high, the other low.

Okay, so I lied to Brennan. It was more like a fib, really. I'd been skeet shooting before. Twice, actually. Speaking of my principled stand, the head of the hedge fund where I'd been general counsel was a huge fan of the sport. I'm sure he must have missed it terribly during his two-year stint behind bars.

Then again, in these white-collar-crime prisons that double as country clubs, maybe the skeet course was next to the tennis courts.

"Who's first?" asked Brennan as we gathered in a semicircle around him. Translation? *Who wants to suck at this first so I'll look that much better when it's my turn?*

There were no takers, which hardly seemed to disappoint Brennan. If anything, he relished the apprehension among his invited male guests.

Finally, he got his volunteer. By choosing him.

"Harper," he said, pointing. "I believe you're the youngest of the firm's partners, isn't that right?"

Poor Harper, whoever he was. The guy stepped forward with a forced smile, taking the shotgun from his boss like a vegetarian picking up a double cheeseburger. Clearly, he was a city boy. Probably the only hunting he'd ever done in his life was for an apartment.

Brennan provided him with a quick tutorial before giving nods in the direction of both traps, each being manned by a guy sporting the universal hired-hand pose: feet slightly spread, arms behind the back, fingers clasped.

Pull!

Harper missed terribly with both shots. On the bright side, he didn't kill himself or any of the rest of us. Same for the other "volunteers" Brennan summoned after him. No one could shoot a lick.

"Your turn, Mr. Mann," I kept waiting to hear, and to be honest, the thought of shattering at least one of those little clay suckers, if not both, was feeling pretty damn good.

Brennan, however, never looked my way. "Perhaps it's time I give it a whirl," he announced instead.

But before he could even reach down into the box of shells by his feet, his wife, Abigail, chimed in with a nod to Title IX and her fellow women. "What about one of the girls?" she asked.

Brennan didn't miss a beat. "Honey, we both know how

much life insurance I have. The last thing I'm about to do is hand you a loaded gun."

"I wasn't talking about me," she said once the laughter subsided. "Perhaps one of our female guests would like to try."

"You're right," said Brennan. What else could he say? "How about it, ladies? I didn't mean to exclude you."

But of course he did. Had I truly been writing a *Times* profile on him, I probably would've noted that less than ten percent of his firm's partners were women.

Still, as with the men, there were no takers. Just silence.

"C'mon, now," he prodded. "I promise you won't break a nail."

Wow, he really just said that, didn't he?

No one was groaning, though. Instead, the guests were too busy turning in search of the voice that had suddenly called out from the patio.

"I'll give it a shot," she said.

CHAPTER 84

ON A scale of one to ten for entrances, it was easily an eleven.

Stepping off the patio and joining the Ralph Lauren ad on the lawn was the quintessential Benetton couple—a stunning all-American blonde on the arm of a handsome Middle Eastern man.

That said, all eyes were on the blonde.

She, too, was wearing a sleeveless sundress, entirely white with a plunging neckline, but amid all the tan and toned arms of the other female guests, hers appeared a little tanner, a little more toned.

"Shahid, you made it!"

Our semicircle around Brennan did a Red Sea part so the couple of the moment could greet the host and hostess. All anyone else could do was watch and listen as the man, Shahid, introduced his plus-one, Beverly Sands.

"Beverly and I only just met, so you need to make me look good," said Shahid with a tug on his royal-blue blazer.

"I think you look pretty good already," said Abigail, linking her arm with Shahid's. This was clearly her signature move.

"Actually, I was going to ask the same of you, Shahid," said Brennan before turning to find me among his guests. I stepped forward. "Trevor Mann, I'd like you to meet a client of mine, Shahid Al Dossari, and his friend, Beverly Sands."

"Very nice to meet you both," I said, shaking their hands.

"So you know, Trevor's writing a profile of me for the *New York Times*," Brennan explained.

Shahid nodded, impressed. So did Beverly. But for a split second, before her nod, I could've sworn there was something else. A sort of look she gave me. A squint. In a word...doubt.

Or, hell, maybe it was just the sun in my eyes.

Whatever it was, it came and went, her attention returning quickly to Brennan. Specifically, the open shotgun nestled over his forearm.

Playfully but with an edge, she asked, "So am I going to shoot that damn thing or not?"

"Hell, yes," said Brennan, snapping to.

As Abigail stepped back with Shahid still looped on her arm, Brennan proceeded to give Beverly the same tutorial he'd given the men, albeit with considerably more care and attention. The more he talked, the more she hung on his every word like a rapt pupil.

"Like this?" she asked, unsure, propping the butt of the gun high against her shoulder.

"Actually, you want to bring it a little lower, sweetheart," said Brennan, guiding the stock down a few inches.

"And I aim by looking through...?"

"You want to line up the front and rear sights," he said, pointing them out.

"So now what happens?" she asked, closing one eye to aim.

"Now you try to shoot one of the clay disks that will be coming out of those little houses to your left and right," said Brennan.

"Just one?"

He chuckled. So did more than half of the other men in the crowd. "Or two, if you'd like," said Brennan. "Feel free to shoot them both. Ain't nothin' wrong with a little optimism."

With that, he looked back at Shahid and gave him a wink.

"Okay, I'm ready," said Beverly.

"Great," said Brennan. "All that's left to do is say—"

But Beverly Sands knew exactly what to say. Among other things.

"Pull!" she yelled.

As fast as the pigeons were released from the traps, they shattered even faster. First the low one, then the high one. Two quick blasts and they were blown to pieces...all over Abigail Brennan's lawn.

Casually, Beverly handed the shotgun back to a stunned Brennan and immediately looked down at her hand.

"What do you know?" she said with a perfect shrug. "I think I broke a nail."

CHAPTER 85

I'D BEEN around a lot of good defense attorneys, and the best of them were always lightning quick on their feet while oozing grace under pressure at all times. They also knew a no-win situation when they saw one.

In other words, there was no way Josiah Brennan was taking his turn with that shotgun.

"All right, then," he said, turning to his guests with the best self-deprecating laugh he could muster. "I think it's lunchtime."

The menu back on the patio was an eclectic mix of upscale and down-home. Next to the grilled New Zealand baby lamb chops were baked beans and corn bread. The napkins were linen, the utensils plastic. If the red velvet cake and the trifle were too rich for you, there was a tray of Rice Krispie treats made by the Brennans' nine-year-old daughter, Rebecca, who looked like a mini-me of her mother.

I figured a half hour to eat and mingle and blend in with the crowd. Then it was time to get lost. As for my permission to wander aimlessly in someone else's home, that was as easy as three words. "Where's the bathroom?"

I made sure to pose the question to Mr. Henchman, since he was the only guy whose job it was to make sure I didn't do what I was about to do. In his mind, at least for a few minutes, I was accounted for inside the house.

"Down the hall, second left," he told me.

Closing the door behind me in the bathroom, I counted to thirty while staring at an equestrian-patterned wallpaper that even Ann Romney would've passed on. In case Mr. Henchman was standing watch, I then flushed the toilet and ran the sink for a few seconds.

But he wasn't standing watch. I was a guest, after all. That would've been weird.

Walking out of the bathroom free and clear, I immediately turned into Monty Hall on speed. *What's behind door number one? And two? And three?*

Pay dirt came with door number four. The mahogany bookshelves, the studded leather couch and matching armchairs, the painting over the marble fireplace depicting a mute of hounds in pursuit of a fox—basically, just the overwhelming stench of testosterone—left no doubt that I was in Brennan's home office.

And sitting atop a huge partners desk the size of a pool table was the whole reason for my being there. Quickly, I reached for my new prepaid cell phone and dialed Owen, who was waiting back at the hotel.

"Okay, I'm standing in front of his computer," I said. "It's a laptop, a Toshiba."

"That'll work," Owen said. "You remember what to do?"

I did. First, I had to install the flash drive he'd given me, only it wasn't a flash drive. It just looked like one. Owen called it a "phantom" because it overrode any and all password requirements—from accessing internal documents to e-mail accounts—and left no trace of the user. It would be as if I had never even been there. A phantom.

"Okay, we're up," I said, staring at the desktop page. Thankfully, it booted up quickly. "We're on his wireless network. Ready on your end?"

"Ready."

I brought up Internet Explorer, typing in the Web address Owen had given me, which was a series of numbers that meant nothing to me until he explained that it was pi multiplied by pi to the tenth decimal. Yeah, that figured, too...

"Do you see it?" he asked.

"Yep."

The "it" was a site he'd named Moonshine, because, according to Owen, it was homemade and always did the trick. The kid was like a Vegas magician, the way he had a name for everything. The difference being, his tricks weren't illusions. They were real.

"Okay, give me about thirty seconds," he said.

In layman's terms, Owen was now hijacking Brennan's hard drive, gaining access to every document he had. In the scheme of things, needing only a half minute to do that was like building Rome in a day. But from where I was standing, it was feeling like forever.

I kept looking at the door, fearing the worst. It would be the next second or the next second after that when someone would turn that handle and walk in on me. Mr. Henchman, or even worse, Brennan himself. Some things you simply can't talk your way out of.

"C'mon, Owen," I said to the beat of the *tick-tick-tick* in my head. "Tell me we're done."

"Just a little longer," he said.

"I'm starting to get a bad feeling."

"That's called paranoia."

"No, it's called empirical evidence," I said. "Have you been keeping a diary this week, by any chance?"

"Good one," he said. "Now do me a favor, will you?"

"What's that?"

"Go back to the party."

Click. He was done.

I pocketed my phone, exiting the browser and powering down the laptop as quickly as I could. All the while, I kept glancing at the door, willing it to remain closed.

But it wasn't the door I should've been worried about. It was the desk.

The desk?

CHAPTER 86

I TOPPLED to the floor so fast there wasn't even time to break my fall. Instead of throwing out my hands, the best I could do was lead with my shoulder. Better a cracked collarbone than a cracked skull.

What the hell just happened? Did I really just get decked by the desk?

Sort of.

Right there under it, and still gripping my ankles, was the Annie Oakley of skeet shooting herself, Beverly Sands. What on earth she was doing there I was certain we'd get to in a moment. But first, it was pure instinct as I tried to kick myself free. I almost did, too, until she grabbed both my shins.

Uh-oh. *My shins.*

The second she felt the holster beneath my pant leg, out came a snub-nosed .38 that was strapped to her inner thigh courtesy of a tricked-out leather garter belt. Very *La Femme Nikita.*

"Who are you?" she demanded. "Why do you have a gun?"

"Right back atcha," I would've said if it hadn't been for the fact that her gun was aimed right at my head.

Instead, "I'm Trevor Mann," I answered, trying to catch my breath. "We met when you arrived, remember?"

"Yeah, but you don't write for the *Times*."

"What makes you so sure?"

"You don't look smug enough," she said. "You're also too nervous to be law enforcement."

"Yeah, well, sorry I can't be more cool for you with a gun in my face."

She was losing her patience. *"What the hell are you doing in here? Who was that on the phone? And what do you want with Brennan's computer?"*

"Jesus, one at a time, will you? Slow down."

She motioned over her shoulder toward the door. "We don't have that luxury."

"Whatever I tell you, you won't believe me," I said.

She was about to respond, her mouth open to form the first word. But she suddenly stopped, pointing at me.

"Trevor Mann," she said, repeating my name as if running it through her memory. "Why does that ring a bell?"

"The NYPD pension fund?"

She nodded. Bingo. "You're that lawyer."

"Yes, I'm that lawyer."

Her finger was still pointing at me, but fortunately the gun wasn't. She lowered it. "Honest to a fault," she said.

"Thank you."

"That wasn't a compliment," she informed me. "But go ahead, I might just believe you now."

There are times to talk and there are times to shut up. Then there are times when you're on the floor with a woman wearing a leather garter-belt holster in the private office of a rich and powerful man who'd be less than understanding, to put it mildly, should he walk in on you.

Whatever you tell her, Mann, make it fast....

With that, I gave the quickest possible summation of what I was doing and why. "We think Brennan is involved with something he shouldn't be."

"Join the club," she said. "But who's *we*?"

"Me and the guy on the phone."

"Were you hacking Brennan's e-mail?"

"Something like that."

"Was it something *more* than that?"

The way she asked the question, she sounded—of all things—*hopeful.*

That was when it clicked, what she was doing underneath the giant desk. I could see the wires running straight down from the top through a grommet-covered hole.

"You were bugging his phone, weren't you? And I walked in on you," I said.

"Something like that," she replied, mimicking me.

"Who are you, then?" I asked.

She thought for a second, weighing the truth versus a possible lie. The truth won out. "My name's not Beverly Sands, it's Agent Valerie Jensen," she said. "I'm with the NSA."

"Since when do you guys have field agents?"

"We don't. Just like we also don't bug phones," she said, standing. Without the slightest hint of modesty, she hiked up her white sundress, reholstering her .38 along her inner thigh. "C'mon, we've got to get back to the party."

I stood up, falling in line behind her. We were ten feet from the door when she suddenly motioned for me to stop.

The next thing I knew, she was kissing me.

CHAPTER 87

BEFORE I could figure out what the hell was going on, the door of Brennan's office opened. The hinges had the distinct sound of a train flying off the tracks.

Immediately, Valerie broke away from me. We'd been caught in the act: our mouths agape, eyes wide with surprise. But between the two of us, I was the only one not acting.

Valerie had heard the footsteps and had seen the turn of the door handle. Talk about thinking fast on your feet. Agent Jensen was even faster with her lips.

"Are you two cheating?" the young girl asked.

Staring at us with her arms crossed, waiting for an answer, was the Brennans' nine-year-old daughter, Rebecca.

"*Cheating?*" asked Valerie.

"You know, like, having an affair? You came to the party with a different man," Rebecca said. "I saw you, don't lie."

"No . . . no, honey," I said, shifting quickly into denial mode. It was pure reflex. "We were just—"

Valerie cut me off faster than a New York City cabdriver. "Yes, you caught us," she said. "We're having an affair."

I looked at her, stunned. *Did you really just say that?*

She really did.

Little Rebecca nodded with the kind of self-satisfied grin kids get when a grown-up treats them like a grown-up. She pointed at me.

"You better be careful, then," she said. "I saw this movie on TV, and when the husband found out, he killed the other guy with a snow globe."

"Ooh, I've seen that movie, too," said Valerie. She turned to me, raising her hands to act it out. "You get hit right in the head with the snow globe—*bam!*—and blood starts gushing down your forehead and—"

"I know, I know!" said Rebecca excitedly. She was rocking from her heels to her tiptoes. "Wasn't it gross?"

"*Totally* gross," said Valerie. "Like, gag me with a giant spoon."

Rebecca giggled. "You're funny," she said. "You're also really pretty."

"Thank you," said Valerie. "I think you're really pretty, too."

"You think so?"

"Yes, and your mother tells me that you go to the Sidwell Friends School, so I bet you're really smart, too."

Rebecca liked every word she was hearing. "Did you know that Sasha and Malia Obama go there?"

"I did know that," said Valerie. "Have you met them?"

"Yeah, they're nice, which is cool because they really don't have to be, I guess."

I kept doing the smartest thing I could do at that point, and that was keep my big mouth shut. Brilliantly, effortlessly, Valerie was bonding with this girl quicker than Krazy

Glue. Sooner rather than later, though, she'd have to ask the sixty-four-thousand-dollar question. *Can you keep a secret?*

But out of nowhere, another question beat us to it. *Oh, no . . .*

"Rebecca, what are you doing?" he asked.

CHAPTER 88

WE ALL froze as Mr. Henchman appeared in the doorway. As he glared at Valerie and me, it was the closest I'd ever come to being able to read another man's mind.

Two random guests where they absolutely shouldn't be. Whatever's going on, it isn't right.

"You know you're not supposed to be in here," he said to Rebecca. There was little doubt, though, that he was talking to all three of us. "You could really get in trouble."

Valerie and I looked at Rebecca, our collective fate now in the hands of a nine-year-old ginned up on the movie *Unfaithful*.

I was starting to think we didn't have a snow globe's chance in Hell.

Especially when Mr. Henchman applied the full-court press. "Well, Rebecca? What am I supposed to tell your father?"

Then again, some kids you can only press so far.

"Geez, Walt, don't have a cow!" she bellowed. "I was just giving them a tour of the house." Both her hands then landed squarely on her hips. "But if you're so desperate to tell my father something, maybe it should be how you like to drink all his liquor when he's not home."

Oh, snap. Out of the mouths of babes...

Never had I seen a guy so big back down so fast. The upper hand now wore pink nail polish with glitter.

And on that note...

"Thank you again for the tour, Rebecca. I think I'll be getting back to the party now," said Valerie.

"Yes, I really should be getting back, too," I added. "But this certainly has been fun."

I followed Valerie out of Brennan's office while "Walt" remained behind to chat a little more with Rebecca. If I had to guess, I'd say he was negotiating a keep-silent agreement with her in order to keep his job.

For a few seconds, at least, Valerie and I were alone again.

"Come here," she said, quickly pulling me over to the wall in the hallway. Next thing I knew, she was moving toward my mouth again.

"What are you doing?"

"Don't flatter yourself, Counselor," she said, her thumb removing a smudge of her lipstick from my lower lip. She was cleaning me up, that was all. "Sometimes a kiss is just a kiss."

She took a step back, making sure she'd gotten it all. A satisfied nod told me she had.

"So now what?" I asked.

"That depends."

"On what?"

"On whether what you suspect about Brennan is true," she said.

"And if it is?"

She smiled. "Then you and me? This is the beginning of a beautiful friendship."

CHAPTER 89

ONE HOUR later, and from one hot seat into another.

I kept shifting around in my chair, trying to get comfortable, but I knew it wasn't the chair. It was me. I had that uneasy feeling, the kind you get when you think you're being watched. Only, in this case, I knew for sure I was being watched.

In the parking lot. In the lobby. In the elevator. In the hallway. And ultimately, in the conference room. There were cameras everywhere. Everything was being recorded.

Welcome to the NSA's headquarters at Fort Meade, Maryland.

"What fun have you brought us now, Valerie?" asked Jeffrey Crespin.

Based on his tone alone, I was fairly certain the word *fun* in that question bore little resemblance to the actual definition of the word. Suffice it to say, Valerie Jensen had never been awarded Employee of the Month.

No wonder, really. When I'd asked her before the meeting why an agent working undercover would risk drawing so much attention to herself with her skeet shooting exhibition on Brennan's lawn, she told me she simply couldn't help it. Quote, "I just hate those penis-measuring contests that men always have."

Crespin, who was introduced to me as a deputy director of some counterterrorism division I'd never heard of, listened patiently in his suit and tie as Valerie—now in sweatpants, a Northwestern T-shirt, and a ponytail—finished briefing him about her Saturday afternoon at Brennan's house, which had necessitated her dragging Crespin away from a charity dinner and into the office on a Saturday night.

The long and short of it? Their ongoing investigation to prove Shahid Al Dossari was helping to launder Saudi money that was ending up in the hands of Al Qaeda operatives had suddenly collided with some Columbia Law School professor posing as a writer with the *Times* and his unseen partner, who were conducting their own little investigation.

"Only it's not so little," said Valerie. That was when she turned to me and nodded. It was my turn to talk.

But before I could get two words out of my mouth, Crespin interrupted me. "Where's this partner, the one you were on the phone with at Brennan's house?" he asked.

"That's part of the agreement," I answered.

Crespin cocked his head at Valerie. He definitely didn't like the sound of that. *"What agreement?"*

"Let's just say the partner has trust issues," Valerie explained. "The agreement I made with Mr. Mann is that he would come here voluntarily in exchange for being able to come alone."

"Do you at least know where this person is?" asked Crespin.

"I don't," she answered. "But Mr. Mann does."

He was staring at me again. "And I suppose that's going to remain your secret, right? Who he is...who he works for?"

"Yes, but I know of a way you could probably get it out of me," I said, grabbing the segue. "That is, if it didn't kill me first."

With that, I took out a flash drive containing the recordings Owen had first shown me, along with the ones from Dr. Wittmer. The stage was mine again. Or, at least, I was making it mine.

Valerie had a laptop booted up and ready to go. This was her second viewing within the hour. I dispensed with any preface and simply clicked Play.

I'd only just met Crespin, but I was hardly surprised to see him stare at the screen stone-faced as he watched. The guy was stoic. Like a doctor. I hardly expected him to recoil at the sight of torture.

But there was something.

It happened at the beginning of one of Wittmer's recordings—the detainee who was cooperating under the influence of the serum but was still killed by it. The very moment the guy's face was visible on-screen, Crespin glanced at Valerie. And Valerie glanced back.

"What?" I asked. "What is it?"

"Nothing," said Valerie.

But I knew the sound of that *nothing*. It was the same *nothing* I'd told Detective Lamont and his partner, McGeary, when they were showing me the recording of Claire's murder on the CrackerJack: the moment when she stuffed her phone behind the seat.

Yeah, that *nothing* from Valerie?

It was definitely something.

CHAPTER 90

"HOW DID you get these?" Crespin asked calmly after the last recording was finished.

It was tempting to joke about the irony. Here was the NSA asking me how I'd gotten information I wasn't supposed to have. Yeah, that's rich.

How did I get these? "The how isn't important," I said. "It's the who."

And not just who was responsible, but also who had been killed along the way. Crespin needed to understand the stakes, the price others had paid.

I explained everything Owen and I knew for sure, as well as what we suspected. We'd been following the money, but we still didn't know whose it was. Brennan, through his law firm, had been moving that money but not supplying it. It had to come from somewhere, though.

As for the serum itself, Dr. Wittmer had implicated Frank Karcher, the National Clandestine Service chief of the CIA, as the man who'd first approached him about transporting—and administering—it overseas.

Finally, there was the photo in Wittmer's house suggesting that Clay Dobson could be involved.

"*Could* be," I stressed.

I wasn't about to try to sell Crespin on the idea of the White House being involved, as I was hardly sold on the idea myself. For starters, we had nothing that linked Karcher to Dobson.

Funny, though, how the world works sometimes.

When I was done, Crespin flipped open a manila folder in front of him and removed a large, folded-up piece of paper. He slid it in front of me.

"What's this?" I asked.

Go ahead, said his nod, *open it*.

I unfolded the paper. It was a copy of the front page of the *New York Times*. Not today's, though. Not even tomorrow's, which would've been the Sunday edition.

No, this was Monday's paper—an editor's mock-up, complete with margin notes and dummy text for a couple of articles still to be inserted.

Instinctively, I looked at my watch. I knew from Claire that weekday editions of the *Times* went to print around ten o'clock the night before, with the "first edition A book," aka the front section, always closing last. We were a full twenty-four hours before that.

It felt a bit like a *Twilight Zone* episode. Crespin was showing me the future.

I stared down at the paper again. I didn't ask, but all I could think was *How did he get this?*

If he wasn't reading my face, he was definitely reading my mind.

"The how isn't important," he said. He then pointed to the first-column story above the fold, the tip of his index finger landing directly next to the name in the headline. "It's the who."

CHAPTER 91

THERE IT was in boldface type.

President Set to Nominate Karcher
As Next CIA Director

Quickly, I scanned the first paragraph. My gut told me there'd be no need to read the second.

Frank Karcher was being dubbed the "unexpected choice," but an "unnamed source within the White House" was certainly bending over backward to describe him as an impeccable candidate.

"It had always been a coin flip between Frank Karcher and Lawrence Bass. Heads or tails, though, it's our national security that wins."

Those unnamed sources sure can spin.

Crespin stood up from the table and walked over to the window. He stared outside, saying nothing. Meanwhile, Valerie had grabbed the laptop, her fingers furiously tapping away on the keypad.

I didn't know what she was doing, but I figured Crespin must be deep in thought, trying to figure out this huge minefield he was suddenly standing in. On a pogo stick, no less.

There was no scenario that didn't entail collateral damage, from the presidency on down. And that was if the White House *wasn't* involved.

And if it was? If the link to Clay Dobson via Frank Karcher proved real?

Then Crespin wouldn't need the front page of the *New York Times* in advance to know what the headlines would be. Independent counsels, congressional hearings, the entire administration upended, if not toppled. The Fourth Estate would have the ultimate field day. A feast for the ages.

Now kick in the foreign policy and national security ramifications.

This wasn't drones or waterboarding or even some extremely ill-advised photos taken by a few guards at Guantánamo Bay. No, this was the coup de grâce, the mother lode.

The single greatest terrorist recruiting tool of all time. Or at least, until the next one came along.

If I'd been Crespin, I would've been staring out the window, too. He had to be wondering what his next move was. He was the NSA, not the FBI. At some point, this was a job for law enforcement, and I was assuming that point was now. On second thought...

He was the NSA, not the FBI.

Crespin turned away from the window. "How much do you know about this building, Mr. Mann?"

"You mean, the actual building?" I asked.

"Yes."

I looked over at Valerie for some help. *Is this a trick question?* But her head was still buried in the laptop.

"I know nothing about it," I said.

Crespin nodded. "You're not alone. And what little the public does know about this building is because we want them to know it. But does that make it true? On Wikipedia, for instance, it says that every wall in this place is wrapped with an ultrathin copper shielding that prevents all electromagnetic signals from getting out."

Okay, I'll take the bait. "Is that true?" I asked.

"It must be," he said. "I read it on the Internet."

Valerie, still fixated on her laptop, smiled. She was listening the whole time. Note to self: The NSA is always listening.

Crespin took his seat back at the table. I wasn't sure what exactly he was talking about, although I got the feeling that was by design.

He continued: "You see, people like to say that information is power. But inside these walls—copper shielded or not—we like to say something else. The real power? It's not information. It's misinformation."

As if on cue, Valerie leaned back in her chair. Whatever she'd been doing, she was done.

"Unbelievable," she muttered.

"What?" I immediately asked. It was simple reflex.

But she wasn't talking to me. Just Crespin. And as he stared back at her, he did something I'd yet to see him do. He smiled.

"Karcher to Brennan or Brennan to Karcher?" he asked.

"Both," said Valerie.

I'd had enough of feeling like the odd man out. "Maybe one of you can tell me what's going on?"

"Sure," said Crespin. "But first I have to ask you something. *How good are you at pretending you're drunk?*"

CHAPTER 92

"WHAT ARE you having?" asked the bartender.

"Second thoughts," I was tempted to say. Instead, "Double Johnnie Black on the rocks," I told him.

This one drink would be my prop, a big ol' glass of whiskey in an unsteady hand to suggest that I'd had plenty more where that came from. The fact that I was already looking pretty ragged from raw nerves and lack of sleep would only add to the effect.

What had Brennan said to his guests on the patio, his quote from Will Rogers? *You never get a second chance to make a good first impression.*

It wasn't quite as catchy, but Jeffrey Crespin had his own saying for what I was about to do. "You only get one shot at this, Mann, so I'll ask you a second time. Are you sure you're up for it?"

"Absolutely," I lied.

From my end seat at the bar in a place called Shadows in

Georgetown, it wasn't Brennan I was waiting for. As hangouts go, this was hardly his scene. Hip and chic, all right, but not enough power brokers. Law students instead of lawyers, congressional staffers instead of congressmen. Plus, way too many Eurotrash guys with one too many shirt buttons undone.

Maybe that was why Shahid Al Dossari had chosen the place: the international flavor. That, and the de rigueur "dark and sexy" lounge lighting. Shadows was clearly saving the owners a ton of money on their electric bill.

All that mattered, though, was that the choice was Al Dossari's. He'd picked the location. He might have gotten suspicious had Valerie led him there.

Excuse me, had "Beverly Sands" led him there.

At the twenty-minute mark, I checked the same prepaid cell I'd used at Brennan's house to see if there was any follow-up from Valerie. Word of a delay or even a change of venue.

Neither, though. No new texts.

Finally, about a half hour after Valerie had first sent me the address, I looked up to see her walking in with him. Right away, I could tell he was really getting off on watching the other men jealously checking out his date. *Yeah, that's right, boys, she's with me. . . .*

Tick-tock. Valerie'd had only an hour after leaving NSA headquarters to get dolled up again as Beverly. This, after initially telling Al Dossari that she had a previous engagement after Brennan's party. No wonder the guy was smiling like the devil. This surprise nightcap was the next-best thing to a booty call. And undoubtedly, in his eyes, the night was still young.

How was Valerie handling that, I wondered? After all, Al Dossari had to have certain *expectations* by this point. Would she ever take one for the team, so to speak, like Joan did on *Mad Men*? No, she'd never. She couldn't, right?

For Christ's sake, Mann, let's keep the focus....

As they passed the bar, I bent down to pick up something I'd pretended to drop. When I straightened up, I glanced over my shoulder to see them grabbing a booth in the back. All according to plan. Give them a little time to settle in with their bottle of champagne—nice and relaxed—and then...

"Hey!" I blurted out, stopping in front of their booth with a double take. "It's Annie Oakley!" For good measure, I raised my arms as if shooting a shotgun, spilling some of my drink in the process.

I watched as Valerie pretended not to recognize me at first. Al Dossari, on the other hand, wasn't pretending. All the better.

"Remember?" I said. "We met earlier today at Josiah Brennan's little soiree. Trevor Mann? The *Times*?"

"Oh, of course," said Al Dossari, sliding out of the booth to shake my hand. "Nice to see you again."

If that were only true. His pained expression was practically screaming, *Of all the damn bars in this town, you had to be in this one? Drunk, no less?*

Make that very drunk.

I turned back to Valerie. "Hey, really, nice shooting today. Just excellent!" I said. "Wait, what's your name again?"

"Beverly," she said. "Beverly Sands."

"That's right, of course! And I'm Trevor Mann."

"Yes, I believe you said that already." Beverly nodded toward my drink with a patient smile. "Are we celebrating something, Mr. Mann?"

"Ha! More like commiserating, I'm afraid. Problem is, I'm down here in DC by myself, so I have no one to commiserate with."

"Well, I'm told I'm a good listener," she said.

God, she's good at this. She makes it look so effortless.

"Oh, it's nothing," I said with a sloppy wave of my hand. "I mean, it's *something*, but I really shouldn't say anything."

"Yes, that's probably best," said Beverly.

With that, I tossed back the rest of my whiskey as if it were liquid courage. No, better yet, a truth serum.

"On second thought, what the hell. It's going to be in all the headlines soon enough," I said, before leaning in to whisper, *"Can you two keep a secret?"*

CHAPTER 93

IT WAS almost too easy. Like pushing a big button.

Suddenly, Shahid Al Dossari wasn't so eager for me to get lost. "Can I buy you another round, Mr. Mann?"

And they say women are gossips.

I happily slid into their booth while Al Dossari flagged the cocktail waitress. As I exchanged glances with Valerie, she broke character for a split second to give me a nod. *So far, so good. Now bring it home.* Or, at least, that's how I took it.

"What were you drinking?" Al Dossari asked me as the waitress arrived with pep in her step. She knew a good tip when she saw one.

"Double Johnnie Black on the rocks," I said.

"Not anymore. Make it a double Johnnie Blue, neat," he said.

I was fairly convinced that his cocksure money-is-no-object upgrade was more for Beverly Sands's benefit than mine, but I wasn't about to object. All things considered, if I was pretending to be loaded, it might as well be with top-of-the-line real whiskey.

"So where were we?" asked Valerie.

"Mr. Mann was about to take us into his confidence," said Al Dossari.

"First of all, Mr. Mann was my father. Call me Trevor," I said. "Second..." I paused for a moment à la an alcohol-induced memory lapse. "Actually, I can't remember what number two was, but in any event, here's why I'm stuck here in DC. Of course, it involves politics. Do you guys follow politics?"

"Sure, a little," said Al Dossari. And by "a little" it was clear he meant "a lot."

I let out a deep sigh. "Stop me if this bores you, but apparently the CIA has invented some new interrogation method that makes waterboarding look like a day at the beach. Problem is, it's killed a bunch of prisoners, hordes of them. Even bigger problem, at least for the president, is that his new CIA director is involved."

"Wait," said Valerie as if confused. "Didn't I see on the news that the new CIA director wasn't going to take the job? I remember because he was standing with his twin daughters and they were adorable."

"That's right, but this is the *new* new CIA director, the one the president is about to announce," I said. "That's on the hush-hush, too. I think his name is Archer."

It was probably more from wishful thinking than anything else that I paused for Al Dossari to jump in and say "Karcher" to correct me. That would be *too* easy, though. He remained silent as the waitress returned with my twenty-five-year whiskey.

"Anyway," I continued, "the *Times* has the story and I've been asked to stay down here to do some interviews on the Hill once it breaks on Monday." I grabbed the lowball of Johnnie

Blue, raising it high. "So, as they say in synchronized swimming...bottoms up!"

Beverly Sands lifted her drink to mine with a laugh. Trevor Mann, the reporter from the *Times* who very possibly had a drinking problem, was nonetheless entertaining. *Right, Shahid?*

She turned to him, her look wondering why he wasn't joining in the cheers. And for the first time, we got a hint of something. He looked distracted. Downright uncomfortable.

"Are you okay?" asked a concerned Beverly Sands. "Shahid?"

"Huh?" He snapped out of it, raising his champagne. "Oh, I'm sorry...cheers."

We clinked glasses, and I waited for some kind of follow-up question from Al Dossari. Valerie was waiting, too. Maybe he needed a command performance from me to be sure of what he'd heard.

Or maybe this was all for naught. The link was only between Karcher and Brennan, and as for Al Dossari, he was simply the CIA's patsy. A sort of post-9/11 Lee Harvey Oswald. Only, in this case, for real.

Suddenly, Al Dossari began sliding out of the booth. "Will you two excuse me for a moment?"

CHAPTER 94

VALERIE AND I both watched as he walked toward the men's room in the back of the bar. We were seeing the same thing. I assumed we were thinking it, too.

"He's not going to the bathroom, is he? He's calling Brennan," I said. "Or maybe even Karcher. One of them, right?"

Valerie grimaced, a twinge of guilt. "No, he really is going to the bathroom," she said. "In fact, he's going to be in there for a while."

"How would you know?"

She nodded first at his champagne glass and then at her purse. "When he stood to shake your hand," she said. "It's like liquid Ex-Lax, only a hell of a lot stronger and quicker."

"Why?" I asked. *Why would she spike his drink?*

"Technically, it's our third date," she said. "In Shahid's mind, it doesn't end with us playing Boggle. This way, he won't even want a peck on the cheek."

"I was wondering about that," I said. "You know..."

Up shot one of her eyebrows. "Whether I'd ever have sex with a mark?"

"Do you guys really call them *marks*?"

"Yeah, strange, right? *Targets of an undercover sting operation never caught on.*"

"So you really haven't—"

"Is that really only your second whiskey?"

"Sorry, I was just curious."

"For the record, the answer's no," she said. "Not to say he didn't try on dates one and two. But love of my country only goes so far."

The cocktail waitress returned to pour some more champagne. Valerie quickly placed her hand over Al Dossari's glass. "I think he's done for the night," she said politely.

I glanced toward the back of the bar as the waitress walked away. "What happens now?" I asked. The plan she and Crespin had concocted only got me to the table.

"What happens now is that you tell me who your silent partner is," she said.

"I meant—"

"I know what you meant. I also know that whoever this guy is, he's CIA, or perhaps ex-CIA at this point. There's no other way you could have those recordings."

"No other way?"

"Prove me wrong."

"If you know he's CIA, what difference does his name make right now?"

Valerie eyed me for a moment. We'd known each other for less than a day, but it was hard to ignore a certain foxhole mentality. Like it or not, we were in this together.

"You want trust? I'll give you trust," she said. "Remember

when Crespin and I looked at each other during one of your recordings?"

"Yes. You tried to pretend it was nothing—"

"But it was obviously something, you're right," she said. "Thing is, it was Karcher who initially tipped us off about our man on the toilet right now, that he was funding a known terrorist. So I became Beverly Sands to cozy up to Shahid Al Dossari, and—lo and behold—we just confirmed it. Shahid's money has been moving in and out of an Al Qaeda operative's account as recently as last week. Bingo, right? Except for one problem. According to one of your videos and the date stamped on the bottom of the screen, that operative has been dead for over a year."

Sometimes you just say the first words that come to your mind no matter how trite. "Holy shit."

"That's right, holy shit," she said. "Pretty goddamn brilliant, too. Developing that truth serum takes big bucks, and it's not like the CIA can go to Congress for it. So what does Karcher do? He uses the hotshot lawyer, Brennan, to make it look like one of his clients is funding a terrorist with Saudi money. Instead, what Karcher's really doing is funding himself."

"But Al Dossari would have to know, right?"

"It would seem that way."

"That's the part I don't get, then," I said. "Wouldn't Karcher be throwing Al Dossari under the bus? Without the recordings from the black site, you guys would still have Al Dossari on funding terrorism."

"Yeah, that's the brilliant part. All the NSA does is provide the proof. Then we hand everything—including Al Dossari—back over to Karcher," she said. "*The CIA will take it from here*, he'll tell us, and then it's out of our hands."

"Then what, though?" I asked. "It's not like Karcher can't drop the ball."

"No, of course not. A few months from now we'd probably hear that Al Dossari has flipped and is now Karcher's newest mole in the Middle East, or something like that. And we'd believe it, too, because we'd have no reason not to."

"But now you do."

"Which brings me back to your friend," she said. "As much as you need to trust me, I need to trust him. And I can't do that if I don't meet him. So tonight, literally . . . *I need you to bring me back to your friend.*"

"What about your date?" I asked. "We just can't leave him."

"Oh, no?" Already she was halfway out the booth. "When he's finally able to leave the bathroom, the last thing he'll want to do is explain what took him so long. Trust me," she said. "We're doing him a favor."

CHAPTER 95

IN TWO minutes flat, we were in the backseat of a DC cab heading off the Beltway past Dulles Airport and out to Arcola. I really should've gotten a to-go cup for that Johnnie Walker Blue.

The driver, whose disposition most closely resembled an ingrown toenail, initially told us that Arcola was out of his territory, especially after midnight. A crisp Ben Franklin later, he suddenly had a brand-new territory. Money is the biggest button of them all.

"Inside or outside doors?" asked Valerie.

I turned to her. *"Inside or outside?"*

"My mother was afraid to fly when I was a kid, so we drove everywhere for vacation. She had this thing, though. We could never stay in a hotel with doors that faced outside," she said. "Too dangerous."

"By any chance, does your mother know what you currently do for a living?" I asked.

"If she were still alive, she wouldn't like it."

"I'm sorry, I didn't realize."

"Cervical cancer. When I was in high school," she explained. "And since we're in the sympathy card aisle, my father then died of lung cancer during my senior year in college."

"Jesus."

"Tell me about it. Of course, if they were both still alive, it's not like I could actually tell them what I do."

"And what is that, exactly? I mean, of all the NSA secrets that Edward Snowden leaked, I didn't hear anything about agents like you."

"Yeah, little Eddie really complicated things, didn't he?"

I waited for Valerie to keep talking and perhaps answer my question. She did neither.

"You're not going to tell me, are you?"

She smiled. "We have to keep some mystery between us, don't we?"

I practically froze. That was exactly what Claire had said to me the night she was killed.

"*What?*" asked Valerie. "What did I say?"

"Nothing," I finally answered.

But she, too, knew the sound of that *nothing*. The look she gave me. Still, she let it go. A touch of woman's intuition, perhaps.

Regardless, the next few minutes for me were inevitable. Memories of Claire came like clicks on the meter in the taxi, one after another, especially from our last moments together.

It's often asked, if you knew this was your last night on earth, what would you do? Had that night with Claire been my last night, though, there was nothing I would've changed. Well, almost nothing. I would've never let Claire go.

"Front or back?" asked the driver.

The question snapped me out of it as I looked up to see him

pulling into the Comforter Motel. Staring at the nearly empty parking lot, it was easy to wonder if the NO in the NO VACANCY sign had ever been illuminated.

"The back," I said.

As he pulled around, I went over the ground rules with Valerie again regarding Owen. We'd gotten pretty good at cutting deals on the fly.

"I go up and explain the situation, tell him you're here waiting in the taxi," I said. "Then I wave you up, okay?"

"Whoa, excuse me?" blurted out the driver.

I'd forgotten about the other deal maker among us. He wasn't liking the way his end was shaking out. "Is there a problem?" I asked.

"You're only paying me to drive you here," he said. "That's the problem."

I reached into my pocket again for more cash, but Valerie stopped me, reaching into her own pocket. She'd had enough of this guy. Money may talk, but a badge shuts them up every time.

"Let's try this again," she said. *"Is there a problem?"*

She was holding her badge so close to his eyes she was practically slapping his face with it.

With a slow shake of his head, he got with the program. No problem.

"You can park over at the end there," I said, pointing to an area near a set of stairs.

There was no other sound beyond the engine idling as I stepped out to the back lot and made my way up to the second floor, or the penthouse, as Owen jokingly called it. We had the first room off the stairs, as well as the one next to it with a connecting door. Once again, the two room strategy. If it ain't broke, don't fix it.

Key card in hand, I eyed the lipstick camera Owen had taped above the sign for the vending machines about twenty feet away.

Then came the last safeguard—the knocking sequence to ensure we were truly alone. I suppose I was fudging that one a bit.

Two knocks followed by one followed by two. The area code of Manhattan. There's no place like home.

Less than a minute later, though, I was back down at the taxi. From the look on my face alone, Valerie knew we had problem. It was the kind no badge could solve.

"What is it?" she asked.

That was part of the problem.

I wasn't sure.

CHAPTER 96

OWEN WAS GONE.

That was the only thing I knew for sure. Both our rooms were empty. Empty of him, at least. Gone, too, was his backpack, his bag of tricks.

But my duffel was right where I'd left it in one of the closets, everything still inside. My guns, the extra cash. In fact, every-thing else in the room looked normal.

"Did they kidnap the maid, too?" asked Valerie, standing in the doorway.

Okay, I said normal, not clean. You put two guys in a hotel on the lam for a few days and it isn't going to be pretty.

But that was the question, wasn't it? Had Owen been taken or had he left on his own? There was a Mobil station with a conve-nience mart a half mile down the road where we'd been picking up some snacks, but the chances of his taking the walk at one o'clock in the morning seemed remote.

"Where are you going?" I asked Valerie. She was headed back out the door, her gun drawn.

"We start with the perimeter," she said.

I understood. Standard police procedure. Start from the outside—in this case, literally—and work your way in.

"His name's Owen," I said.

"What about a last name?"

I must have looked like a stumped contestant on a game show. All this time together and I'd never found out his last name. "Huh" was all I managed.

"Don't worry about it," she said, turning again to leave.

"Wait, don't you want to know what he looks like?"

She stopped just long enough to make me realize that while trust was one thing, the whole truth was another.

"He's tall, slender, with brown hair, shaggy. Does this with his hands from time to time," she said, doing a perfect imitation of his dry wash routine. "Oh, and for the record, his last name is Lewis."

She walked out.

I stood there in shock, wondering how Valerie knew all that, and equally confounding, why she hadn't just told me in the first place. There were no quick answers. What there was, though, was something in my eye line. Owen's laptop.

He had it linked to the lipstick camera outside, our makeshift surveillance system. Since the moment he'd first hooked it up, it had been sitting atop the crappy-looking credenza featuring the TV, plastic ice bucket, and the Yellow Pages.

Now the laptop was in the middle of the queen bed closer to the bathroom. I mean, right in the middle. As if the bed were its pedestal. The only thing missing was the neon sign over it that was blinking, *Look at me, Trevor!*

I walked over and tapped the space bar, waking up the

screen. I expected to see the same running image that had been there for days, the walkway outside both our rooms. Only, now there was something in front of it. A picture.

No, make that a message. But only for me.

In a pop-up window was an illustration off Google Images, one of those goofy clip-art signs that read GONE FISHING.

Now I just had to figure out what it was supposed to mean. *Fishing for what?*

"What are you looking at?" came Valerie's voice by the door. She was back.

I had a split second to make a decision. Given our track record, telling her it was nothing was off the table. It had to be something. But did it have to be the whole truth?

This trust thing was getting a bit tricky.

"Behind you," I said. "That's what I'm looking at."

I spun the laptop around, but not before clicking the illustration closed. What remained was the feed from the outside camera.

"Clever," she said, tracing the angle to the sign for the vending machines. "Owen's doing, I assume?"

"It seems you'd know that even better than me," I said.

That got me a smirk but nothing more. She was far more concerned with taking one more lap around both rooms to see if there was something she'd missed the first time. There wasn't.

"All right, grab your stuff," she said. "Let's get going."

"Going?"

"You didn't still think you'd be staying here, did you?"

Actually, I hadn't thought anything. But Valerie obviously had.

"Where are we going?" I asked.

"Someplace with inside doors," she said.

CHAPTER 97

"GOOD MORNING, Mr. Mann, how did you sleep?" asked Jeffrey Crespin, my human alarm clock. He'd taken it upon himself to shake me awake at six a.m.

How did I sleep? It's the crack of dawn.

"Sparingly," I was tempted to answer. But it was too early and I was too tired for glibness. "Fine," I said instead.

He was sitting on a folding metal chair at the end of my cot, wearing a blue blazer and jeans. I guess the jeans were how he unwound on a Sunday. "Would you like some coffee?" he asked.

I looked over his shoulder to see Valerie in the doorway, taking a sip from a mug, the string from a tea bag hanging over the edge. She was wearing the same Beverly Sands outfit she'd had on four hours ago, which answered the question of where she'd spent the night. It was here.

Wherever the hell that might be.

Not only didn't I know, I was never supposed to know. Hence the Bruce Wayne and Batcave routine after leaving the motel in

Arcola. Valerie'd had the taxi take us to an underground parking garage in Fort Meade, where we got into an unmarked van, but only after she put a sack over my head. For real.

Then again, I guess that's why they call it a safe house.

"Yeah, some coffee would be good," I said. "Cream, if you have it. No sugar."

"I'll see what they have," said Valerie before disappearing into the hallway.

Crespin leaned back in his chair, crossing his legs. "I suppose there's also tea, but I figured you more for coffee," he said.

"You figured right."

"Funny thing, though. Do you know who *never* drinks coffee?"

"I give up."

"Frank Karcher."

I immediately liked where this was going, and Crespin could tell. For only the second time, I saw him smile.

"Al Dossari called him?"

"Late last night," he said. "When he was finally feeling better, I presume."

"What did he say?"

"Everything you told him at the bar."

"But as soon as he heard my name..."

"That was the best part. You'd think Karcher would've told Al Dossari he'd been played by you, but he didn't. He just thanked him for the heads-up."

"It actually makes sense," I said. "Karcher knows I don't work for the *Times*. The paper doesn't have the story."

"And speaking of stories that aren't real..."

Of course. "Al Dossari must have told Karcher how he first met me."

"Exactly," he said. "After Karcher hung up from Al Dossari, he immediately woke up Brennan. Naturally, Brennan made sure to call him right back from the secure line in his study."

Only, thanks to Valerie's handiwork, the NSA could listen in on that conversation, too.

"I can only imagine Brennan's reaction," I said.

"To tell you the truth, I think he was more upset about not actually being interviewed for the *Times* than he was at the prospect of spending the next ten to fifteen years folding laundry."

"That's a lawyer for you," I said. "Prison is what happens to other people."

"We'll see. In the meantime, nice work last night. Valerie tells me you play an excellent drunk."

"I've had some practice."

"She also told me about Owen, that he's suddenly gone missing."

"First things first, if you don't mind. Why didn't you guys just tell me you knew who he was?"

Crespin didn't hesitate. "When gauging an asset, it's always good to know up front if what he's telling you is true."

"I take it I'm the so-called asset in that sentence?"

"It's just the way we do things."

"So you can probably guess my next question."

"Yes," he said. "But the answer to that one makes things a little trickier."

CHAPTER 98

A LITTLE trickier? Did he really just say that?

I'd spent the night, what was left of it, sleeping in the NSA's version of inside doors. I was in a safe house somewhere in DC on the heels of a road trip taken with a boy genius from the CIA who thought he was curing Alzheimer's, only to discover he was really helping to create what would've been the ultimate interrogation tool if it weren't for the fact that it happened to have a fail rate of forty percent. And by *fail*, I mean fatally.

Which would explain why the men responsible for all this were going to such extreme lengths to ensure they were never found out. And by *extreme*, I also mean fatally.

But now, so I was being told, things were about to get...wait for it...*a little trickier.*

I stared back at Crespin. "No, it's actually simple," I said. "You either can or can't tell me how you know about Owen."

"I admire that, I really do," he said, once again without any hesitation. "Despite everything you've been through, you're still capable of seeing the world in black and white."

"Not everything is gray."

He cocked his head. "Look around you, Mr. Mann."

I was surrounded by cinder-block walls and concrete floors. There was the metal chair Crespin was sitting in, as well as my metal cot. Even the blanket I'd been given. All gray.

And Crespin wasn't even being literal.

"Are you trying to change the subject?" I asked.

"No, I'm only giving it perspective," he said. "I know about Owen Lewis because of your friend Claire Parker."

He looked at me as if he'd just thrown a verbal grenade into our conversation. But I wasn't sure why. After all, "I also know about Owen Lewis because of Claire Parker," I said.

"Yes, I realize that. So now comes that trickier part I promised you." He uncrossed his legs, his back straightening. "Claire worked for the NSA."

Ka-boom.

It was as if all the blood had been suddenly flushed from my head. I felt dizzy, the room spinning. A big, gray blur.

"Excuse me?" I said.

"I don't think I need to say it again." No, he didn't. "To be very clear, Claire was everything you thought she was, a national affairs reporter for the *New York Times*. She was a gifted journalist who only wrote the truth. But as I'm sure you're aware, doing that—especially doing it at her level—takes sources."

"You were one of her sources?"

"No, not me personally. Someone else within the NSA. The division is called Tailored Access Operations, if that means anything."

"And in return?"

"You mean, what did she do for them?"

"Give something, get something . . . right?"

"Not exactly," he said. "At least, not in the way you're worried about. I think you know that Claire would never burn any of her sources. That's not what she did for us."

"Then what exactly did she do?"

Before Crespin could answer, though, we were both looking at Valerie leaning against the doorway again. She was back.

In one hand was a piece of paper, in the other a laptop.

So much for a cup of coffee.

"You need to see something," she said.

CHAPTER 99

I ASSUMED she was talking only to Crespin, especially when she walked right past me to hand him the piece of paper. He read it, glanced up at Valerie, and read it again.

Instead of handing it back to her, however, he handed it to me.

The reason was as clear as the e-mail address in the upper left-hand corner. It was mine. I was looking at a printout of an e-mail sent to me by Brennan, except I'd never seen it before.

That was when I noticed the time stamp: 5:34 a.m. Brennan had only sent it a half hour earlier.

Trevor, change of venue for our interview today if that's ok. Too many distractions here at house. Mallard Café at 33rd and Prospect at 11? They do a mean Sun brunch.—JB

"There's your answer, by the way," said Crespin.

Answer to what? "What was the question?" I asked.

"What Claire did for us," he said. "You're looking at it."

That hardly cleared up anything, and he knew it. The guy had coy down to a science.

Valerie to the rescue. "Josiah Brennan didn't send the e-mail," she explained.

I looked down again at the paper. There was Brennan's e-mail address underneath mine, the same address he'd been using since first confirming our supposed interview.

"If he didn't send it, who did?" I asked. But I already knew the answer before the words had even left my mouth. "Karcher?"

"Yes," said Crespin. "And Brennan has no idea."

"How do you know?"

"Karcher used a certain spyware virus. As soon as you read an e-mail from him, he can then assume your identity, basically controlling your entire e-mail account. The reason we know this is because we use the same virus."

"I still don't get the connection to Claire," I said.

Valerie looked over at Crespin as if to say *Go ahead, boss, you're the one who brought it up.*

Crespin thought for a moment. Finally, "Imagine you're in London to interview a certain cleric before he's deported from the UK to Jordan," he said. "The cleric has little trust in an American journalist—or any American, for that matter—but he's eager to speak his mind. The international stage can be in-toxicating, and no one serves up the limelight better than the *New York Times.* A neutral location is agreed upon, almost always a hotel, and the cleric has one of his body men search you even though they're not quite sure what they're looking for. A recording device? It's an interview. Of course you have a recorder. And as far as they can tell, it looks exactly like any other recorder they've ever seen."

"But it's not," I said.

"No, instead it hacks the hotel's Internet service and then hacks the cleric's cell phone. And, here's the key, it does all of it *wirelessly*. Which means Claire didn't really have to do a thing."

"Except give her consent," I said, unable to hold back my smirk.

Crespin nodded. "But this wasn't just any cleric, was it?"

No, it wasn't. This was a guy who'd been jailed repeatedly in London without ever receiving a trial. Over a bottle of Brunello one night, Claire had argued with me that he deserved one, and I'd argued back that according to the antiterrorism laws passed in Britain after 9/11, he didn't. This was the night before she flew to London to interview him.

"Here," said Valerie, giving me the laptop in her other hand. "You need to log on to your e-mail and cancel on Brennan."

"*Cancel?*"

"Unless, of course, you'd prefer your last meal to be eggs Benedict. This is Karcher setting you up," she said.

"Yes, the same Karcher responsible for Claire's death," I shot back. Forgive me for sounding a little testy.

"Listen, I get it," said Valerie. "You want revenge, who wouldn't? But this isn't you pretending to be drunk with some jet-set, skirt-chasing international playboy. This is a guy who wants to kill you."

"Which is exactly why I'll be at the Mallard Café at eleven o'clock," I said, as sure as I'd ever been about anything in my life. "Karcher wants to kill me, all right, but he can't. He won't. At least, not right away. And that's an opportunity we can't pass up."

I was ready to explain, to argue my case. Yell and scream, if I had to.

But I didn't have to. Valerie and Crespin both had that look on their faces, the kind I used to see on juries during the closing argument of every case I'd ever won. It was as if I knew exactly what they were thinking.

This guy might actually have a point.

Now all we needed was a plan.

CHAPTER 100

"CAN I get you anything while you're waiting?" asked the waitress, a quick tilt of her head acknowledging the empty chair across from me. Her name tag read BETSY.

If there had been more time, more options, more everything, this young woman with rolled-up sleeves would've been Claire undercover, and in addition to having her hair tucked into a ponytail, she would've had a Beretta tucked behind the white apron with the big green *M* that all the servers at the Mallard Café wore.

But sometimes you just have to make do.

"I'm good for now," I said. "Thanks, though."

This was clearly music to Betsy's ears. One less thing she had to do. My very real waitress had that harried look of having a few too many tables in her section. As far as I could tell, she was the only one tending to all the outdoor seating that lined the front of the café.

Betsy shuffled off, while I kept waiting, not that I'd expected to be doing anything different. Karcher would absolutely make sure I arrived first. After that, it was anyone's guess. Including whether it would even be Karcher who showed. The guy had a history of letting others do his dirty work.

"Stop fidgeting," came a voice in my ear.

I mean, literally *in* my ear. Crespin had outfitted me with what had to be the world's tiniest transmitter. Smaller than the head of a tack, it was fully out of sight inside my ear canal.

"Sorry," I said, only to realize that I'd just broken one of his two rules.

"What did I tell you about talking to me?" came his voice again. *"And don't answer that."*

Rule #1? Don't talk into the mike, otherwise known as the third button down on my new NSA-brand shirt. Fifty percent cotton/poly blend with a five-hundred-foot range. If Karcher— or whoever he might send—was scouting me, I could ill afford to be seen talking to myself. The wire was so Crespin could hear what I heard.

"It's going to be fine, Mann," he was now assuring me. "Everything's going to be—"

The way his voice suddenly cut out, my first thought was that the transmitter in my ear had failed. But Crespin was just seeing what I couldn't.

"Don't turn around, don't even flinch," he said. "He's approaching you from behind at twenty feet…fifteen…ten…"

A voice boomed over my shoulder. "Is this seat taken?"

It was now.

Frank Karcher sat down before I could even look up. Jesus, he had a big head. It was even bigger in person.

I feigned surprise as best I could. I was supposed to be waiting for Brennan, after all.

"Excuse me, I think you have the wrong table," I said.

Karcher broke into a wide grin. "No, this is definitely the right table. You just picked the wrong fight," he said, glancing at his watch. "The only question now is how long you'll pretend you don't know what I'm talking about."

Said question hung in the air as I pretended to be thinking it over. But I already knew my answer. So far, we were right on script.

"I know exactly what you're talking about," I said finally. "I know who you are and what you've done. I also know it's all about to end."

Again with the grin. Those had to be veneers. "Interesting choice of words," he said. "Do me a favor, though, will you, Mr. Mann? Take a good look under the table."

"I don't need to," I said. "You're not the first person this week to point a gun at me."

"You're right," he said. "But I am the last."

CHAPTER 101

IT WAS my turn to smile, forced and short-lived as the smile was. You can only pretend for so long that you don't have a gun aimed at your crotch.

"If the only thing you wanted was me dead, you would've killed me by now," I said. "We both know that."

And there it was, the only way I'd been able to convince Valerie and Crespin that I wouldn't be a complete sitting duck, if you will, at the Mallard Café. Karcher desperately wanted Owen—"the kid"—and I presumably knew where he was.

Fitting irony that I actually didn't.

Not that Karcher was about to be told that. As long as he thought I knew Owen's whereabouts, he believed there was the chance he could get it out of me.

That's the folly of arrogant men, isn't it? They always overestimate their talents.

"Are you really that much of a hero, Mr. Mann?" he asked. "I don't know what the kid told you, but it's not what you think."

"No, it's exactly what I think," I said. "Somewhere along the line, you convinced yourself that you're above the law, that you get to decide who lives and who dies. But the biggest lie of them all? It's when you claim you're simply protecting freedom."

"*Freedom?* Just where the hell have you been this century? We should be so damn lucky," he said. "That's what you self-righteous pricks have never understood, not ever."

"Then why don't you enlighten me?"

"*Why don't you shut the fuck up?*"

"Easy now . . ." came Crespin's voice in my ear.

Crespin was right. On a risk scale of one to ten, I was already pushing eleven. My letting Karcher lose his temper was upward of just plain dumb. Sure, maybe he'd slip up and admit everything. Or maybe he'd just get pissed off and kill me right there at the table.

I leaned back in my chair, hoping to let a little air out of the moment. Diffuse the tension. But it was too late. Karcher was revved up, and like a pit bull, he wasn't about to let the point go.

"Do you know what I remember most about that day? It's not the image of the towers coming down. Not even close. What's seared into my brain, what will stick forever, are the people on the street watching it happen," he said. "And do you know what they were all doing as they were looking up in horror? They were all mouthing the same three words. *Oh, my God.*"

"I was one of those people," I said. "I was there."

It was as if he didn't hear me. "Now, I'm a devout Christian, but I know for a fact that the God they were all invoking that day wasn't there. And for those who say he was, and that his job is not to intervene, I ask . . . *whose job is it?* If God won't prevent the next time, who will? And trust me, there will be a next time."

"So that's it, then?" I said. "You're now God's understudy? It doesn't matter who you kill—a reporter for the *Times*, a doctor with a guilty conscience, or even other people from your company picnic—because it's all part of a bigger plan, one that the rest of us couldn't possibly understand?"

"Every war has casualties, Mr. Mann. But I'm guessing you've never fought in one, have you?"

"That makes me lucky, not brain-dead," I said. "What's your excuse?"

Damn. Wrong button.

Karcher's face flushed red in an instant, the veins in his stumplike neck bulging out above his collar.

"You know what? Fuck the kid," he said. "I don't care if you know where he is, you can take that to your goddamn grave."

But all I really heard was Crespin's panicked voice in my ear. *"Quick, tell him you know where Owen is!"*

Crespin didn't need to see the deranged look in Karcher's eyes. He could hear the craziness in his voice, the way he referred to my grave as if it were imminent.

I needed to stall.

But again, it was too late. With the slightest flinch—small but telling—I'd just broken Crespin's second rule. *Whatever you do, don't look like you've got someone talking in your ear.*

"Jesus Christ," said Karcher. "You're not alone, are you?"

CHAPTER 102

"NO, HE'S definitely not alone," she said.

I turned to see Valerie pulling up a chair to our table. She couldn't play the waitress, but her being seated nearby was the next best thing. And with her mirrored sunglasses and jet-black wig, there was no way Karcher would've recognized her.

He still didn't.

The Beretta in her lap, however, he spotted instantly, and it sure as hell wasn't pointed at me.

Give the prick some credit, though. Karcher barely blinked. "Friend of yours, Mr. Mann?" he asked coolly.

"One of many," said Valerie. "Which is why you need to wrap your weapon in that napkin and place it slowly on the table."

Karcher looked down at the napkin in front of him like it was a piece of enriched plutonium. He had no intention of touching it.

"Thank you for the suggestion, young lady, but I think I'll pass," he said. "It might be a good idea for you to do it, though."

Those should've been the words of a madman, a last-ditch

effort to buy some time in this chess match, using little more than misdirection and a touch of outright confusion. Call it Karcher's Gambit.

But the tone was more cocky than confused. He was too sure of himself. He knew something we didn't, and I couldn't stop the feeling of pure dread that was suddenly spreading from the pit of my stomach.

I looked at Valerie, and for the first time, she took her eyes off Karcher to look back at me, if only for a split second. But that was all the time it took.

"Shit," she muttered.

Karcher smiled. "Looks like I've got some friends, too," he said.

"Show him," came Crespin's voice in my ear, only he wasn't talking to me. Valerie was wearing the same transmitter. With her eyes locked back on Karcher, she removed her sunglasses so I could see what the hell was going on.

"Shit," I muttered.

Staring back at me in the mirrored lenses was a new addition to my forehead. The small red dot of a laser sight. I was one squeeze of a trigger away from having my brains blown out, which somehow managed to trump getting shot in the crotch. Either way, it was suddenly a lose-lose.

We were definitely off script now. . . .

"I know you, don't I?" asked Karcher, staring straight back into Valerie's naked eyes.

"Maybe," she answered. "Or maybe not. But I definitely know you."

"What about Mr. Mann here?" he said. "How much do you really know about him?"

"Enough to be sitting here," she said.

"*Keep stalling him,*" came Crespin's voice in our ears.

"I suppose you know more, though?" Valerie tacked on.

"He shot a federal agent in Manhattan, for starters, and got a detective up there killed as well."

Karcher looked at me to see if I'd take the bait and try to argue otherwise. All along, he'd been defending himself without admitting to anything. Now he was hoping I'd trip myself up in the heat of the moment so he could build some semblance of reasonable doubt.

But I gave him the best comeback I could. Silence.

Not Valerie, though.

"What about outstanding parking tickets?" she deadpanned. "Does he have any of those as well?"

"No, but he does have a dead guy in his bathtub. I forgot to mention that," Karcher said, his voice tinged with what could only be described as glee. Extra creepy on a guy his size. "The police searched his apartment yesterday."

"You know, if there was only some way I knew you were telling the truth, some type of method," she said. "Wouldn't that be something? I mean, what wouldn't we all give for that?"

Karcher deflected her with a chuckle, but it was quickly drowned out by something else I was hearing.

My head was suddenly filled with footsteps, only they were more than steps. They were strides. Crespin was running, his breathing heavy as if he were in a full sprint. I knew Valerie could hear it, too, but she kept right on talking to Karcher. Stalling him.

Then, out of the corner of my eye, I saw something that I really, truly wished I hadn't.

CHAPTER 103

NO! NO! NO!

I wanted so desperately to signal her somehow, wave my hands and tell her she had to stop. But I was helpless; I knew I couldn't. It would be like yanking the pin on a grenade.

The waitress. Betsy. Ponytail and rolled-up sleeves. She was heading to our table.

"Huh, looks like we have a party of three," she said, pulling up between Karcher and Valerie. She was half distracted, clutching her order pad while searching for a pen in the deep pocket of her apron. "If you'd like, I can move you all to another table."

"No, that's okay, I was just saying hello to these guys," said Valerie, flashing a polite smile. "I'll be getting up in few seconds."

But from the moment I felt the tap on my foot underneath the table, I realized this wasn't just a figure of speech. Valerie was giving me a signal. In a few seconds, she really was getting up, and the reason was right in front of me. Literally.

Our waitress, Betsy, was directly in the line of fire.

I stole a peek at Valerie's sunglasses now folded on the table, the lenses angled up toward my face.

The only question was whether or not Karcher had noticed, too.

Asked and answered.

Karcher's eyes lit up as he glanced at me. He saw it. Or, rather, he didn't see it. The red dot on me from the laser sight was gone, blocked by the—

"Now!" yelled Valerie.

She had Karcher in no-man's-land, his hand swinging. For a fraction of a second, he was undecided where to aim his gun.

A hell of a lot can happen in a fraction of a second.

Valerie lunged for Karcher as I sprang from my chair, the sound of Crespin in my ear, still sprinting, matching the pounding of my heart.

Betsy had no idea what was happening; she immediately jumped back based on nothing but reflex and fear of the unknown. I was heading right for her, no stopping, the *M* on her apron the target of my dive.

I could feel the wind being knocked out of her as I tackled her to the ground, the crack of a rifle shot from only-God-knows-where splitting the air above us. But nothing more.

Small comfort. Oswald's first shot in Dealey Plaza missed, too.

I turned my head, looking up to see Valerie still struggling with Karcher, each with a hand on the other's gun. He outweighed her by nearly a hundred pounds, but she'd gotten to her feet first and had the leverage. For how long, though?

"Stay down!" I barked at Betsy, as if there were a chance in the world she was about to get up.

No, that was my job now.

Palms down, I began to push off the ground, my eyes trained

on Karcher. His face and neck were a mishmash of muscle and tendon straining for all the strength he had. Slowly, his gun was moving back toward Valerie. She had about six inches to live.

That was when I saw it. The only thing that could make things worse. And only one word came to mind to warn her.

"Red!" I yelled.

I don't know what came next, what I heard or what I saw. But Valerie knew what I meant and knew her geometry, and as the second shot echoed in my ears I saw her step back and take Karcher with her, the dot jumping from her back . . .

To his.

The only red now was blood. Lots and lots of it. Karcher fell to the ground faceup and only inches from Betsy, who shrieked in horror as she caught sight of the gaping hole in his barrel chest from the exit wound.

"Drop it! Drop your weapon right now!"

Valerie and I turned to each other and then up to the rooftop down the street. It was Crespin in our ears. He was done running. I don't know if God actually knew where the shots were coming from. But now Crespin did. He'd reached Karcher's sniper.

"I got him . . . it's over," he said, catching his breath. "It's over."

Of course, if that were only true . . .

BOOK FIVE

TRUTH OR DIE

CHAPTER 104

FRANK KARCHER had been the master of making all sorts of things disappear. People. Problems. His moral compass. But the one thing he couldn't cover up was his own death.

Instead, others were going to do it for him. At least, that was the way it was playing out.

There were a dozen witnesses to what happened outside the Mallard Café, and they all knew what they'd seen. When the police arrived and a couple of detectives fanned out to ask what had happened, each and every one had an answer.

But none of them knew *why* it had happened. Same for every news outlet that rushed to the scene. Karcher's death was the stuff of headlines and lead stories, but the whole truth hadn't gone public yet.

The question now was whether it ever would.

"I feel like a kid waiting outside the principal's office," I said.

Valerie leaned forward, glancing at the closed door to our

right. "Yeah, and your parents are already in there having the adults-only talk, right?"

"Exactly."

She nodded. "Par for the course, I'm afraid. The only way to know your worth in this town is the level of classified info you're allowed to hear. The whole loaf or just a slice."

"Or in my case, only a few crumbs," I said.

"Hey, I'm not in there, either. That makes us both a couple of muzjiks," she said.

"Muz-*whats*?"

"Peasants. The word for Russian peasants, actually."

"Of course."

"Also, one of the highest-scoring words in Scrabble."

"Now you're just showing off," I said.

"Scrabble was big in our house growing up. My father played it every Sunday with my sister and me to build our vocabularies," she said. "That's one reason why I know the word."

"Muzjiks, huh?"

"Yep. Use it on your first turn and it's worth a hundred and twenty-eight points."

I waited for her to continue. She didn't.

"And a second reason?" I asked. She'd said that was *one* reason why she knew the word.

With the look she gave me, I suddenly realized this wasn't mere idle chitchat. Valerie was finally answering the question I'd asked when we first met. *Who are you?*

There was no one around us in the hallway. Still, she looked both ways as if crossing the street. "I was stationed in Moscow," she said.

But the way she said it, I knew. "CIA?"

She nodded.

"How long ago?" I asked.

344

"It feels like forever."

"What happened?"

"Someone decided to tell the world our deepest, darkest secrets because he didn't like the way we got them. Consequences be damned."

So that was who she was. Valerie Jensen had been an undercover CIA agent. "And you were exposed...."

"Hundreds were, all over the world," she said. "More than a few were killed, too. Not that it ever made the news. I was lucky. It wasn't like a woman could ever be in Tehran or Kabul."

"Still," I said. "Moscow." Putin had never struck me as the forgiving type.

"Thankfully, money will pretty much get you anything you need there, including a way out through Finland in the middle of the night," she said. "Funny, though. After all that, where does our whistle-blower first gain asylum?"

Russia.

"So how did you end up with the NSA?"

"It was a bit like the Island of Misfit Toys. No one else had any use for us. All the covert training and nowhere to use it," she said. "Except here at home, of course."

"Another thing that will never make the news," I said.

"That depends, I suppose."

"On what?"

"On how well you can keep a secret."

I had to laugh. "Imagine that," I said. "You're not even the best secret I've got going right now."

"All the more reason why we're sitting here."

"Yep. A couple of muzjiks."

Valerie laughed back, and for a minute, it was as if we were able to forget where we were and why.

Actually, it was only like ten seconds. Right up until the door opened next to us and an older woman with gray hair stepped out and peered over her horn-rimmed glasses with a perfunctory smile. She was Clay Dobson's assistant.

"You two can come in now," she announced.

CHAPTER 105

THE ONLY way I ever thought I'd set foot in the White House was on a guided tour with a bunch of people wearing fanny packs. Shuffling along the velvet ropes, I'd stare into all the capital *R* rooms. The East Room. The State Dining Room. The Blue, Red, and Green Rooms decorated by Jackie Kennedy.

Still, when the tour was over, the closest I'd ever get to the Oval Office was a postcard in the gift shop.

Now I was literally a few feet away from it in the West Wing—the office right next door. The office of the president's chief of staff.

And if Owen was right, the man ultimately responsible for the deaths of Claire and our unborn child, as well as countless others.

But that was a big if. As in, if only there were some actual evidence.

"Ian, do me a favor and scoot over on the couch there for Mr. Mann," said Dobson, orchestrating from behind his huge desk. Make no mistake. This was his office, his meeting, his seating chart. He'd already motioned for Valerie to take the other arm-chair next to Crespin.

Ian—as in Ian Landry, the president's press secretary—promptly scooted over on the couch to make room for me.

"There you go," he said. "Best seat in the house."

It was a little strange to see Landry out from behind the podium of the Brady Room. To watch him take questions from the press was to know there wasn't anything he couldn't spin. It was a talent all the more remarkable given that, unlike previous press secretaries, Landry didn't hide behind the façade of plausible deniability. Rather, he'd claimed from day one that he knew everything that happened in the White House.

After all, President Bretton Morris had won election by promising to level with America at all times. "Hard truths, and no easy fixes," he was fond of saying in his campaign commercials. And with nearly a billion dollars spent on advertising, he'd said it an awful lot.

"Would either of you like any coffee?" asked Dobson.

"No thanks," Valerie and I answered in unison.

"All right, then. Let me start by telling you what I told Jeffrey," Dobson said, pointing to Crespin in his charcoal-gray suit. "The president has no knowledge of this meeting. If he did, it would never be happening. Instead, Ian would be in the press room telling the world everything about Operation Truthseeker, or whatever stupid name this damn thing probably had."

Seamlessly, Ian Landry chimed in. "The president would sooner sacrifice a second term than try to sweep something like this under the rug."

"And trust me, that's not hyperbole," said Dobson. "Unfortunately, though, this is about more than just favorability ratings and politics. This is about national security. And Frank Karcher has seriously threatened it."

I listened very carefully to what came next.

Dobson explained the protocol of what happens after the death of active CIA personnel, especially someone on Karcher's level as the National Clandestine Service chief. Basically, anything and everything having to do with his life gets searched, reviewed, raked over, and then raked over again.

"The problem in this case," said Dobson, "is that it's like having the fox guard the henhouse. We don't know how deep this runs at the CIA—who was involved and how many—but if the guy shooting at you from that rooftop yesterday is any indication, it doesn't bode well."

"He's an agent with the Special Activities Division, Karcher's former unit within the CIA," explained Crespin.

"Then, of course, there's the young man at the center of all this." Dobson looked down at an open file as if searching his notes for Owen's name. "Yes, Owen Lewis," he said. "Who, as of right now, is nowhere to be found."

Damn, Skippy, nowhere to be found. Where the hell are you, Owen, and what's with the secret fishing expedition? You're up to something, but what?

I waited for Dobson to look at me in light of his mentioning Owen, but he didn't. Instead, he reached for another file on his desk, this one featuring a bright red stripe across it.

"But back to Karcher and the issue of national security," he continued. "I'm pretty sure I could lose my job, if not worse, for what I'm about to share with you, but since that's the least of my problems this morning, we'll be making an exception." He paused to take a sip of coffee, staring at us over the lip of the mug. First at Valerie. Then at me. "Besides, according to Crespin here, if it weren't for the two of you, things could've been a lot worse."

And with that, Dobson opened the file.

CHAPTER 106

THE FIRST thing he held up was a color photograph, measuring roughly eight by ten. It could've been a head shot for a leading man, albeit one more suited for Bollywood than Hollywood.

"This is Dr. Prajeet Sengupta," said Dobson, his exaggerated diction suggesting just a trace of xenophobia. He then read from the file in bullet-point fashion. "Born in India, educated here in the States. Stanford undergrad, Harvard Medical School. Currently a staff neuroscientist with the New Frontier Medical Institute in Bethesda, specializing in ionotropic and metabotropic receptor manipulation in the human brain." Dobson paused, looked up. "If anyone knows what that actually means, be my guest."

I didn't. Not exactly. Still, it wasn't hard to see where this was heading.

Sure enough, according to Dobson, Prajeet Sengupta was the missing link to the serum, the guy Karcher had used to turn

Owen's research into an injectable polygraph machine. One question, though, and I didn't hesitate with it.

"How do you know this?" I interrupted.

Dobson nodded slightly as if he'd expected me to ask that. "Again, this isn't for broadcast, but before the CIA could do its reconnaissance on Karcher's apartment, including his hard drive, I got in there first." He corrected himself with a raised palm. "Not me personally, but a special investigator with the FBI. Working unofficially, of course."

All the while, Dobson was still holding up the picture of Sengupta. It was a posed photograph, most likely taken on behalf of the medical institute where the doctor worked. I could picture the website, complete with a glowing bio underneath his good looks and warm smile. Nowhere would his moonlighting efforts be mentioned.

Then—*poof!*—he was gone.

Dobson lowered the photo, only to lift another one from the file. Exhibit B, apparently.

"Now meet Arash Ghasemi," he said.

The only thing the two pictures had in common was the size. Instead of a posed head shot, this one was courtesy of a zoom lens from an angle that suggested the photographer was somewhere in the Middle East he really shouldn't have been. Black-and-white and a bit grainy, it was still clear enough to tell that Ghasemi was the opposite of Sengupta in the looks department. More to the point, Ghasemi had pretty much been hit by the ugly stick. Repeatedly.

Again, Dobson read from the file. "Born in Iran, educated in the States. Stanford undergrad; MIT graduate program, nuclear science and engineering. Then, days after accepting a job with General Atomics in San Diego, he suddenly split town and returned to Iran."

The subtext of that last sentence was crystal clear. Arash Ghasemi was now working for the Iranian nuclear program.

Less clear was whether it was by choice. And even less clear than that was what this Iranian nuclear engineer had to do with Sengupta, the Indian neuroscientist.

Until I replayed Dobson's descriptions of the two in my head. Word for word. And the one word—the one school—he'd mentioned twice.

"Stanford," I said.

"Very good, Mr. Mann. You win the Samsonite luggage," said Dobson. "You see, this is a tale of two roommates."

CHAPTER 107

HE HAD it all right there in the file, right down to the actual dorm where they first met freshman year. Arroyo House in Wilbur Hall.

Prajeet Sengupta and Arash Ghasemi had become fast friends at Stanford. Put them most anywhere else in the world and they had little in common. Under the bright glare of a California sun, however, they might as well have been brothers. Two strangers thrown together in a strange land.

By sophomore year they had become roommates, all but inseparable, including rushing Sigma Chi together.

"And if you're looking for a reason why Ghasemi trusted Sengupta so much—even twenty years later—look no further than that fraternity," said Dobson.

The handsome and more gregarious Sengupta had been tapped to pledge. But Ghasemi had been passed over. That is, until Sengupta made it very clear that they were a package deal. Sigma Chi couldn't get one without the other.

Of course, who the hell was some pledge to be making a demand like that?

"A pretty damn clever one," said Dobson. "In true frat-boy fashion, Sengupta challenged the rush chair to a drinking contest—shot for shot, last man standing. If Sengupta won, Ghasemi could become a brother. And if he lost? That was the clever part. The rush chair outweighed the skinny kid from Bangalore by nearly a hundred pounds. It wasn't a fair fight. How could he ever lose?"

But he did.

Dobson smiled. "Like I said, it wasn't a fair fight. Sengupta, who was premed at the time, had injected himself with a derivative of a drug called iomazenil. Apparently, it binds the alcohol receptors in the brain. In other words, it's a binge drinker's dream come true." Dobson pointed at me. "Okay, now this is where you ask me that question again, Mr. Mann. *How do I know this?*"

For sure, I was about to. Not Valerie, though. She'd been around the block a few times in the world of intelligence gathering. All she could do was sigh in a way that had only one translation. *We live in a very complicated world.*

"CIA or NIA?" she asked Dobson.

"Both," he answered. Then he explained.

Not long after Ghasemi returned to Iran—against his will—to work for the Iranian nuclear program, Sengupta was recruited by the National Investigation Agency of India, the NIA. This was at the urging of the CIA based on the greatest shared interest the US and India have as two nuclear powers: making sure Iran doesn't become one as well.

"Sengupta knew that his good friend Ghasemi was miserable back in his homeland of Iran," Dobson continued. "Iranians might despise what they see as US hegemony, but they do so having never spent time in this country. But Ghasemi had. We weren't the enemy."

I listened to Dobson, almost dizzy. It was hard enough to keep track of the names, let alone the motives and inferences.

Valerie might have had the pole position, but I was finally up to speed.

Ghasemi was giving Sengupta, his good friend and former roommate, Iranian nuclear secrets.

Dobson took another sip of coffee before leaning forward, his words coming slowly. "I understand you've lost someone very close to you, Mr. Mann, and that undoubtedly you want justice. I sure would. But I'm afraid justice means exposing Sengupta, and that would mean no more connection with Ghasemi. Thanks to that relationship, our government currently knows more about the Iranian nuclear program than the Supreme Leader himself. And I wish it were hyperbole when I say that the fate of the world could very well depend on that relationship continuing."

Yes, indeed. *We live in a very complicated world.*

I wasn't sure what I was going to say, only that it was something. Perhaps a feeble attempt to strike some sort of "justice bargain," the way I used to with prosecutors after I went to the dark side, as Claire liked to call it, and became a defense attorney.

But before I could even push out the first word, the door of Dobson's office opened. It was his secretary.

"I'm sorry to interrupt, but there's—"

Dobson cut her off. "I said no calls, Marcy."

"I know, but it's not for you. It's for Mr. Mann," she said. "Apparently, it's an emergency. Someone named *Winston Smith*?"

That got everyone staring at me. Although, with Dobson, it was more like glaring. If looks could kill. "No one outside this room is supposed to know you're here, Mr. Mann," he said.

Immediately, Crespin cleared his throat. Maybe he could just sense it, that something was up and I desperately needed a lifeline. Or maybe it was more than a sense. Perhaps he, too, had read *1984*.

"Sorry, Clay, my bad," said Crespin. "Mr. Mann's sister is being operated on this morning, and that's his nephew calling to let him know how it went. For obvious reasons, Mr. Mann ditched his cell phone once this whole ordeal started."

I watched and listened to Crespin with nothing short of amazement. He was so calm, so convincing. The guy could probably fool a polygraph, if he had to. He had to be the best liar I'd ever met.

Actually, make that the second best.

Dobson nodded to his secretary. "Put it through."

As she disappeared back to her desk, he handed me his phone. The longest two seconds of my life followed as I waited for the call to be transferred.

Click.

"Winston, is that you?" I asked.

"Yes, it's me," said Owen. "And what Dobson just told you is bullshit."

CHAPTER 108

THE QUESTIONS were bouncing around in my head so fast and deliriously I could feel my brain smushed up against my skull just trying to contain them all.

Where has Owen been? How did he know I was in Dobson's office, let alone what was being said? And who's the "new friend" he went on to mention, the one he wants me to meet?

The only thing close to an answer—or, better yet, what would get me closer to all the answers—was the address Owen gave me before hanging up. But not before first telling me I had to come alone. "For real, Trevor. I mean it. Just you."

Of course, that went over like a fart in an elevator with Valerie and Crespin. Especially Crespin. He and his Spidey sense had bailed me out in Dobson's office, and this was how I repaid him? *I'm off to go meet the kid, but you can't come?*

"I'll be back, I promise," I said. "And I'll do everything I can to have Owen with me."

It was either detain me or let me go. They let me go.

Almost one hour to the dot after saying good-bye on the phone in Dobson's office to my nephew, Winston Smith, I arrived at Fifteenth Street NW and Madison Drive.

If the *Jeopardy!* category is Well-Known Washington Addresses, I'll admit that I tap out with 1600 Pennsylvania Avenue. Besides, who really needs to know the address of the Washington Monument? All you have to do is look up, right?

"Father, I cannot tell a lie," came a voice over my shoulder.

I turned to see Owen, smiling at his own cleverness about the line and our location, although I knew he hadn't chosen it for the irony. Just because I thought I'd come alone didn't mean I actually had. The flat, sprawling grounds of the Washington Monument, with nothing but a circle of skinny flagpoles for cover, were his way of making sure that even if I had been followed, no one was within earshot.

Speaking of hearing things on the sly...

Owen pivoted to his right. "Trevor, I'd like you to meet Lawrence Bass," he said.

I pushed aside what was now the latest question in the long queue—*How the hell did these two ever meet up?*—and shook the man's hand.

I knew exactly who Bass was. Namely because of what he wasn't—the next director of the CIA. Owen and I had watched him withdraw his name on television, standing in the East Room, flanked lovingly by his wife and two young daughters. We'd listened to him explain that he wanted to spend more time with his family. And we'd both known he was lying.

"Wait a minute," I said, turning back to Owen. Gone fishing? Lawrence *Bass*? "This is where you went?"

"No one just walks away from being named CIA director," Owen said. "There had to be more to it, not that I was really expecting Lawrence to divulge anything. But as it turns out, he was doing some fishing of his own."

True to his military background, Bass took the cue and didn't dillydally. Nor was there much emotion. The guy seemed to have everything wrapped in a blanket of calm and measured.

"Last week, I paid a visit to Clay Dobson in his office," he said. "And I never really left."

With that, Bass reached into his pocket and held out an iPhone. I recognized the app he tapped; it was the same one Claire always used to edit and organize her interviews. Voice Recorder HD.

Let the answers begin.

CHAPTER 109

OWEN DIDN'T bother saying the actual words. That would've been redundant. One glance at him, the look on his face, was all it took.

What did I tell you, dude?

All I could see in my mind was the picture of Dr. Wittmer and his good ol' college chum, Clay Dobson. And all I could hear now was Dobson's voice telling someone in his office that Wittmer should've been killed sooner.

Of course, that someone was Frank Karcher—or Karch, as Dobson kept calling him in between rounds of cursing him out. For two guys in cahoots with each other, they sure weren't seeing eye to eye on much. Cover-ups are a bitch.

"Jesus," I said. "How...?"

"Well, I was the director of intelligence programs with the NSC," said Bass, who somehow managed to convey that without a hint of bravado. It was merely fact. Same for the way he claimed he'd been able to hide the bug in Dobson's office. "I just dropped it in his pencil holder when he wasn't looking."

Bass fell silent again so I could keep listening, but all I had were more and more questions.

"What about Landry?" I asked. Was the press secretary involved as well?

"Best we can tell, no," said Owen. "There's at least a half dozen times when the two are alone in Dobson's office together and nothing ever comes up."

"Anybody else?"

"Just Prajeet Sengupta," said Owen.

The Indian doctor? "I thought you told me that was all bullshit."

"Not all of it. Like with any good lie, there's always a bit of truth. Sengupta exists, he's a real person," said Owen. "Come to think of it, the Iranian guy from Stanford is real, too."

I clearly didn't follow. Bass paused the recording, his thumb shifting to another file. He pressed Play.

For the next minute, with the flags around the monument whipping in the wind above us, I listened to Dobson on the phone with Sengupta asking about his friends in college, specifically if there was anyone from the Middle East.

"Sengupta was Dobson's man for the serum, botched as it was," said Owen. "Turns out, Sengupta has a brother back in India doing twenty years for drug trafficking. Or at least, he was until Dobson intervened with Indian intelligence officials. The serum in exchange for time served. The brother's now a free man."

"So Dobson discovers an Iranian roommate and invents the story about him," I said.

"Yeah, and of all things, the guy—Ghasemi—actually did go back to Iran. According to Stanford alumni records, he owns a software company in Tehran—but of course, that wouldn't prevent him from moonlighting for the nuclear program, right? Dobson had all the angles covered," said Owen. He then turned to Bass. "Except one."

Bass raised his palms as if to deflect the credit. "I knew nothing about this serum, but I couldn't shake the feeling that something was up. Especially when I heard Karcher's name to replace me."

"You were right. Hell, you were both right," I said, giving Owen his due.

So why didn't they look happier about it? Or even happy at all?

That was when I realized what they had already figured out. And to think, I was the only one with the law degree.

CHAPTER 110

"DAMN," I muttered.

Owen nodded. "Yep."

The recordings. "They're inadmissible. Not only that, they're illegal," I said.

Owen nodded again. "Yep."

"I don't care," said Bass.

"He really doesn't," said Owen. "Believe me, I've tried to talk him out of it."

"Out of what?" I asked.

Bass shrugged. "So maybe I risk doing a little time. It will be worth it to implicate Dobson. And once the investigation starts, something else will have to turn up," he said. "The truth will come out."

I had every intention of making a great counterargument, beginning with the reason why Owen hadn't wanted to go public in the first place. He wanted Dobson dead to rights. We both did now. But I'd just come from the guy's office, where I'd seen up close and personal Dobson's ability to construct an alternate reality. Dobson was good at it. Too good. Without the recordings from his office, the odds of his seeing the inside of a jail cell were anything but a sure thing. He'd be ruined politically, but he'd probably still go free.

Yeah, that was the argument I was about to make. Point by point.

Instead, all I could do was listen to the echo of Bass's last sentence in my head. The truth will come out, he said.

The truth will come out.

I turned to Owen. "You still have the notebook from the lab, right?"

It took him a second to figure out what I was asking, but only a second. The kid was a genius, after all. And when I saw him smile, it was suddenly as if he could hear the same echo.

"I'd say three days. Two, if I don't sleep," he answered. "But then what? How?"

I reached into my pocket. Never had a prepaid cell phone been put to better use.

"Yes, Operator, could I please have the main number for the *New York Times*?"

Sebastian Cole couldn't take my call fast enough.

"Jesus Christ, you're alive!" he said. "I was starting to wonder."

"You and me both," I said. "But yes, I'm alive. Very much so. Now, do you remember that envelope I gave you? The one you were only supposed to open if I wasn't?"

"Are you kidding me?" said Sebastian. "I've been staring at it every day since you left. I was planning to kill you myself just so I could open it."

"I'll save you the time," I said. "Go ahead...open it."

"Are you serious?"

"As the Queen Mother," I said. "And as you read what's in-side, I want you to keep one thing in mind."

"What's that?"

"You ain't seen nothing yet."

CHAPTER 111

INSIDE THE White House, dead presidents are nothing more than old paintings. The real currency is the almighty favor, and I'd just done a big one for the Morris administration.

"Thank you again, Trevor, for making this happen," said Dobson.

He had left the West Wing for the Westin and Sebastian Cole's corner suite, where I greeted him at the door with a firm handshake and the assurance that "this"—as in, this meeting and what it was in exchange for—was in everyone's best interests.

The deal I'd brokered was simple. I told Dobson that I'd already gone to Sebastian at the *New York Times* with the recordings of the serum being used at the black site in Stare Kiejkuty. But a lot had changed since that visit, most of all the revelation by Dobson that the CIA had a mole in the Iranian nuclear program who stood to be exposed. With Karcher now dead and his draconian operation disbanded, there was a choice to be made.

A bombshell of a story for the *Times* versus our country knowing whether Iran had the bomb.

What was an American patriot to do?

Convince the *Times* editor to stand down, that was what. And in return, Sebastian got unfettered access to the president and his full cooperation for an unprecedented series of in-depth interviews culminating in a book detailing his first term in office. Guaranteed bestseller on the *Times* list itself. Number one with a bullet.

This meeting was simply to iron out the details.

"Can I get you something to drink?" I asked. I pointed over at a credenza. "They just brought up some fresh coffee, if you want."

Of course he wanted it. Death, taxes, and Dobson chugging caffeine. "Sure," he said. "Black, no sugar."

Right on cue, Sebastian came over to shake hands, launching immediately into a conversation with Dobson about the last time they'd seen each other. It was last year's White House Correspondents' Dinner, just a few months after President Morris took office. Jimmy Fallon was hilarious.

"I thought the president was in good form, too," said Sebastian, or something like that. Whatever it took to keep Dobson occupied.

"Here you go," I said, returning moments later with the coffee. "Black, no sugar."

Dobson took a sip. He shot a glance at the mug.

"I know, it's a little strong, isn't it?" I said. "Too strong?"

Which was like asking a guy if your handshake was too strong. What's he going to say?

"No, not at all," he said. "It's good."

"Good," said Sebastian. "Shall we sit down?"

He led the way over to the hotel's modernist take on a living room area—one couch opposite two armchairs, a black lac-quered table in the middle. There were no place cards, but once Sebastian sat down in one of the armchairs, it was only natural that Dobson would take the couch. Better yet, he sat right in the center. Center stage, if you will.

"Nice room," said Dobson, looking around.

You should see the other one, dude.

Or, at least, that was what I pictured Owen saying through the wall while watching on his laptop.

The kid really had a thing for adjoining rooms.

CHAPTER 112

FROM THE other armchair, I watched and listened as Dobson laid out in detail the ways in which Sebastian would be able not only to conduct the one-on-one interviews with the president but also to travel with him once he began his reelection campaign.

"Not the press bus, Cole," said Dobson. "I mean shotgun, right there next to the man. We're talking the kind of access that would make Bob Woodward shit his pants with jealousy."

Sebastian smiled and nodded. In fact, that was pretty much all he allowed himself as he deftly used the cover of his proper British upbringing to come off as agreeable as possible. Owen had made it very clear.

Faster than aspirin but slower than eye drops.

"Clay, do you want some more coffee?" I asked. Five minutes in and I'd already poured him one refill.

Dobson shook me off. "No, I'm all set," he said.

We'll see about that, I so wanted to say.

Instead, I simply peeked at my watch and shot a glance over at Sebastian. Finally, and once and for all.

It was time to hear the truth.

"So, any questions so far?" Dobson soon asked. It was clear he was only being polite. This was his end of the bargain, the quid to Sebastian's quo, and he was sure he'd delivered in spades.

And, in fact, he had. Desperate men know no boundaries.

Sebastian sat back in his armchair, folded his legs, and used the few seconds of complete silence that followed to make it very clear that, yes, he actually did have some questions.

"Have you ever told a lie?" he asked.

Dobson's reaction was as expected, his eyes narrowing to an incredulous squint. "What kind of a question is that?"

"A rather simple one," said Sebastian.

Dobson looked at me for help with this suddenly crazy British journalist for the *New York Times*. I was the broker of this deal, after all.

But I was also a former prosecutor.

"Had you ever met Claire Parker?" I asked.

"*What?*" said Dobson. "Who?"

"Did you not hear me or do you not know the name?"

"I know the . . . I mean, I know who she is."

"You mean *was*, right? You're aware that she was murdered in Manhattan a little over a week ago, aren't you?"

I watched as Dobson looked over my shoulder at the door. It was his way out. Escape. Freedom. From what exactly, he wasn't sure yet. But it couldn't be good.

That is, for a lesser man.

And in that moment, right there, a lifetime of ego and arrogance—of Dobson always thinking he was the smartest guy in the room—did exactly what we thought it would. It kept his ass seated square on that couch. Complete and utter inertia.

"Yes, it was all over the news," he said calmly. "Claire Parker, the writer for the *Times*, was shot to death in the back of a taxi."

"Do you know why she was murdered?" I asked.

"It was reported as a robbery," said Dobson.

"Do you think that's what it was?"

"Why wouldn't it be?"

The smug expression, the self-satisfaction . . . he looked like a kid who'd just figured out a board game without reading the rules.

"I don't know, you tell me," I said. *"Do you know why she was really murdered?"*

Dobson opened his mouth to answer, but it was as if the hinges of his jaw had suddenly jammed. Every muscle in his face and neck snapped to attention as if somewhere in his brain a switch had been flipped. And indeed it had.

"No," he managed to push past his lips, but as soon as he did, it was as if the word had turned around and punched his lights out, his head jolting back and his legs shaking as if the couch had just become an electric chair.

His eyes darted to the table in front of him, the coffee table. He stared at his cup, the realization sinking in. He couldn't believe it. He didn't want to believe it. But he had no choice. He was getting the ultimate taste of his own medicine, and it was going down hard.

So was he.

CHAPTER 113

"DID YOU instruct Frank Karcher to have Claire Parker killed?" I asked, and immediately repeated the question, full-throated, over the sound of Dobson desperately trying to fight against the pain. *"Did you. Instruct. Frank Karcher. To have Claire Parker killed?"*

Even if he wanted to leave now, he couldn't. His body wouldn't let him.

But he also had no intention of answering. Forget every word, it was every syllable that had become a struggle—and yet he somehow managed to string two together after sucking in a gasp of air.

"Fuck you!" he bellowed.

From the corner of my eye, I saw the flat-screen against the wall light up. Dobson turned to look, only to realize he was looking at a live feed of himself. Feeling pain was one thing, watching yourself feeling it added a whole new component. Owen was playing for keeps. We all were.

Fuck you back, Dobson. Have you forgotten how your serum works?

Only this wasn't his serum.

This was the one he'd wished he had from the start. The one that didn't kill people even if they were being honest. Better yet, it didn't need to be injected. It could be absorbed into the bloodstream without being compromised by stomach acids.

The only thing Owen couldn't do was make it tasteless. But strong black coffee was a pretty good masking agent.

I leaned forward, staring into Dobson's eyes, which had turned red from burst blood vessels. He looked like a demon.

"The only thing that will stop the pain is telling the truth," I said.

But as I looked at him, his body convulsing so violently it felt as if the entire room were shaking, I realized we both knew that wasn't true. There was something else that could stop the pain.

Sebastian looked over at me, worried. I could read his face. *Is Dobson that deranged? Is he crazy enough to do it?*

I shook my head, but it was too late. Dobson had seen Sebastian. And of all things—as his eyes began to leak with red tears, his fists balled so tight I thought they would both snap off at the wrists—he did something that for the first time made me think that, yeah, maybe he was that sick in the head.

He smiled.

I turned away, only to see him again on the television, the smile seemingly wider. He wanted us to know. *If I'm going down, I'm taking you all with me.*

No. He was bluffing, I was sure of it. Sebastian, on the other hand, wasn't. He was more than looking at me now. He was pleading.

"Do it," he said. "Please."

I put my hand in my pocket, feeling for the cylinder. I knew it was there; I must have checked it twenty times before Dobson arrived. But I had no intention of taking it out, let alone using it.

"Do it!" Sebastian repeated. He was scared to death. Or, more specifically, scared of the murder charge that would be slapped on all of us.

In the cylinder was the antidote. A small syringe with a spring-loaded needle and the ability to negate the effects of the serum in a matter of seconds. "Just in case," Owen had said.

As in, just in case Dobson would sooner die than confess.

But I wasn't having it. Or maybe I was simply too angry, too consumed by the desire to see him own up to what he'd done.

Suddenly, I heard the door flung open behind me, the sound of Owen bursting into the room. As fast as he was moving, he managed to keep his voice calm.

"Trevor," he said. Just my name. That, and all the subtext that went with it. *Are you sure you know what you're doing?*

And for the first time since this whole nightmare had started, I was.

I stood and walked slowly over to Dobson, sitting on the coffee table directly in front of him. There would be no more yelling from me, no more demanding that he come clean.

He simply needed to know that I was fine with his decision either way. He had everything to lose, and I had nothing.

"She was pregnant," I told him. "She was pregnant with my child."

And with that, I stood up and walked out of frame. The choice was his now, and only his.

Truth or die?

EPILOGUE

CHAPTER 114

IN THE world of newspapers, the term is *shirttail*, a short and related story that's added to the end of a longer one.

Of course, I only know that because of Claire. She was my go-to for journalistic lingo, and I was hers for all things legal. Between the two of us, we always had a leg up on the Sunday crossword.

Suffice it to say, Dobson's confession was all the rage for a couple of weeks. All the more so given how it was obtained. But that was the whole point, wasn't it? Owen never denied that the serum had the potential to foil a terrorist plot that could kill hundreds, if not thousands or more. The question was, who got to decide whether or not we used it? So let the public debate begin, because that's how a democracy is supposed to work. In the words of Lincoln at Gettysburg, *"government of the people, by the people, for the people."*

It was only fitting, then, that Owen gave the recording of Dobson to the DC police, the FBI, and the entire world, via the

Internet, all at the same time. First, though, he gave a private screening to Agent Valerie Jensen and Jeffrey Crespin. That was the first of a few deals I negotiated.

Ethics and morality exist on an ever-shifting scale. The trick, I thought, was keeping perspective. Somewhere along the line, there always needed to be a clearly established definition of right and wrong. Black and white. As long as you had that, you could proceed to deal with the gray areas.

At least, that was what I used to teach my students at Columbia Law. But then this past summer happened. I don't teach them that anymore.

"Look around you, Mr. Mann," said Crespin. It's *all* gray.

Which would explain why he was ultimately fine with my other two deals. They needed his approval.

One was regarding Josiah Brennan.

Jesus himself could've returned to defend Brennan in court for money laundering, but there was still no way he could avoid jail time entirely. That is, if the NSA chose to cooperate with law enforcement and pursue charges against him.

All I could picture, though, was Brennan's nine-year-old daughter, Rebecca, getting frisked every time she went to visit him behind bars. The same Rebecca who could've easily ratted out Valerie and me in her father's office. So I had a different suggestion, and Crespin went for it.

It was time for Brennan to launder some of his own money.

Detective Dave Lamont didn't have a nine-year-old daughter, but he did have three teenage sons with his wife, Joanie. They also had a mortgage, school tuitions, and orthodontist bills. NYPD death benefits only go so far. His additional life insurance policy, even less far.

So Brennan was charged with something else instead: looking after the Lamont family financially. Also, setting up a special

IRA for Lamont's partner, McGeary. Was it a rich man buying his freedom? Maybe if he'd thought of it first. But he didn't. Money doesn't always have to be the root of all evil.

Which was the same rationale I used regarding Shahid Al Dossari, the other deal that needed Crespin's consent.

Personally, I didn't care one way or the other what the NSA wanted to do with him. He had skedaddled back to Saudi Arabia the split second Dobson was arrested, and the fact that he wasn't a US citizen presented a far more complicated legal challenge, especially given his wealth and influence.

But there it was again. *Wealth and influence.*

"Might as well put it to good use," I told Crespin.

"Just what do you have in mind?" he asked.

It was actually what Owen had originally had in mind.

CHAPTER 115

I THOUGHT I was curing Alzheimer's....

That was what he'd told me from the start. Now maybe he will.

Of course, I couldn't really blame Al Dossari for making a counteroffer to the "strongly" suggested contribution to Owen's newly founded research facility. Twenty million dollars is a lot of money, after all. Even for a Saudi banker.

Then again, everything is relative. Assuming he was able to fight extradition and avoid trial in the States, he'd still be the Roman Polanski of poker and gambling here. No more trips to Vegas. No more trips anywhere in the United States, his favorite place to be.

In the end, Al Dossari figured that was an even greater price to pay.

God bless America.

And Godspeed to Owen. "I've got my work cut out for me," he said when the facility officially opened in the fall.

"Well, then," I said. "You better get busy...dude." For good measure, I rubbed my hands together as if doing a bit of his dry wash routine.

You meet a lot of people in your lifetime, many of whom will have an immeasurable impact on you. Then there are those who literally change who you are. You can generally count those people on one hand. And fittingly, Owen Lewis will always be one of them. In the wake of everything that happened, all the sadness and despair and mayhem, he managed to give me something I would've never thought possible. Optimism.

Crazy to think...I still can't even buy the kid a drink.

So that was that. All the deals I'd cut after Dobson's confession. As for the one made before it, I'm fairly certain Sebastian has no regrets. In fact, I'm positive of it.

Sebastian Cole may be the last journalist on earth whom President Morris—with his twenty-one-percent approval rating—will actually grant an interview to, but Sebastian's first-hand account of what happened in that hotel room, including a very revealing Q&A with Dobson while he was under the influence of the serum, gave him the scoop of a lifetime.

Throw in the exclusive interviews Owen and I guaranteed him in return for his cooperation, and Sebastian all but owned the front page of the *Times* for an entire month.

But the best part—at least for me—was the class he displayed throughout it all. The byline of every article he wrote covering the story read the same. *By Claire Parker and Sebastian Cole.*

"You're a far better man than I first gave you credit for," I told him.

"Likewise," he said.

It's been moments like that when I've missed Claire the most. That's when I usually hop in my car and make the drive up to

Wellesley, west of Boston, and the Woodlawn Cemetery, where all Parkers have been buried for over a century. Only once, though, have I fallen into the cliché of talking to her tombstone. She would've laughed at the sight of that. And who knows? Maybe somewhere she is laughing, and doing that little crinkle thing with her nose that, in a weird and wonderful way, always made her look even prettier.

I know that as time goes on, those trips to her gravesite will happen less often. But not because I'll miss her less. No, eventually what will happen, maybe amid a gust of wind through the branches of a nearby northern red oak, is that I'll hear that tombstone of hers talk back to me.

"It's okay, Trevor," she'll say. "Now get on with it, will you? Maybe even ask out that gorgeous agent from the NSA. *Though between you and me, she might be a little out of your league.*"

Claire always told it like it was.

Though, for the record, Valerie Jensen and I did manage to have dinner together when she was in Manhattan before the holidays. We even went back to her hotel afterward. "Your move," she told me.

Of course, that was during the game of Scrabble we played in the bar off the lobby. She'd brought the game all the way up from DC. And of course, she kicked my ass but good. Her father also taught her poker, she said. "Maybe we'll play after the trial."

Which brings us fully up to date. Dobson's trial. And me sitting in the first row waiting my turn. It couldn't come soon enough.

"The prosecution calls Mr. Trevor Mann."

It felt strange to be back in a courtroom after all these years, and even stranger to be taking the witness stand. I'd always been in front, asking the questions, not actually sitting in the stand.

Place your left hand on the Bible, raise your right hand...

No serum needed here. We were kickin' it old school.

"Do you solemnly swear or affirm that you will tell the truth, the whole truth, and nothing but the truth, so help you God?"

You better believe it.

"THIS IS NOT A TEST" — EVERY NEW YORKER'S WORST NIGHTMARE IS ABOUT TO BECOME A REALITY.

ALERT

FOR AN EXCERPT, TURN THE PAGE.

AT 3:23 A.M., the two Supervac trucks turned off their head-lights and pulled off the northbound FDR into a junk-strewn abandoned lot beside the Harlem River across from the Bronx.

After he put the first truck into park, Tony took a quart of or-ange Gatorade from the cooler they'd brought, cracked its lid, and commenced gulping. His stubbled face was filthy, and he was sweating exuberantly, had in fact sweated through the back of his heavy coveralls.

"Hey, you want some of this, Mr. Joyce?" said Tony, coming up for air.

"No. All yours, Tony. Truly, you broke your butt down in the hole. I'm proud of you," Mr. Joyce said.

It was true. Tony had some heft on him and could use a few hygiene suggestions, but no one could say he wasn't a worker. He'd been going at it hard for the last three hours between the two manholes, really hustling. He'd been Johnny-on-the-spot for every task with the equipment without a word of complaint.

They were finally done now. At least with the prep work. It had gone off without a hitch. The truck tanks were empty now, and the manholes were closed. Everything was set up and ready to go.

"How's the link?" Mr. Joyce called into the radio he took from his pocket.

"Crystal clear," Mr. Beckett in the other truck replied.

They had hacked into the MTA internal subway video feed, and Mr. Beckett was now monitoring the security cameras at every 1 Line station from Harlem to Inwood.

"OK, I see it," Mr. Beckett said over the radio a second later. "It's pulling out of 157th in the northbound tunnel. There. It's all the way in. You have the green light, Mr. Joyce."

Mr. Joyce took the cheap disposable cell phone from the left breast pocket of his blue coveralls. It was a Barbie-purple slide phone made by a company called Pantech, a training phone one would buy a suburban girl for her middle-school graduation. He turned it on and scrolled to the phone's only preprogrammed number.

Theory becomes reality, he thought, and he thumbed the call button, and the two pressure cookers planted in the train tunnel ten stories beneath Broadway twenty blocks away detonated simultaneously.

THE INITIAL EXPLOSION of the pressure-cooker bombs, though great, was not that impressive in itself. It wasn't meant to be. It was just the primer, the match to the fuel that the two trucks had been pumping into the air of the tunnel for the last three hours.

The tunnel was semicircular, seventy-three feet wide at its base, twenty feet high, and a little less than four miles long. Within seconds of the blast, a powerful shock wave raced in both directions along its entire length. There were no people on the subway platforms so late, but in both stations the wave ripped apart vendor shacks and MTA tool carts and wooden benches.

As the wave hit the south end of the 181st Street station, a three-ton section of the vaulted tunnel's roof tore free and crashed to the tracks, while up on Broadway, the fantastic force of the blast set off countless car alarms as it threw a half dozen manhole covers into the air.

South of the main blasts, in the tunnel between the 157th Street station and 168th Street, the shock wave smashed head-on into the approaching Bronx-bound 1 train that Mr. Beckett had spotted. The front windshield shattered a millisecond before it tore loose from its moorings, killing the female train driver instantly.

As the train derailed, its only two passengers, a Manhattan college student couple coming back from a concert, were knocked spinning out of their seats onto the floor of the front car. Bleeding but still alive, they had a split second to look up from the floor of the train through the front window at a rapidly brightening orange glow. It was strangely beautiful, almost like a sunset.

Then the barreling twenty-foot-high after-burn fireball that was behind the shock wave slammed home, and the air was on fire.

Back at the Harlem River shore, Mr. Joyce had to wait seven minutes before he heard the first call come in on the radio scanner he had tuned to the fire department band. He clicked a pen as he lifted his clipboard.

"We did it, Tony," he said, giving the driver a rare grin.

"Phase one complete."

MORE BLUE AND red emergency lights than I could count were swinging across the steel shutters and Spanish billboards of 181st Street and St. Nicholas Avenue when I pulled up behind a double-parked FDNY SUV that morning around 4:30 a.m.

I counted seven fire trucks, an equal number of police vehicles and ambulances. As I hung my shield around my neck, I saw another truck roar up. Rescue One, FDNY's version of the Navy SEALs. Holy shit, was this looking bad.

I found the pitch-black subway entrance and went down stairs that reeked of smoke. All I could hear were yells and the metallic chirp of first-responder radio chatter as I swung my flashlight over the tiled subway walls.

The initial report I received from my boss, Miriam, was that some kind of explosion and a subway tunnel fire had occurred. One memory kept popping into my head as I hopped a turnstile toward the sound of radios and yelling.

Don't tell me this is 9/11 all over again!

I went past a token booth and almost knocked over the white-haired, blue-eyed fire chief, Tommy Cunniffe, thumbing something out of his eye.

"Chief, Mike Bennett, Major Case NYPD. What the hell happened?"

"Massive tunnel explosion of some kind, Detective," Cunniffe called out in a drill-sergeant baritone. "Two stations, 168th Street and here at 181st Street, are completely destroyed. We have the fire almost under control here, but there's colossal structural damage, a large cave-in at the south end of this station. It's like a mine accident down there. We're looking for bodies."

"Is anybody dead?"

"We don't know. I heard over the horn there was a train that got fried a little south of 168, but everything is just nonsense still at this point. I got two engine companies down there working this water line that we had to feed seven stories down through the elevator shaft. It's an unbelievable disaster."

"Chief," came a voice from his chest-strapped radio. "We got movement. A heartbeat on the monitor."

"Coming from where?" Cunniffe yelled back.

"Up near you in one of the other elevator shafts."

"Downey, O'Keefe, get me a goddamn halogen!" Cunniffe screamed at two firemen behind him.

I ran over with the firemen and helped them pry open the door to one of several elevator shafts. When we got the doors open, three huge firemen the size of rugby players appeared out of nowhere and tossed a rope.

"Hey, Danny, what the hell are you doing? It's my turn," said one of them as the biggest clicked his harness onto the rope and lowered himself into the darkness.

"Screw you, Brian," the big dude said. "You snooze, you lose, bro. I got this. Watch how it's done."

I shook my head. These guys were amazing. Tripping over themselves to help. No wonder they called them heroes.

"Send down the rig," said the fireman in the shaft a minute later. "We got two, a mom and a daughter. They're OK! They're OK!"

Everyone started cheering and whistling as a pudgy Hispanic woman, clutching her beautiful preschool-aged daughter, was pulled up out of the shaft into the light.

"OK, good job, everyone. Attaboys!" Cunniffe bellowed as EMTs took the mother and child up the stairs. "Now get the eff back to work!"

An hour later, I was deep underground ten blocks south in full-face breathing apparatus and a Tyvek suit as I toured the devastation that had been the 168th station with FBI bomb tech Dan Dunning, from the Joint Terrorism Task Force.

"This is unbelievable," he said, swinging the beam of his powerful flashlight back and forth over the vaulted ceiling.

"Which part?" I said.

"This was one of the grandest stations of the whole subway system, Mike. See the chandelier medallions next to the cave-in, and the antique sconces in that rubble there? This used to be the station for the New York Highlanders, who went on to become the New York Yankees. A part of history. Now look at it. Gone. Erased."

"Could it have been a gas leak?"

"Not on your life," Dunning said. "Gas and electric are surface utilities. These are the deepest stations in the system. Ten stories down. Whatever blew them up was intentionally put here. I can't say for sure yet, but you ask me, these goddamn bastards set off a thermobaric explosion."

"A what?"

Dunning pulled off his mask and spat something.

"Thermobaric explosions occur when vapor-flammable dust or droplets ignite. They rely on atmospheric oxygen for fuel and produce longer, more devastating shock waves. As you can see, when they occur in confined spaces, they are catastrophic. They pumped something down here and lit it up. A gasoline mist maybe, is my guess. Just like in a daisy cutter. I mean, look at this!"

We hopped down off what was left of a platform and walked over the incinerated tracks toward a blackened train. As crime-scene techs took pictures, I could see that one of the train's plastic windows had melted and slid down the side of one of the cars like candle wax. Inside, the driver was burnt pulp, the two other bodies in the front car skeletal and black like something from a haunted house.

"Look at that," Dunning said, pointing his light at a charred sneaker in a corner.

"Wow, the shock wave must have knocked them out of their shoes," I said.

"Worse, look at the sole of it. It's almost completely ripped off. That's how powerful this bomb was. It separated the sole off a sneaker! Think of the incredible violence that would take."

I shook my head as I thought about it, breathing in the sweet gasoline smell of burn that the respirator couldn't filter out.

What is this and where is it going?

THREE HOURS LATER, our command post shifted four blocks north to the NYPD's new 33rd Precinct building at 170th and Edgecombe Avenue.

When I wasn't answering my constantly humming phone, I was busy upstairs in a huge spare muster room helping a couple dozen precinct uniforms set up a central staging area for what was obviously going to be a massive investigation into the explosion.

Everywhere I looked throughout the cavernous space were stressed-out, soot-covered MTA engineers, FDNY arson investigators, and FBI, NYPD, and ATF bomb techs talking into phones as they tried to get a grip on the scope of the disaster.

The biggest development by far was the discovery of shrapnel in two separate sections of the tunnel. Preliminary field reports seemed to indicate that the metal shards were from some sort of pressure-cooker bomb placed at the two main blast sites. We hadn't released anything to the press as of yet, but it was looking like this was in fact a bombing, a massive and deliberate deadly attack.

At 6:05 a.m., the mayor had made the call and canceled the city's subway service system-wide. It was a huge, huge deal. For the first time since 9/11, eight million people now had to find a new way to get to and from work and school. A mega meeting at the precinct command post had been called for nine-thirty. The mayor and commissioner were on their way as well as head honchos from the city's federal law-enforcement agencies and the MTA bosses who ran the subway.

I'd managed to get ahold of my first coffee of the morning and had just declined a third call from some annoyingly persistent *New York Times* reporter when I looked up and saw Chief of Detectives Neil Fabretti come through the command post door. I almost didn't recognize him in his stately white-collar uniform. At his heels was a tall, clean-cut white guy in a nice suit whom I didn't recognize.

"Detective, I can't tell you how much I appreciate you being all over this since this morning," Fabretti said, giving my hand a quick pump. "I already spoke to Miriam. NYPD has the ball on this, and I want you to head up the investigation. The rest of Major Case is now at your disposal as well as any and all local precinct investigators as you see fit. How does that sound? You up for it?"

"Of course," I said, nodding.

"Do you know Lieutenant Bryce Miller? He's the new counterterrorism head over at the NYPD Intelligence Division," Fabretti said, introducing the sleek, dark-haired, thirty-something cop at his elbow. "Bryce is going to be involved in this thing from the intelligence angle, so I wanted you guys to meet. You're going to be working together hand in glove, OK?"

I'd actually heard about Miller, who was supposed to be something of a hotshot. He'd been an FBI agent and Department of Justice lawyer linked closely to the Department of Homeland Security before being hired splashily to show the new mayor's seriousness in fighting the terrorists who seemed to love NYC for all the wrong reasons. But hand in glove? I thought as I shook Miller's hand. I was in charge, but I also had a partner or something? How was that supposed to work? And who was to report to whom?

Miller quickly took back his hand as if he didn't want my soot-stained jeans and windbreaker to muss his dapper, streamlined gray suit.

"Hercules teams have been deployed to Times Square and Wall Street," Miller said in greeting. "The helicopters are up, and there are boats in the water. Just got off the phone with the Commissioner. We're going full court press in Manhattan, river to river."

I assumed Miller was talking about the Intelligence Division's tactical units used to flood an area to show any potential attackers the NYPD's lightning-quick response capability. But weren't such shows of force supposed to be used to prevent attacks?

"Now what is this thermobaric-bomb stuff I keep hearing?" Miller continued. "That's crazy speculation at this point, isn't it? Something like that would take an incredible amount of technical know-how and meticulous planning. We would expect a blip of chatter activity from surveillance before such a large-scale attack, and my team and my contacts in Washington are reporting exactly nada. Couldn't this just have been a utility screwup?"

"I don't know about any of that, Bryce," I said eyeing him. "I was actually just with the bomb guys and saw the shrapnel from what looked like pressure-cooker bombs in two separate locations."

My phone hummed again as I took a black piece of something out of the corner of my eye with a pinkie nail.

"No matter how little anyone wants to say or hear it, this was definitely no accident. We just got hit again."

ABOUT THE AUTHORS

JAMES PATTERSON is one of the best-known and biggest-selling writers of all time. Since winning the Edgar™ Award for Best First Novel with *The Thomas Berryman Number*, his books have sold in excess of 300 million copies worldwide and he has been the most borrowed author in UK libraries for the past eight years in a row. He is the author of some of the most popular series of the past two decades – the Alex Cross, Women's Murder Club, Detective Michael Bennett and Private novels – and he has written many other number one bestsellers including romance novels and stand-alone thrillers. He lives in Florida with his wife and son.

James is passionate about encouraging children to read. Inspired by his own son who was a reluctant reader, he also writes a range of books specifically for young readers. James is a founding partner of Booktrust's Children's Reading Fund in the UK.

HOWARD ROUGHAN has co-written several books with James Patterson and is the author of *The Promise of a Lie* and *The Up and Comer*. He lives in Florida with his wife and son.

14th Deadly Sin

James Patterson
& Maxine Paetro

**A new terror is sweeping the streets of San Francisco.
And the killers look a lot like cops...**

As Detective Lindsay Boxer investigates whether the perpetrators
are brilliant impostors or police officers gone rogue, she receives
a chilling warning to back off.

On the other side of the city, an innocent woman is murdered in
broad daylight in front of dozens of witnesses. But there are no
clues and no apparent motive.

With killers in disguise, a maniac murderer on the loose, and
danger getting ever closer to Lindsay's door, could this be one
case too many for the Women's Murder Club?

CENTURY

Burn

James Patterson
& Michael Ledwidge

**Detective Michael Bennett is coming home to New York.
And a world of unimaginable evil awaits.**

Having brought an end to the vengeful mission of the ruthless
crime lord who forced the Bennett family into hiding, Michael is
finally back in New York City.

However, Bennett is thrust straight back into a horrifying case: a
witness claims to have seen a group of well-dressed men holding
a sickeningly depraved and murderous gathering in a condemned
building.

The report reads like the product of an overactive imagination.
But when a charred body is found in that very same building, the
unbelievable claim becomes all too real...

CENTURY

THE *SUNDAY TIMES* BESTSELLER

Hope to Die

James Patterson

I am alone, I thought. Alone.

Pain knifed through my head. I sank to my knees, bowed my head, and raised my hands towards heaven.

'Why?' I screamed. 'Why?'

Detective Alex Cross has lost everything and everyone he's ever cared about.

His enemy, Thierry Mulch, is holding his family hostage. Driven by feelings of hatred and revenge, Mulch is threatening to kill them all, and break Cross for ever.

But Alex Cross is fighting back.

In a race against time, he must defeat Mulch, and find his wife and children – no matter what it takes.

THE END-GAME HAS BEGUN.

CENTURY

Invisible

James Patterson
& David Ellis

My nightmare: it's the same every time. I'm trapped in my bedroom with an inferno blazing around me.

It started eight months ago, when my sister was killed in a house fire. Her death was written off as an accident, but I know she was murdered.

There have been dozens of 'accidental' fires across the US over the past year that are all too similar to be coincidental.

I've never been more sure of anything.

One of the worst serial killers of all time is being ignored.

And it's up to me to stop him.

arrow books

NYPD Red 3

James Patterson
& Marshall Karp

A chilling conspiracy leads NYPD Red into extreme danger.

Hunter Alden, Jr has it all: a beautiful wife, a brilliant son and billions in the bank. But when his son goes missing and he discovers the severed head of his chauffeur, it's clear he's in danger of losing it all.

The kidnapper knows a horrific secret that could change the world as we know it. A secret worth killing for. A secret worth dying for.

New York's best detectives, Zach Jordan and Kylie MacDonald, are on the case. But by getting closer to the truth, Zach and Kylie are edging ever closer to the firing line . . .

CENTURY

Private India

James Patterson
& Ashwin Sanghi

When Santosh Wagh isn't struggling out of a bottle of whisky, he's head of Private India, the Mumbai branch of the world's finest investigation agency.

In a city of over thirteen million he has his work cut out at the best of times. But now someone is killing seemingly unconnected people, strangled in a chilling ritual, with strange objects placed carefully at their death scenes.

As Santosh and his team race to find the killer, an even greater danger faces Private India – a danger that could threaten the lives of thousands of innocent Mumbai citizens…

arrow books

Also by James Patterson

ALEX CROSS NOVELS

Along Came a Spider • Kiss the Girls • Jack and Jill •
Cat and Mouse • Pop Goes the Weasel • Roses are Red •
Violets are Blue • Four Blind Mice • The Big Bad Wolf •
London Bridges • Mary, Mary • Cross • Double Cross •
Cross Country • Alex Cross's Trial (*with Richard DiLallo*) •
I, Alex Cross • Cross Fire • Kill Alex Cross •
Merry Christmas, Alex Cross • Alex Cross, Run •
Cross My Heart • Hope to Die

THE WOMEN'S MURDER CLUB SERIES

1st to Die • 2nd Chance (*with Andrew Gross*) •
3rd Degree (*with Andrew Gross*) • 4th of July (*with Maxine Paetro*) •
The 5th Horseman (*with Maxine Paetro*) • The 6th Target (*with
Maxine Paetro*) • 7th Heaven (*with Maxine Paetro*) •
8th Confession (*with Maxine Paetro*) • 9th Judgement (*with
Maxine Paetro*) • 10th Anniversary (*with Maxine Paetro*) •
11th Hour (*with Maxine Paetro*) • 12th of Never (*with Maxine Paetro*) •
Unlucky 13 (*with Maxine Paetro*) • 14th Deadly Sin (*with
Maxine Paetro*)

DETECTIVE MICHAEL BENNETT SERIES

Step on a Crack (*with Michael Ledwidge*) •
Run for Your Life (*with Michael Ledwidge*) •
Worst Case (*with Michael Ledwidge*) •
Tick Tock (*with Michael Ledwidge*) •
I, Michael Bennett (*with Michael Ledwidge*) •
Gone (*with Michael Ledwidge*) •
Burn (*with Michael Ledwidge*) •
Alert (*with Michael Ledwidge, to be published September 2015*)

PRIVATE NOVELS

Private (*with Maxine Paetro*) • Private London (*with Mark Pearson*)
• Private Games (*with Mark Sullivan*) • Private: No. 1 Suspect (*with
Maxine Paetro*) • Private Berlin (*with Mark Sullivan*) • Private Down
Under (*with Michael White*) • Private L.A. (*with Mark Sullivan*) •
Private India (*with Ashwin Sanghi*) • Private Vegas (*with
Maxine Paetro*) • Private Sydney (*with Kathryn Fox,
to be published August 2015*)

NYPD RED SERIES
NYPD Red (*with Marshall Karp*) •
NYPD Red 2 (*with Marshall Karp*) •
NYPD Red 3 (*with Marshall Karp*)

NON-FICTION
Torn Apart (*with Hal and Cory Friedman*) •
The Murder of King Tut (*with Martin Dugard*)

ROMANCE
Sundays at Tiffany's (*with Gabrielle Charbonnet*) •
The Christmas Wedding (*with Richard DiLallo*) •
First Love (*with Emily Raymond*)

OTHER TITLES
Miracle at Augusta (*with Peter de Jonge*)

FAMILY OF PAGE-TURNERS

MIDDLE SCHOOL BOOKS
Middle School: The Worst Years of My Life (*with Chris Tebbetts*) •
Middle School: Get Me Out of Here! (*with Chris Tebbetts*) •
Middle School: My Brother Is a Big, Fat Liar (*with Lisa Papademetriou*) •
Middle School: How I Survived Bullies, Broccoli, and Snake Hill (*with Chris Tebbetts*) • Middle School: Ultimate Showdown (*with Julia Bergen*) •
Middle School: Save Rafe! (*with Chris Tebbetts*)

I FUNNY SERIES
I Funny (*with Chris Grabenstein*) •
I Even Funnier (*with Chris Grabenstein*) •
I Totally Funniest (*with Chris Grabenstein*)

TREASURE HUNTERS SERIES
Treasure Hunters (*with Chris Grabenstein*) •
Treasure Hunters: Danger Down the Nile (*with Chris Grabenstein*)

HOUSE OF ROBOTS
House of Robots (*with Chris Grabenstein*)

KENNY WRIGHT

Kenny Wright: Superhero (*with Chris Tebbetts*)

HOMEROOM DIARIES

Homeroom Diaries (*with Lisa Papademetriou*)

MAXIMUM RIDE SERIES

The Angel Experiment • School's Out Forever •
Saving the World and Other Extreme Sports • The Final Warning •
Max • Fang • Angel • Nevermore • Forever (*to be published May 2015*)

CONFESSIONS SERIES

Confessions of a Murder Suspect (*with Maxine Paetro*) •
Confessions: The Private School Murders (*with Maxine Paetro*) •
Confessions: The Paris Mysteries (*with Maxine Paetro*)

WITCH & WIZARD SERIES

Witch & Wizard (*with Gabrielle Charbonnet*) • The Gift (*with Ned
Rust*) • The Fire (*with Jill Dembowski*) • The Kiss (*with Jill Dembowski*) •
The Lost (*with Emily Raymond*)

DANIEL X SERIES

The Dangerous Days of Daniel X (*with Michael Ledwidge*) •
Watch the Skies (*with Ned Rust*) • Demons and Druids (*with Adam Sadler*) •
Game Over (*with Ned Rust*) • Armageddon (*with Chris Grabenstein*) •
Lights Out (*with Chris Grabenstein*)

GRAPHIC NOVELS

Daniel X: Alien Hunter (*with Leopoldo Gout*) •
Maximum Ride: Manga Vols. 1–8 (*with NaRae Lee*)

For more information about James Patterson's novels, visit
www.jamespatterson.co.uk

Or become a fan on Facebook